TO STEAL AN EARL

The Sisterhood of Independent Ladies
Book Three

by Maeve Greyson

ARE YOU SIGNED UP FOR DRAGONBLADE'S BLOG?

You'll get the latest news and information on exclusive giveaways, exclusive excerpts, coming releases, sales, free books, cover reveals and more.

Check out our complete list of authors, too!

No spam, no junk. That's a promise!

Sign Up Here

www.dragonbladepublishing.com

Dearest Reader;

Thank you for your support of a small press. At Dragonblade Publishing, we strive to bring you the highest quality Historical Romance from some of the best authors in the business. Without your support, there is no 'us', so we sincerely hope you adore these stories and find some new favorite authors along the way.

Happy Reading!

CEO, Dragonblade Publishing

Additional Dragonblade books by Author Maeve Greyson

The Sisterhood of Independent Ladies Series
To Steal a Duke (Book 1)
To Steal a Marquess (Book 2)
To Steal an Earl (Book 3)

Once Upon a Scot Series
A Scot of Her Own (Book 1)
A Scot to Have and to Hold (Book 2)
A Scot To Love and Protect (Book 3)

Time to Love a Highlander Series
Loving Her Highland Thief (Book 1)
Taming Her Highland Legend (Book 2)
Winning Her Highland Warrior (Book 3)
Capturing Her Highland Keeper (Book 4)
Saving Her Highland Traitor (Book 5)
Loving Her Lonely Highlander (Book 6)
Delighting Her Highland Devil (Book 7)
When the Midnight Bell Tolls (Novella)

Highland Heroes Series
The Guardian (Book 1)
The Warrior (Book 2)
The Judge (Book 3)
The Dreamer (Book 4)
The Bard (Book 5)
The Ghost (Book 6)
A Yuletide Yearning (Novella)
Love's Charity (Novella)

Also from Maeve Greyson
Guardian of Midnight Manor (Novella)

CHAPTER ONE

London, England
June 1817

"I DO WISH you would have allowed me to resolve this, *Maman*." Sophie Redwell, daughter of the deceased third Earl of Rydleshire and sister to the entirely fabricated fourth, stared out the carriage window at the dreary streets of rainy London. The weather matched her spirits. Why could Maman not have been more patient? She fixed as stern a look as she dared on her mother. "There was no need to bring this to Her Majesty's attention. No need whatsoever."

"The last threat we received specifically targeted the queen as well as the two of us." Nia Redwell, dowager Countess of Rydleshire, repeatedly tapped her closed fan atop her knee, revealing her agitated state. "If the blackmailer focused solely upon ourselves, I would have allowed you to address this issue however you saw fit." Her usually calm visage hardened into a furious scowl. "But the assassin now threatens Her Majesty. It is our duty to inform her." She drew in a deep breath, snapped open the fan, and furiously fanned herself, leaving no doubt that she dreaded this visit as much as Sophie did.

Sophie fiddled with the beaded strings dangling from her reticule, willing the dismal day to either encourage them with sunshine or storm so fiercely they would be forced to take shelter. The latter was her preference, of course—anything to delay what would undoubtedly be a very unpleasant audience with the queen.

She glanced down at the delicate brocade purse in her favorite shades of purple. It held the missives from the dangerous individual who had made it quite clear that they were not merely interested in selling their silence for a good deal of blunt. No, indeed. Whoever had discovered the truth about the fake fourth Earl of Rydleshire had decided they not only wanted to see Maman and Sophie hanged for the elaborate scheme but also wished to name the queen as an accomplice in perpetuating a false peer to keep the title and its entailments from reverting to the monarchy and becoming a treat for Mad King George, and now Prinny, to bestow upon one of their pets.

How the fiend had discovered that the queen did indeed know about the twenty-five-year ruse was beyond Sophie's imagining. This newfound enemy was more dangerous than any she had ever encountered. They knew entirely too much. Names. Dates. Details so intimate that she believed the miscreant had to be either a former servant from her birthplace in Calais, France, or someone from the nearby village. She should never have shared the letters with Maman until after she resolved the matter and had the fiend permanently silenced by whatever means required. Then this visit with the intimidating monarch would be entirely unnecessary.

The fact that the queen had ordered them to join her at her secluded cottage near Kew worried Sophie even more. Very few received invites to Queen Charlotte's favorite sanctuary. In this case, the invitation was likely to be dire. The uneasiness in her middle churned and sloshed to the point of making her swallow hard and clear her throat to keep from becoming ill. "Did you make Her Majesty aware of *all* the details of the threats?"

Maman snapped her fan shut and tucked it inside her reticule. "My letter to her consisted of nothing but our code word. I considered that safest, considering the circumstances."

Periculum: Latin for danger, insecurity, peril. Sophie cleared her throat again, thankful she had taken nothing more than a weak cup of tea before departing from their townhouse in Mayfair. If she had bothered to eat a morsel or drink her usual chocolate, no doubt existed in her mind that she would be casting up her accounts while hanging her head out the window of the carriage. She hated feeling all jittery and sick. It was utterly ridiculous, considering her usually fearless viewpoint on most things. She was an exemplary archer. Her swordsmanship was quite impressive, and her ability to untangle secrets had always made Maman quite proud. It was a rare thing that made her nervous or instilled fear within her. Queen Charlotte was one of those things.

A shrill squeak escaped her as the carriage jerked to a halt in front of the cottage.

"Sophie!" her mother hissed with an exasperated glare. "Do compose yourself."

"Forgive me." She repaired her nervously chewed lips by reapplying a sparing amount of rose lip salve, then quickly tucked the tin back into her reticule before following Maman out of the carriage by way of the regally carpeted steps held in place by an unsmiling servant.

Two more of the queen's footmen, who were of the exact same height and dressed in their elaborate livery of crimson coats with gold braiding, knee breeches, stockings, and powdered hair, stood at attention, flanking the doorway to the left of the cottage's large center window. Neither smiled nor made eye contact, but both left Sophie with the distinct impression that they never missed the simplest detail or quietest whisper.

Another stoic man, whom Sophie remembered from a prior visit as the queen's secretary, opened the door before they reached it. He offered them a formal bow. "Lady Rydleshire. Lady Sophie. Her Majesty awaits you in the drawing room. Follow me, please."

He led them up a curved staircase to a room with a vaulted ceiling that softly draped at the apex with a gently curved arch.

Delicately painted vines blooming with a multitude of colorful flowers crisscrossed the curves overhead and ran down the corners where the walls met. The background for the vines on both the walls and ceiling was a pale, earthy green that reminded Sophie of springtime. Even though the day was rainy, natural light streamed in from the large center window identical to the one on the first floor centered between the two doors at the front of the cottage.

As soon as they entered, both Sophie and her mother halted and offered their deepest curtsies.

"Your Majesty," the dowager uttered in a reverent tone while keeping her head bowed.

"Come. Sit." Regal and somewhat terrifying with her astonishingly high, upswept hair and lavish gown of pale blue silk embellished with pearls and lace, Queen Charlotte eyed them with the vigilance of a royal falcon about to descend upon its prey.

Sophie remembered the monarch hardly if ever smiled—and when she did, one better brace oneself, because a royal command that would be neither easy nor pleasing was almost always forthcoming.

"Leave us," the monarch ordered her secretary. "And close the door behind you."

"But Your Majesty—"

The queen had but to lift a brow to send the man scurrying on his way. The door closed with a soft thump behind him. One of her beloved dogs, a tiny, fluffy thing of the purest white, gave a haughty yip, as if to remind the secretary to never question Her Majesty again.

"Thank you, Phoebe." Her Highness scratched the little Pomeranian behind its pointed ears and cuddled it closer. "I am quite certain he took your instruction to heart."

Her other furry companion, a Pomeranian colored the shade of fresh honey, placed its tiny paws on her lap, threw out its chest, and trembled with an almost laughable growl.

"Now, now, Mercury. Jealousy is most unbecoming." After resettling her precious pups back among the lavish folds of her gown that covered the settee on either side of her, the queen fixed an unnerving glare first on Sophie and then on the dowager countess. *"Periculum?"*

Lady Rydleshire straightened her back and squared her shoulders. "Yes, Your Majesty. We have been discovered and are threatened."

The queen ratcheted her brows higher. "We?"

Sophie's mother bowed her head. "I am afraid so. You were included in the most recent threat to expose the truth about the Rydleshire title."

The monarch's expression hardened as her piercing gaze slid back to Sophie. "Details, girl. As I assume you were the one who received these threats and brought them to your mother's attention. It has not escaped my notice that she has been quite busy at King Louis's court." She cast a sour look back at the dowager countess, and her mouth puckered as though she smelled something foul. "I mean, really, Nia? You have always possessed a much more discriminating taste than that. I am very disappointed in you."

The dowager opened her mouth to speak, then closed it and once more bowed her head. "Yes, Your Majesty."

"If you continue trembling and groveling like a traitorous subject, I shall soon doubt our friendship. Cease such behavior immediately."

"I am concerned for your safety, my precious queen. And if anything dire comes of this, I shall never forgive myself." Lady Rydleshire drew a lacy handkerchief from her reticule and pressed it to the corners of her eyes.

Sophie ached for her mother's distress, knowing how much dear Maman treasured her close friendship with the queen—not because of the power such a relationship entailed, but because she truly adored Queen Charlotte. Sophie straightened her spine and sat taller, determined not to cower. "The blackmailer is not only asking for money, Your Majesty. They want Maman and me hanged, and your knowledge about the Rydleshire title made public and brought before Parliament." She brought forth the threatening letters and gently slid them onto the table in front of the queen. "They have names, dates, and details. I cannot help but feel that this person once worked in our household in Calais."

The queen expelled an irritated hiss and looked even more displeased. "But you have yet to find this scoundrel and silence them?"

"I have not, Your Majesty, but I know I am close."

"How close?"

The queen *would* ask that. Sophie swallowed hard and tried to remember to breathe. She didn't dare lie. Queen Charlotte seemed to possess the ability to peer into one's soul. "I have worked on this for some time now," Sophie said, trying to sound more confident than she felt. "I know I am quite close."

"How. Close?"

Her Majesty was not known for her patience, and Sophie sensed she had reached its end. She relented and blew out a heavy sigh, consigning herself to the possibility of being beheaded. Well, that was doubtful. But the queen's displeasure, along with Maman's, was just as unpleasant as an execution. "I do not know, Your Majesty. Not yet. But I will not rest until I find them. Make no mistake."

The royal rolled her eyes, then turned back to Sophie's mother. "You assured me this would never happen, Nia."

"I never believed that it would." The dowager gave a sad shake of her head. "And unfortunately, I cannot use my usual resources due to the sensitive nature of this matter."

"Agreed," the queen said. "I would not wish this particular assignment given to any of your current apprentices or the associates from your past life." Her irritated scowl made Sophie fear the beheading might actually become a reality. "Have you recently dismissed anyone from your household in Calais?"

"No, Your Majesty." Sophie fidgeted in the chair, cringing

when it creaked. "Most of our servants have been with us since I was born. Even those with the fewest years of service have been in our employ for well over five years."

"Then your suspicion of the blackmailer being a former member of your staff is illogical." Queen Charlotte dismissed Sophie with another impatient roll of her eyes and focused on the dowager. "Have you taught this child nothing? You were once my very best agent, Nia."

Sophie's mother reached over and patted Sophie's arm. "My daughter is now the best, and I trust her implicitly. It was she who trained the spy who uncovered the plot to assassinate the prince regent."

The queen hissed again, sounding like a sputtering teakettle. "Heaven only knows we would never wish any ill upon my dearest Georgie, now would we?"

Sophie bit the inside of her cheek to keep from smiling. Her Highness's tone suggested that she and the prince regent had still not overcome their discord over who should rule in the king's stead when His Majesty had become permanently incapacitated by madness.

"Our concern is now for you," the dowager countess said. "Sophie and I can manage our part in this as long as your safety—both physically and politically—is secured."

"Obviously, you cannot manage this situation in any manner at all." The queen leaned forward and, with the tiniest silver spoon, scooped up a portion of dark brown dust from a small crystal bowl. She sprinkled the snuff onto the side of her hand beside her thumb and inhaled it up her nose with a sharp sniff. "You have come here to warn me of this unpleasantness, and yet you possess absolutely no information other than the miscreant's written demands. Not only that, but you offer no resolution." She shook her head. "I am very disappointed in you, Nia." She turned to Sophie. "And with you, child, I am most unimpressed. Did it never occur to you that this entire situation could have been avoided if you had debuted several years ago? At an *appropriate* age, I might add. Then you could have married well to make this all go away. Why was that not done, I ask you?"

"We could not possibly risk it," Sophie said, perhaps a little sharper than she should have. "Not with the secret of the title hanging in the balance." She had known this meeting would be unpleasant, but to be told by the queen that she was not only most unimpressive but also a mindless spinster cut her to the quick. "Your Majesty, you must—" Queen Charlotte's narrow-eyed glare silenced her and dared her to continue. Sophie was not so dimwitted as to take that dare.

"Be that as it may," the queen said, sharply biting out each word, "if today does not come to pass as I have deemed it shall, the two of you shall return here tomorrow at precisely the same hour." Her irritated scowl darkened even more. "Unless, of course, I have a prior commitment to another of those unpleasant receptions with Georgie." She drew herself up like an insulted peahen. "I should refuse all such engagements after that incident in April. The audacity of them jeering at the queen. After my many years of service. How dare they?"

"Most unforgivable," the dowager countess hurried to say.

"You should have ordered them beheaded." Sophie clamped her mouth shut. She should not have said that.

The queen did not smile, but definitely appeared to be more pleased than she had since their arrival. "Perhaps you are not so unimpressive after all, dear girl."

A timid pecking on the door interrupted them, followed by a hesitant "Your Majesty?"

"Did I not dismiss you from this room, Edwards?"

The secretary kept his head bowed as he opened the door wider. "Yes, Your Majesty, you did. However, you also wished to be informed of his arrival." He offered another apologetic dip of his chin. "Sir Nash Bromley is here."

Indignance and age-old fury roared in Sophie's ears, preventing her from hearing another word, even though it was the queen greeting their new guest. Nash Bromley. That arrogant, priggish, self-serving, poor excuse of a churl she should have impaled when they were both at Rydleshire Academy. If her practice sword had been steel rather than wood, she would have relieved this earth of a most insufferable individual and then danced on his grave.

"Sophie!" her mother said in a snappish whisper.

A barely audible chuckle behind her brought Sophie to her feet and made her turn. She clenched her teeth and curtsied, so intent on reining in her grudge over ancient insults and slights that she failed to look up at the man standing before her. Instead, she stared at the floor, concentrating on cooling the angry blush burning her cheeks.

"Sir Nash," she forced out in a barely civil tone while keeping her gaze downcast.

"Lady Sophie."

His voice was much deeper than she remembered.

"It is indeed wonderful to see you again after such a long while," he said. "What has it been, my lady? Ten years?"

Ten years too little, she wanted to snap, but Maman stood close enough to pinch her if she didn't behave, and she had already made a less-than-desirable impression on Her Majesty.

"It has been some time," she forced out, then decided to look into the eyes of her arch-nemesis. A gasp almost escaped her.

The arrogant Nash Bromley she had last seen when she was naught but ten and five and he was twenty had been handsome enough to make her young heart yearn for him to be kinder and treat her with the same admiration he offered the older girls. But the man before her was so…changed. She realized her mouth was hanging open and snapped it shut.

Somehow, he had transformed into an even more striking figure whose dark blue jacket made his broad shoulders appear so wide it was a wonder he didn't pass through doorways by turning sideways. His legs were no longer tall, gangly sticks but impressively muscular, stretching his snug pantaloons in the best sort of way. All that seemed familiar about him was the shade of his hair—a ripened wheat color that wasn't really blond, but neither was it auburn. And those eyes. Those were the same too. The iciest blue that had always mocked her and flashed with lightning whenever she had bested him in archery or swordplay. But currently, those piercing eyes gleamed with amusement.

She tipped her chin higher and glared at him. So the abrasive yet handsome cub of twenty had matured into a breathtaking man who could be a god descended from Mount Olympus. What of it? It mattered not to her. He surely had remained the same obnoxious cove.

With an insultingly smug smile, Nash gallantly bowed his head in her direction before turning to her mother and offering a respectful bow. "Lady Rydleshire. If not for your exemplary training, I fear I would not have survived to once again enjoy the pleasure of your company today."

"Yes, well," the queen interrupted before Sophie's mother could respond. "You three shall have plenty of time to reacquaint yourselves with one another." She tipped a pointed glance at the chairs, and each of them immediately sat. "When I read the word *periculum*, I foresaw the need to take control of whatever prompted such a message. Sir Nash, you shall take up residence with Lady Rydleshire and Lady Sophie at Rydleshire House in London."

Sophie bit the inside of her cheek to stop the unreasonable outburst about to break free of her. She consoled herself with the whiteness of the man's knuckles as he tightened his grip on the arms of his chair. His reaction enabled her to manage a serene, albeit slightly wicked, smile. He didn't want this any more than she did. Since Her Majesty seemed to hold him in such high regard, maybe he could convince her of the plan's folly.

"Take up residence at Rydleshire House?" he repeated, leaning forward slightly as if to improve his hearing. "Your Majesty?"

Queen Charlotte smiled, and that was when Sophie knew they were all doomed.

"Remember yourself, Sir Nash," the queen warned. "Yes. You shall move into their residence this very day." With another sly smile that chilled Sophie to the bone, the monarch gracefully fluttered her hand at both Sophie and her mother, as if bestowing a regal blessing upon them. "These ladies are two of my dearest friends, and they are in danger. You are to secure their safety and assist them not only in capturing the vile creature wishing to do them harm, but you will also silence that creature forever. Am I quite clear?"

Nash's squared jaw flexed, revealing to one and all that he sat there gritting his teeth.

The queen hiked a brow. "Well? When your queen asks a question of you, it is in your best interest to answer."

He jerked his head downward as if trying to nod but suddenly discovered his neck was stuck in place. "My obedience to Your Majesty goes without saying. But to protect these fine ladies with the expediency which I am certain you require, I shall need as many details as possible—and living with them, Your Majesty? Shall I pose as a groom in their stable or as a household servant?"

"You shall not be a servant but an esteemed guest. At least for a little while." The monarch scooped up her fluffy dogs and cuddled them closer—and then she smiled. Again.

Sophie's nape tingled, and she knew without a doubt that every tiny hair on the back of her neck stood on end. Another unpleasant regal command was headed her way. The air reeked of it.

The queen eyed the dowager countess smugly, then gave an almost imperceptible nod. "To prevent this issue from ever arising again, the fourth Earl of Rydleshire shall be pronounced expired without an heir, and I shall see to it that Georgie bestows the title upon none other than Sir Nash Bromley, the husband of Lady Sophie—well, the husband as soon as the banns are read." She paused and tipped her head, as though pondering the details of her plan. "Or should we acquire a special license?" She nodded, slow at first and then a bit faster. "Yes. I would take great pleasure in seeing this over and done with immediately. Edwards will see to it that the archbishop understands my wishes, and the special license shall be ready within days. And do not fear—Georgie will not dare cross me on this. Shall we just say that my inclinations are *always* honored by him now?" Queen Charlotte appeared uncharacteristically pleased as well as proud. "We should have done this ages ago. Do you not agree, Nia?"

"Yes, Your Highness." The countess reached over and rested her hand on Sophie's forearm in a silent plea for her to keep quiet.

"But if you proclaim the fourth Earl of Rydleshire dead, Maman and I will be in mourning. How could I possibly marry while in mourning?" Sophie couldn't breathe, nor could she remain quiet as her mother wished. She would rather endure the queen's wrath than marry Nash Bromley. She despised the man and knew he felt the same about her. He had to. Why else would he have been such a mean-spirited wretch the entire time they trained at the academy all those years ago? "It might raise questions, Your Majesty. And with a blackmailer already making threats, we risk overplaying our hand."

The queen kissed each of her pups on the tops of their little heads and returned them to their perches on either side of her. Once again, she sprinkled a bit of snuff on her hand and inhaled it with a long, appreciative sniff. After returning the tiny spoon to the crystal bowl and replacing the silver lid on it with a quiet click, she leveled a stern but still pleased-with-herself gaze on Sophie. "The two of you shall marry before the earl's death is announced, of course. Do not doubt me, girl. The only thing I have ever left to chance is allowing you and your mother to handle this situation yourselves for the past twenty-five years. It is high time I remedied that. Do you not agree?"

Sophie couldn't speak, couldn't breathe, couldn't swallow. All she could do was stare at the queen.

"Do you not agree, Lady Sophie?" the monarch repeated in a tone that brooked no argument.

"Of course she agrees, Your Highness," Sophie's mother hurried to say, and gave Sophie's arm a warning squeeze.

Queen Charlotte slightly narrowed her eyes and slid her gaze to Nash. "And you?"

"Your Majesty," he began, his deep voice suddenly stricken with a strained raspiness.

"Yes?"

He sucked in a deep breath, scrubbed a hand across his mouth, then deflated with a gusting exhale. After casting a disgruntled look in Sophie's direction, one she resented and shot right back at him, he bowed his head. "I am ever obedient to you, Your Majesty. As always."

"Excellent. Today has proven to be just as satisfying as I had hoped." The queen lifted a silver bell and rang it, causing both her dogs to bark. "Now, now—decorum, Mercury and Phoebe. We must always maintain proper decorum."

As soon as her secretary opened the door, she gave a nod. "My guests are ready to leave, Edwards. Show them out, then we have much to accomplish and little time in which to accomplish it, so do not dawdle."

"Yes, Your Majesty." Edwards stepped aside and opened the door wider while casting an expectant look Sophie's way.

She assumed the others were included in his unspoken invitation to leave the premises, but at the moment she didn't really care. All she knew for certain was that she needed to get out of the queen's presence so she could scream. With her teeth clenched so tightly that her jaws ached, she rose and gave the monarch a deep curtsy. "Your Majesty."

Queen Charlotte gave a dismissive nod.

Or, at least, Sophie thought she did. With her mind and emotions in such a turmoil, all she knew for certain was that she needed to escape so she might figure a way to free herself from becoming leg-shackled to the most irritating man in all creation. She snatched up the letters from the blackmailer and stuffed them back into her reticule.

She rushed past Edwards, skimmed down the stairs, and shoved through the door out into the rain, not giving the slightest care if she became soaked to the skin. She ran up the path toward

Kew instead of getting into the carriage.

"Sophie!" her mother called out. "Sophie, you must stop this instant!"

A strong hand closed around her arm and, gently but firmly, pulled her to a stop. "Lady Sophie, this is folly. You risk becoming quite ill by running off into the rain."

"At least then we would both be free of a marriage that neither of us wants." She yanked her arm free, wishing she had a sword to challenge him to a duel. Everything in her screamed to battle for the world she had worked so hard to protect all these years.

Nash stared down at her, his expression unreadable. "Come back to the carriage. To your mother."

"No."

He glanced back at the queen's cottage, then turned to her again. "Do you want the queen to see you behaving like this?"

"She already thinks I am an unimpressive, mindless spinster. I hardly think I can descend much lower in her esteem." For the first time that day, Sophie was thankful for the rain. It hid the hot tears streaming down her face. "Leave me in peace, Sir Nash. We may be forced to marry, but that hardly means we must tolerate each other's company."

His still-unreadable expression hardened into an irritated scowl. "You forget, my lady. I am charged with ensuring you are kept safe."

Before she could respond, he picked her up and threw her over his shoulder as if she were a sack of grain. *How dare he!* "You will put me down this instant!" She pelted blows across his back, knocked off his hat, pulled his hair, and twisted his ears. She contemplated biting him but decided against it. Instead, she squirmed and battered him with every ounce of rage, insult, and hurt feelings he had ever foisted upon her all those years ago.

Nothing fazed him. He marched back to the carriage and unceremoniously tossed her inside. She landed on her bum in the floor between the seats. Before she scrambled to her feet, he slammed the door, latched it, and banged on the side for the driver to take off.

She fought her way to the window and hung out of it, shaking her fist at him. "I hate you!" she roared. "And I always will!"

He didn't bother reacting, just marched to his horse after retrieving his hat, mounted up, and followed them.

"That was quite the display," her mother remarked in a calm tone, as if speaking about the weather.

Flopping back into the seat, Sophie glared at her. "Prepare yourself, Maman. That was only the beginning."

CHAPTER TWO

THE SCRAWNY, FIERY-HAIRED duckling who had annoyed him to no end ten years ago had become an intoxicatingly beautiful swan. Nash stared at the back of the carriage while rubbing his ear that still stung from the vicious twisting she had given it.

Gads, but Sophie was incomparable. If he had known she would bloom into such a desirable woman, he would not have shooed her away like the annoying little buzzing bee she had been. The thought gave him pause. Apparently, by teasing, nettling, and, more often than not, completely ignoring her, he had created quite the fierce enemy that the past ten years had done nothing to mellow. And now she was to be his wife. A wife who not only despised him but swore they would never be in each other's company if she had her way about it.

Never in all his days had he ever feared becoming leg-shackled in such a manner—ordered by Her Majesty, no less. While it was true his family was landed gentry, he was naught but a mere knight who currently owned nothing but his horse. At least, not until his father passed and grudgingly left everything to him because there was no other son, daughter, or cousin to leave things to. Still, being hunted by marriage-minded mamas had never been a problem. What mother wished her daughter saddled with the likes of him?

He snorted as the fault in his reasoning became clear. The

mother hadn't wanted him for her daughter. The queen had. But the queen had also said he would soon be the next Earl of Rydleshire. To resolve whatever mysterious problem endangered Lady Rydleshire and Lady Sophie. He shook his head. The more he thought about it, the more muddled everything became.

Another disgruntled snort escaped him as he recalled the rest of what the queen had said. *Have the fourth Earl of Rydleshire pronounced expired without an heir.* Was the man already dead, or was that Her Majesty's subtle way of ordering the earl's demise? And was he supposed to do it? What had the man done to displease the monarch so? The third Earl of Rydleshire had been assassinated by an enemy spy, but before his death, the man had been lauded as one of the best agents of the Crown.

Nash resettled the reins and scrubbed his face with one hand. Queen Charlotte had never been subtle before. Why would she be so secretive now? The monarch had said he and the lovely ladies would have plenty of time to reacquaint themselves, but with a special license being obtained, *plenty of time* took on quite the abbreviated meaning. Perhaps Lady Rydleshire would be good enough to enlighten him, since it was obvious that his future wife would rather spit in his eye than speak to him.

A hearty chuckle rumbled free of him. He had always loved a challenge.

The carriage's slower pace pulled him from his thoughts. They were nowhere near Mayfair, where the queen's secretary had earlier informed him that the ladies resided. Now that he knew who they were, he recalled Lady Rydleshire once mentioning a townhouse on Curzon Street when he had trained at her academy in Calais. Since the woman and her husband were renowned spies, he had considered it an honor and a privilege to receive such exemplary training at the behest of Queen Charlotte as a reward for his father recovering three of her little dogs when they escaped her coach. The queen had been quite impressed when his sire refused a reward of gold. His father had informed the queen it was his honor to be of service to his monarch.

Determined to express her gratitude, she had sponsored Nash's training at Lady Rydleshire's elite school, which was anything but affordable to a family of his father's means.

He closed the distance between his mount and the carriage, rounding it to discover a broken-down wagon in the middle of the road. "Driver—stay alert."

The man nodded and drew out a firearm.

The queen had said to keep the ladies safe. That meant danger could come from anywhere. Nash edged his mount closer to the side of the coach and spoke to them through the window. "A wagon blocks the road. We shall have to take another route. Secure the door on the other side and draw those shades. I shall remain on this side."

Lady Rydleshire nodded and hurried to do as he requested. Sophie glared at him, then pulled a pistol out from the compartment beneath the seat opposite her and her mother.

"Let them come," she said, in a fearless tone that should have angered him but instead stirred his admiration and much more.

Well, admiration or not, they would discuss her behavior in the future. He would keep the lady safe whether she wished him to or not. That part of their relationship was not negotiable.

The remainder of the trip proved uneventful, but Nash neither relaxed nor secured his weapon until the ladies ascended the front steps of the residence and disappeared inside. He relinquished his mount to the groom and watched as the carriage and his horse disappeared around the corner to the mews behind the townhouse.

With a last quick glance up and down the street of the upper-class area, he bounded up the steps and entered as if he owned the place. A rueful smile came to him. According to Her Majesty, he soon would.

A tall, stern-faced man of some years increased his long-legged stride to meet Nash in the entryway. With a curt tip of his gray head, he held out his hand. "I am Thornton, sir. The butler here at Rydleshire House. May I take your things?"

"Thank you, Thornton." Nash handed over his hat, gloves, and greatcoat. "I am Sir Nash Bromley, by the way."

"Yes, sir. We are aware that you are soon to be the new master of the house. Welcome to Rydleshire. Her ladyship awaits you in the parlor, if you would be good enough to follow me."

"Well, the lady wasted no time," Nash said under his breath as he followed the butler. He was quite certain it was Lady Rydleshire waiting for him. His lovely swan had probably retired to her rooms to plot his demise. As he entered the decidedly feminine sitting room done in delicate shades of rose and pale blue, Lady Rydleshire turned away from the window and faced him.

She offered him a somewhat unhappy smile. "Welcome to your townhouse, my lord. I took the liberty of ordering tea, along with a decanter of brandy that originated from a lovely area near your holdings in France. I thought it appropriate, considering today's events."

A sense of guilt flooded him even though he wasn't quite certain why. "Lady Rydleshire—please know I had absolutely no knowledge of the queen's intentions when she summoned me to her cottage." He offered what he hoped was a compassionate demeanor. "And I am not lord of the manor yet. I am simply *Nash*. Your most grateful student who has always held you in the highest esteem."

Her gracious nod did little to ease the uncomfortably stifling sensation of the unfairness of it all. She seated herself and tipped a hand toward a nearby chair. "Please. Sit. I am sure you have more than a few questions."

He chose a different chair. One that did not make him vulnerable by placing his back to the door. He noticed the countess's amused look. "Forgive me, my lady. Old habits and your lessons, actually. Never sit with your back to the door, remember?"

"I do, indeed." Her smile appeared to come easier to her. "And I am honored you continue to take the lessons to heart."

He eyed the doorway. "Will Lady Sophie be joining us?"

The dowager's amusement disappeared with a long-suffering sigh. "Lady Sophie felt the need to take refuge in her workroom." She tightened her mouth as if tasting something tart. "It is probably for the best—at least for now."

"Probably so." Nash pulled in a deep breath and decided to barrel forward with complete candor. "I fear Lady Sophie still harbors ill feelings about my thoughtless behavior when we were both much younger and far less mature."

"A young girl longing to be noticed and treated like a woman is easily wounded. Those wounds sometimes never heal." Lady Rydleshire startled and jerked her focus to the doorway. "Ah…tea. At last."

Nash pondered the dowager's nervousness. He hadn't recalled her as being a lady inclined toward jumpiness, but it had been an uncomfortably surprising day.

The butler hurried in, his footsteps silenced by the lush Turkish rug of the sitting area. "Shall I pour, my lady?"

"Please do, Thornton."

The man turned to Nash. "Tea or brandy, sir?"

"Tea for now. No sugar, lemon, or milk, thank you." He would forgo alcohol until later. One's wits must be kept sharp. He accepted the cup and waited for the butler to leave before resuming the conversation. "While I make no excuses for my thoughtless behavior toward Lady Sophie when we were both so young, it is my hope she and I can somehow achieve harmony now that we are both older and wiser."

"That is my hope as well."

He took the doubtfulness in the countess's tone as a challenge. Somehow, he would make peace with Lady Sophie. After all, he rather enjoyed sleeping with both eyes shut, and in the lovely swan's current mood, relaxing at all could be detrimental to his wellbeing. In fact, when he retired, not only would he keep his door locked, but a dagger under his pillow might not go amiss. "We will sort this between us, my lady, I assure you. All will be well."

Rather than answer, Lady Rydleshire merely glanced aside and sipped her tea. A determined air settled across her as she slid the saucer and cup to the table and lifted her chin as though about to issue a challenge. "I assume the queen's announcement that the earl would be deemed expired without an heir concerned you."

"I am not certain the word *concerned* properly describes my initial feeling. Confused would be more accurate." He set his drink aside as well, glanced at the door, then leaned toward her. "Does she wish him *expired* by my hand?"

Lady Rydleshire studied him for a long moment, her expression impossible to read. "If she does?"

His mentor's coldness about her own son's life seemed greatly out of character for her. This was not the stern yet caring teacher he remembered. "My loyalty to Her Majesty is, as always, unquestionable," he answered quietly. "Forgive me if that disturbs you, my lady." Although, in truth, the woman did not seem disturbed at all.

"Rest easy, young Bromley." She interrupted herself with a soft laugh. "Forgive me, sir. I still think of you as that ambitious youth in what now seems so very long ago. In my mind, you are still my most prized yet impetuous student. Young Bromley."

"I took no insult, my lady." In fact, when *young Bromley* had slipped from the dowager's lips, it had hit him like a mother using a pet name for a cherished child.

"I am glad." She resettled herself in her chair, stiffening her spine and sitting taller. "The queen does not require you to eliminate the young earl. Her command was directed at me."

"She wishes you to assassinate your son?" That thought disturbed him no small amount. A mother ordered to end her own child's life? If the act indeed had to be done to protect queen and country, he would handle it himself to spare the dowager countess as much as he could. "Permit me to accept the order in your stead, my lady. I understand it will not keep you from losing your son, but at least he will not die by your hand."

Lady Rydleshire closed her eyes, as though fighting to hold her composure.

"Shall I send for Lady Sophie, my lady? To help calm you?" He was at a loss, inexperienced in dealing with overwrought women. Saving or seducing them? Easily done. Catering to their unsteady emotions, absolutely not.

The dowager countess opened her eyes and smiled. "No, thank you. I assure you I am quite...gathered." She laced her fingers together and primly folded her hands in her lap. "Announcing the earl expired with no heir will end the charade I created twenty-five years ago to prevent the title from reverting to the monarchy and becoming a bargaining tool for King George. Thereby leaving my precious Sophie and me almost destitute and dependent upon the charity and kindness of others."

Nash stared at her, trying to take in the enormity of what she suggested.

"Your jaw is quite slack, young Bromley," she said. "Close your mouth and breathe."

"But...but provisions for you in case of...your marriage contract. Was your dowry not set aside in the case of such an unfortunate event as the death of your husband?" He clenched his teeth to stop his nonsensical babbling. "You are telling me that the fourth Earl of Rydleshire, Lady Sophie's brother, never existed?"

"Only in the minds of those in which he needed to exist." The lady released a weary sigh, took another sip of her tea, then returned the cup to its saucer. "Sophie's father and I loved each other with a ferocity that sometimes frightened us both. And while we were proud to be the queen's best agents, we were quite poor at handling finances or forming contingency plans in case something ever happened to David." Her faint smile held no happiness as she stared off into space. "We were young and full of our own perceived self-importance. We thought ourselves invincible." Her voice softened. "Then David was murdered a month before Sophie was born."

Nash found himself sitting on the edge of his seat. "But how did you do it all these years? How did you manage to invent a person and make the world believe he was real?"

"Determination. Loyal servants. And my dearest friend and ally, Queen Charlotte." She offered him a thoughtful look. "And when Sophie reached an age to help, things became much easier. She is quite brilliant, if I do say so myself."

"Could the queen not simply—"

"I did not wish the queen implicated any more than she already was. Her knowledge of my rather delicate situation was dangerous enough for her." Lady Rydleshire rose and returned to staring out the window. "King George was more stable back then, but still not quite…right. It would have been difficult and perilous for her to attempt anything more than what she had already done for Sophie and me."

"And yet now she has ordered the title to revert to the monarchy and be given to another," he said. "The precise situation that prompted you to create the farce in the first place."

"Yes," the dowager said, without facing him. "It appears that the past twenty-five years were for naught."

"I am sorry, my lady."

Lady Rydleshire turned and eyed him, her expression hard and unyielding. "Do not apologize for the error of my ways, young Bromley. But know this—if you do not protect my Sophie with all your being, I will make you sorry you were ever born."

He rose from his seat and returned the lady's fierce stare. "You will both be kept safe, my lady. Make no mistake."

"Then I suggest you go to Sophie," she said. "She has the letters, the threats, in her possession. That would be a good place for you to start."

"Lead the way, my lady."

She remained beside the window, framed by the day's dreary, wet grayness. "I would prefer Thornton showed you the way." She nodded at the doorway. "Do be good enough to ring for him. I have a great deal on my mind." Then she turned back and stared out the window once more.

Nash felt the dismissal as keenly as if she had shouted for him to get out. He didn't bother to answer, just did as she requested and yanked down on the tapestry bellpull hanging beside the door.

The butler appeared so quickly that he wondered if the man had been eavesdropping in the hallway. Probably so. First rule of discovering anything about a household was to befriend the servants. They knew everything. Another reason that the Rydleshire earldom scheme seemed so unfathomable.

"Take me to Lady Sophie's workroom, please," he told the butler.

"This way, sir."

Nash followed, noting each turn into a different hallway and the short flight of steps that took him deeper into the bowels of the home. When they reached the bottom of the stairs, Thornton extended his hand and directed Nash to a short hallway ending at a dark mahogany door.

"The Lady Sophie's workroom, sir. Will there be anything else?" The butler arched a bushy gray brow.

Prayers, Nash thought, but decided not to voice the request. "Nothing, Thornton. Thank you. That will be all."

After the shuffling of the man's retreating footsteps faded away to silence, he stepped forward and knocked.

Nothing but silence answered. The lack of sound or response became deafening.

He knocked again, hard enough to rattle the heavy door's hinges.

"If you insist—then enter! But do so at your own risk."

Nash smiled but quickly wiped it from his face before pushing open the door. "Lady Sophie? Your mother suggested I join you, so I might familiarize myself with the threats."

"Then my mother values your life very little." She didn't spare him a look from where she sat at the end of a long worktable, studying what looked to be several letters with the benefit of an oversized quizzing glass and several brightly burning oil lamps.

A chandelier wrought of black iron also burned overhead, and every sconce attached to the sturdy posts inset between the many bookcases had also been lit. Light flooded the large workroom, but what Nash noticed most was the way it enhanced the silky sheen of the lady's rich, coppery curls she had freed to tumble down her back.

He risked moving closer but remained alert in case the delightful swan attacked. "I apologize for the past, my lady. Surely you can find it in your generous spirit to chalk up my behavior to the foolhardiness of youth?"

She slowly passed the glass over the nearest letter, studying it while ignoring him.

"Lady Sophie?"

Without granting him the courtesy of looking him in the eye, she straightened and set the magnifier aside. As prim as an elderly matron, she folded her hands in front of her and rested them on the table while staring straight ahead. The pink fullness of her pout and the flicker of her heartbeat pulsing at the base of her throat made him wet his lips.

She pushed up from the bench, went to a bookcase on the right, and ran a finger along the spines of the many tomes filling the shelves. After making her selection, she eyed it while cradling it in one hand and slowly flipping the pages. "A blackmailer has so far sent five letters, demanding ridiculously low sums for the price of their silence. I paid them each time, hoping to trap the fiend, but so far have had no success. The last and most recent letter did not demand payment. Instead, it stated that within a month's time, Queen Charlotte would be revealed as part of the Rydleshire scandal and brought to ruin before Parliament and the *ton.*"

He edged closer, determined to force her to confront and overcome her obvious dislike of him that she had formed at the tender age of five and ten. Perhaps a bit of goading was in order.

"I should not have ignored you back then, Lady Sophie. Nor teased you or so soundly trounced you in the classroom or on the practice fields. I apologize. Such behavior was most ungentlemanly. I truly wish you could find it in your heart to forgive me so we might achieve harmony in this household."

Her head snapped up, and her rich mahogany eyes flashed with fury. "Your memory is quite poor, Sir Nash. Not once did you trounce me in the classroom or on the practice fields, even though you were five years my senior."

He refrained from smiling but couldn't resist jutting his chin higher. "Have you forgotten the agility field, my lady? If memory serves, you ended up in the mud with Monsieur Sorbonne's swine."

"That was your fault, and you know it." She bared her straight white teeth as though ready to sprout fangs and rip him to shreds.

With a dismissive shrug, he sauntered closer and allowed himself a smile he knew would annoy her. "It was part of the test, my lady. Do you truly believe the enemy would refrain from tripping you just because you were a female child?"

"I was not a child!" She slammed the book down on the table and sent the parchments fluttering in all directions. With the color riding high on her lovely cheeks, she scooped up the quizzing glass and headed for him, brandishing it like a weapon. "I was a young woman. Almost ten and six. And you cheated that day." She poked him in the chest with the pointed beadwork at the top of the magnifying glass's frame. "You not only hurled that staff between my ankles but also rolled the log."

She jabbed his breastbone again. Hard. "You were a cruel, dismissive churl determined to make my life miserable." She bared her teeth again, her gorgeous dark eyes gleaming with angry, unshed tears. "Get out of my workroom!"

He snatched hold of her wrist before she could stab at him again. When she swung at him with her free hand, he caught that one too, yanked her against his chest, and held both her hands behind her back.

She reared back and puckered, obviously about to spit.

"Do not do it, my lady," he warned, pinning her arms tighter behind her and forcing her closer still. "I did not realize I had made such an enemy of you, and again, I apologize for my boorish behavior that created such deep wounds. But you and I are bound now by royal command. You do not have to love me. Even liking me is not required. But you will treat me with the civility I deserve, and I shall do the same for you. Now, what shall it be between us, Lady Sophie? A constant dredging up of past hurts that neither of us can change, or working together to find the devil determined to destroy you, your mother, and the queen?"

Her chest heaved against him, making it increasingly difficult to concentrate. She smelled of jasmine and hot-tempered, furiously irresistible woman. She was the perfect height for a passionate, blood-warming kiss. He would only have to bend his head the slightest bit to taste those lips that had unleashed so much hatred. With more restraint than he ever knew he possessed, he refrained from closing his mouth over hers and burying his fingers in the silkiness of her wild mane. He shoved her away before his control broke.

"Well, my lady?" he growled. "What shall it be?"

She resettled her hold on the quizzing glass as if trying to decide whether to throw it at him. "We shall work together to capture the fiend, but we will be man and wife in name only." She pointed the glass at him and narrowed her eyes. "Am I quite clear, Sir Nash? You would do well to remember my prowess with a blade. Both at a distance and close range. I assure you, my skills have only improved with age."

Her skills weren't the only thing about her that had improved, but he doubted very much if voicing that observation would be wise at the present moment. He offered a gentlemanly bow instead. "You and I shall be partners, my lady, associates combining forces for the greater good."

She appeared to relax—at least somewhat. But leeriness still shouted from her. The lovely swan did not trust him as far as she could throw him. She remained silent, watching him like a cornered animal.

He blew out a heavy sigh. "I swear to never dishonor you. Nor will I ever cause you any additional misery than I already have. Whether or not you believe it, you may trust me. After all, yours is not the only freedom that was curtailed this day."

Her dark eyes flared wider. "Maybe so, but you gained a title you did nothing to deserve, while I lost everything I worked to protect my entire life. I daresay the borders of your *freedom*, as you call it, will only widen with your advancement to the peerage. After all, you always were one of those men who possessed a very loose definition of fidelity. I feel sure that hasn't changed."

"When I give you my word, Lady Sophie, it is sacred and kept no matter what." Her insult thrummed through him, heating his blood to boiling. "You obviously know little about me."

Her smile chilled him to the bone. "I believe Lady Margaret Shireton would disagree, sir. Did she not find you with Lady Withrington a mere night after you had promised her your love for eternity and beyond? Or was it that once your word served its purpose and unlocked her bedchamber door, it was no longer valid?" The coy tilt of her head both angered and fascinated him. "Does your word spoil after a while, sir? Like a piece of overripe fruit?"

"You—" He cut himself off. The lady had him dead to rights, and he would not insult her intelligence by denying it. He threw up his hands in surrender. "What would you have me say, Lady Sophie? What might I do, other than drop dead at your feet, to make this untenable situation more bearable for you?"

She glared at him. Her irritated pout made him resolve to steal that kiss the next time the opportunity arose. After all, she already hated him.

"Lady Sophie?" he prodded. He would not leave this oppressiveness hanging between them.

"Do not make promises you have no intention of keeping." She jutted her chin upward and took a step closer. "And when you feel the need to wander, as I am sure you will, at least do me the courtesy of being discreet."

"Anything else?" He chose not to tell her that wandering would not be necessary if she would allow him to show her how much they could enjoy each other in bed.

"Pick a house."

"Pick a house?"

"Yes. Wherever you choose to live, I shall live elsewhere, on a different Rydleshire property."

He allowed himself a haughty snort. "I will not agree to that stipulation, my lady. Wherever I live, there you shall also be. I am sure Her Majesty would back me on that requirement in our marriage."

Sophie narrowed her eyes. "You would not dare tell her."

"Oh, I would, my lovely swan. So quickly that it would make that pretty little head of yours spin."

"You are the scaliest cove I have ever had the misery of knowing."

He pulled her into his arms, buried his fingers in her tumble of curls, and tilted her face up to his. "I am also about to be your husband, my lady. Whether or not you like it—and I intend to do my damnedest to make you like it."

He took her mouth and poured his fury into the kiss, reveling in the soft sweetness of her lips. His heart lurched when she responded in kind, clutching him tightly and kissing him back as though starved for his attentions. She molded her lush curves against him, driving him to the point of madness. A groan escaped him before he could stop it. He slid his hands down her back and squeezed her bottom with both hands.

Then she shifted with a quickness that caught him off guard and buried the sharpness of her knee into his groin with a hard thrust that doubled him over and dropped him to the floor.

"Damn it, Sophie!" He rocked on his knees while cupping his tortured man parts. The pain threatened to make him cast up his accounts all over her workroom floor. He coughed and swallowed hard to keep from shitting through his teeth. "What the blazes did you do that for?"

"To remind you that I also far surpassed you in self-defense training, and to underscore that you will never so much as touch a hair on my head without my permission first. Is that understood, Sir Nash Bromley?"

"Understood without a doubt, my lady," he answered with a strained groan.

CHAPTER THREE

S OPHIE STORMED OUT of her workroom, leaving Nash balled up on the floor. It served him right, taking such liberties with her as if she had no choice in the matter. She headed upstairs toward the main entry hall. She had to escape this madness and speak with someone who wouldn't look at her with pity and tell her nothing could be done.

One of her dearest friends, her sister by choice, Frannie, the Duchess of Lionwraith, was not available. She was still in her confinement at Lionwraith Estate in the Lake District after giving birth to twins. But Celia, the Duchess of Hasterton, Sophie's other trusted sister by choice, lived across the way, within easy walking distance of Rydleshire House. Celia would not only provide sound advice but also sympathy. After all, she understood the direness of the situation, since she had been the first daughter of the Sisterhood of Independent Ladies to survive the same sort of troubled waters.

Sophie growled and increased her pace at the thought of their common enemy: *heirs male to the body primogeniture.* For all three of them, only firstborn sons could inherit their fathers' titles, entailments, and wealth. As firstborn daughters, the laws felt they deserved nothing unless their parents' marriage contract provided some negligible income to help them survive until they married well and became the responsibility of their husbands. To overcome the outrageous unfairness of it all, their mothers had not only created the Sisterhood of Independent Ladies as a support system but also fabricated imaginary sons to hold on to everything that should have been rightfully bequeathed to their daughters if only the law allowed.

Rather than depend on the kindness and generosity of others or cast aside their widowhood and capture a husband willing to accept the financial burden of another man's daughter, their mothers built their own empires behind the façades of their imaginary sons. And Sophie's empire had just been snatched away and given to the beastly man who had not only broken her heart all those years ago but had also been too pigheaded at the time to realize it.

"May I be of some assistance, Lady Sophie?" Thornton called out as she barreled past him.

She skidded to a stop. "Yes. If it is still raining, I shall need my umbrella." She glanced down at her bare hands. *Drat it all.* She would have to go upstairs and fetch a pair of gloves too. Heaven forbid anyone should see her outside the house without them. "I don't suppose my gloves from earlier are still down here, are they? Has Marie already taken them up?"

"I shall recover them for you, my lady. And yes, it is still raining. Shall I have Marie select a cloak for you as well, and should I also summon the carriage?"

"No. No carriage. And thank you, Thornton, it would be lovely if you could see to my gloves and a cloak. I shall wait in the library." She didn't want to be discovered fidgeting in the hallway by the abominable Nash or Maman. The parlor would be just as hazardous, but surely the library would be safe. She hurried inside it and thumped the door shut behind her.

"You cannot hide from him," her mother said from somewhere deep within the multi-level room.

Sophie caught a hand to her chest and sagged back against the door. "Maman, really? Today has been filled with enough startling surprises without your adding to them." As the pounding of her heart calmed, she pushed away from the door and squinted around the dim interior. "Where are you, and why are you sitting in the dark? Is this your hiding place as well?"

A heavy sigh came from the vicinity of the windows. It helped Sophie locate her mother's silhouette against the soft gray day outside. "Maman?"

"I am not hiding. Merely thinking. Did you compare the handwriting on each of the letters? Have you discovered any additional information?"

Sophie joined her mother and stared out at the drizzly day. "They all came from the same author, but I cannot discern if the writer was male or female."

"And still no sign of the marked banknotes you included in each of the payments?"

"No. And I was so certain that would be the way to discover the blackmailer. Even Mr. Anderly at the bank thought it a brilliant trap."

"What did young Bromley think?"

Sophie chewed on her lip and wished Thornton would hurry and return with her cloak and gloves so she could make her escape.

"Sophie? He found you, did he not? I had Thornton show him to your workroom."

"Oh, he found me."

"Your tone suggests something ill is afoot. What have you done?" Maman shifted her attention away from the rainy street and pinned it on her. "Answer me, young lady."

"I merely kneed him in his manly pride and left him writhing on the floor."

"Sophie."

The disappointment in her mother's voice made her heart hurt. Maman had always been so proud of her, so loving and supportive, but at the moment, she was not pleased.

"I had to," Sophie said. "He kissed me without my permission."

The dowager exhaled another long-suffering huff and started

massaging her temples. "If he brutishly forced himself upon you, then you should have shot or stabbed him as you have been trained to do. I assume that since you merely took him to the floor, his behavior was not entirely unwelcome." She dropped her hands to her sides and leveled a burning glare on her. "In other words, you set a trap for him."

"I did not."

"Then I shall go shoot him myself."

As her mother stepped away, Sophie caught her by the arm. "Do not shoot him. He might have been slightly provoked. I made him a little angry."

"And so he channeled that anger into a kiss rather than striking at you?"

Sophie recalled the moment, and a hot surge of *oh dear heavens* flashed through her, making her wish she had her fan. Thankfully, the room was dim enough that Maman could not see the furious blush burning across her cheeks. "I believe that is what he did. Yes, indeed. Kissed me in anger."

Maman shook her head, and even in the low lighting, Sophie could tell she rolled her eyes. "Nash Bromley is to be your husband. Do you truly wish to live the rest of your life in a state of constant conflict?"

"The queen had no right to command that!" It was the same thing she had bemoaned all the way home from Kew, but maybe, just maybe, saying it while standing on Rydleshire property might make her mother finally agree. "She took it all and gave it to him. To *him*, Maman. He deserves none of it! All he deserves is what I gave him in my workroom."

"You once loved him."

And there it was. Out in the open between them. Sophie swallowed hard, her throat aching with tears of anger that frustrated her to no end. Why in heaven's name did she always cry whenever she got angry? She sniffed and squared her shoulders. "I was a love-struck child smitten with an older boy. A ridiculous infatuation that was never returned, and thankfully, I outgrew it."

"You cried into your pillow every night," Maman said. "For him. My heart ached as you softly wept his name over and over into the darkness."

"How could you possibly know that?"

Her mother caught hold of her shoulders and turned her. "My darling daughter. My precious late bloomer. The brilliant child fathered by the love of my life. Do you not understand how I noticed your suffering? Your sweet antics to get young Bromley's attention? Your efforts to get him to take the slightest notice of you? I silently watched over you at night from the darkest corners of your room because I was so afraid you would try something foolish you might not recover from."

"I did think of sneaking into his room once," Sophie softly admitted.

Maman nodded. "I know. Why do you think I hastened his training so he could leave?"

Sophie stared down at her fists clenched against her middle. "That was the past. I am a great deal wiser than that awkward girl of almost ten and six. I intend to find a way to either avoid or change this command from the queen."

"You know that cannot be done, my girl. We owe Her Majesty a great deal for all she did for us after you were born. It would be most rude, and also very unbecoming of genuine friends, to ignore her wishes or go against them."

"But—"

"Do you wish Queen Charlotte publicly shamed, or for her to suffer something possibly even worse because you defied her, and the blackmailer got the upper hand?"

Sophie wanted to scream. This was so unfair. So damned unfair. She pulled in a deep breath, held it to the count of five, then allowed it to ease out. "No, Maman. You know I would never wish Her Majesty to suffer because of us."

A light tapping came from the library door, and then it opened. "Your things, Lady Sophie," Thornton said from the doorway.

"Running away, child?" her mother asked, sarcasm dripping from every word.

"I need to speak with Celia." She curtsied and rushed out before Maman shared an observation regarding that.

After donning her gloves and cloak, she stepped out onto the front step and opened her umbrella. At least it was just drizzling enough to make everything unpleasantly damp. She gathered up her skirts and gingerly crossed the way to Celia's townhouse. As soon as she clacked the bronze knocker, the door swung open. "Good afternoon, Gransdon. Is Her Grace receiving today?" she asked before the butler could formally greet her.

The older man hurried her inside with one of his rare smiles. "Her Grace will always receive you, Lady Sophie. Do come in." He took her cloak and umbrella and handed them off to a cheerful maid. "Properly attend to the dampness of Lady Sophie's things, Miss Anna."

The maid dipped a quick curtsy. "Yes, Mr. Gransdon."

He turned back to Sophie and led her toward the library. She wasn't at all surprised. At this hour, Celia was probably reviewing her business ledgers. He tapped on the door, then quietly opened it. "Lady Sophie to see you, Your Grace."

"Sophie! Thank goodness. These columns have grown quite wearisome today." Celia, more formally known as the Duchess of Hasterton, rose from behind a desk littered with papers, ink-stained quills, and open ledgers. She rounded the desk while reaching for both of Sophie's hands. After catching hold of them, she turned and nodded to the butler. "A lovely tea, if you please, Gransdon. Here in the library."

"Yes, Your Grace." He excused himself with the barest tip of his head.

"I was so hoping you would come straight away and tell me what happened." Celia tugged her deeper into the library, leading her to a pair of wingback chairs in front of the hearth. "Was it terribly awful? How was the queen?" Her dark brows arched higher over her ever-widening eyes. "And how is your mother now? Is everything all right? Do tell me all will be well. I am so worried about the both of you, what with those terrible threats."

Sophie waited for her cherished friend to calm down and allow her to get in a word. She folded her hands in her lap and tilted her head while waiting.

"Sorry," Celia said. "I am going on a bit. Aren't I?"

"Just a bit."

"Shall we need brandy with our tea?" The duchess went to the bookcase behind the desk and opened the cabinet to display several decanters.

"Most definitely." Sophie sagged into the depths of the sumptuous leather chair and blew out a very unladylike huff. "Queen Charlotte did not receive us at Kew. She met with us at her private cottage."

"Oh dear." Celia hurried over with a glass of brandy for each of them, then returned to the cabinet and fetched the decanter, setting it on the low, bandy-legged table in front of them.

Sophie fortified herself with a sip, then unleashed another frustrated huff. "Her Majesty has commanded that I marry Sir Nash Bromley by special license. She has also commanded that the fourth earl be proclaimed dead without an heir, and has sworn to order Prinny to bestow the Rydleshire title upon Sir Nash—thereby giving him all the fruits of Maman's and my twenty-five years of endeavors."

"Oh my." Celia stared at her in open-mouthed dismay, then her astonishment shifted to bewilderment. "Sir Nash Bromley. Why do I know that name?"

"Ten years ago," Sophie replied. "When I wrote to you about that insufferable cove who refused to acknowledge my existence."

"Oh dear," Celia repeated.

"Is that all you can say? *Oh my. Oh dear.* I came here for your help! How can I avoid marrying that infuriating whore bird?"

Celia refilled her glass just as Gransdon entered with the tea.

"Set it on the table, Gransdon, thank you."

The butler placed the tray on the table beside the brandy and hurried back out.

"If the queen herself has commanded this, I fear that you have no recourse, dear sister." Celia settled down into the chair beside Sophie but perched on the edge of its seat. "You must admit, doing so will disarm the blackmailer. If he persists in following through with his threats and publicizes the truth about the Rydleshire title, very few would believe it once you have done everything the queen ordered."

Sophie slid her glass to the table, leaned back into the comfortably supportive wing of the chair, and propped her head in her hand. "I never thought you would side against me."

"Do not be precious. I am not siding against you, and you know it. I am merely voicing what you yourself already know to be true. You have been well and truly snared." Celia poured them each a cup of tea and sweetened it with a hearty slosh of brandy. "What does the whore bird say about all this—or does he know yet? And why him? How has he curried such favor with the queen? An earldom given to a mere knight?" She frowned. "You did say he came from landed gentry, did you not? It has been quite some time since I read your letters about him."

Sophie glared at her, willing Celia to stop firing off questions without taking a breath. "Initially, I do not think he wanted the leg-shackling any more than I did. But now that he has had time to ponder it and all he stands to gain, I believe he's quite warmed to the idea." The burn of his kiss still simmered deep within her, demanding she acquiesce without a fight. But she couldn't. He had been so...so *mean* to her all those years ago, when she had loved him with all her heart.

"Well, of course he warmed to the idea." Celia thoughtfully pursed her lips as she held her teacup aloft while cradling its matching saucer in her other hand. "And why did Queen Charlotte choose to gift him with such a prize? Any idea?"

"According to Maman, Sir Nash brilliantly handled some sort

of delicate matter within the royal household some years ago, and ever since, Queen Charlotte thinks him quite the darling.”

“Something to do with Mad King George, I’d wager.” Celia tipped a glance at the decanter. “More brandy? I daresay you deserve it.”

“No. Becoming muddle-headed is something I can ill afford right now.” Sophie gave a sad shake of her head. “Maman refuses to consider anything less than doing exactly as the queen has commanded.”

Celia set her saucer and cup on the table and scowled off into the distance before shifting her attention back to Sophie. “I am so sorry, dear sister. But I do not see a way out of this, especially since your mother insists that it must be done.” With a soft *tsk*, she offered Sophie a sympathetic pout. “Have the years turned him into a disgusting toad?”

“Quite the opposite, in fact. If anything, he is even more handsome than I remembered.”

“Well, there is that, then.” Celia reached over and rested her hand atop Sophie’s. “I am sorry, dear sister. Truly, I am.”

“As am I.” After a disheartened groan, Sophie pushed up from the chair. “I suppose I should return home and attempt to be civil.”

“At least there is the silver lining that this might assist you in catching that fiendish blackmailer.” Celia rang a bell on her desk, then led Sophie into the hallway.

“I suppose.”

Celia kissed her on the cheek. “I should be proud to be a witness for your wedding, and I am sure Elias would as well. Name the date and time, and we shall be there.”

“I will.”

“Promise?”

Sophie forced a smile as she accepted her cloak and umbrella from Gransdon. She turned back to Celia, struggling to keep her smile from faltering. “I promise.”

Her dear friend squeezed her arm. “Take heart, sister. If I

think of absolutely anything that can be done, I shall hurry right over."

With a defeated nod, Sophie headed back outside and opened her umbrella. It was raining harder. An ominous sign, indeed. By the time she made it back inside Rydleshire House, her slippers and stockings were soaked through. She had managed to keep the hem of her dress from getting too muddy, but it was quite soppy as well.

"If anyone asks for me, I have retired for the day, Thornton," she told the butler as she slogged up the stairs. She didn't bother waiting for his standard *yes, my lady*, knowing the man's loyalty to be unquestionable. As soon as she entered her private sitting room, she perched on her favorite chair with the decorative brass inlays and removed the cloyingly wet footwear and hosiery. Marie would have readily come at her call to handle the task, but for now, she simply wished to be alone with her troubled thoughts. Just as she was about to enter her bedchamber, a sharp knock on the sitting room door made her jump.

"Who is it?" she snapped.

"Nash."

A combination of disgust, resentment, and an absolutely unreasonable longing for another kiss surged through her. She started to shout *go away*, but admittedly that would hardly be considered civil. Bracing herself for what she felt certain would be another unpleasant encounter, she strode across the room and yanked open the door, but stood so as to bar his entry.

"How can I help you, sir?" She clenched the door latch so tightly it was a wonder it didn't bend.

He stared at her, the muscles in his square jaw twitching. His focus then shifted to the dripping slippers and stockings she held aloft in her other hand. "Thornton informed me you had retired for the day. Are you unwell?"

"I have enjoyed as much of today as I can possibly stand, Sir Nash," she forced out so sweetly she nearly gagged.

His light blue eyes seemed even icier than before, unblinking and sharply watchful. "You and I must eventually come to an accord if we hope to capture the assailant who caused this day. You do understand that, do you not, Lady Sophie?"

"Contrary to what appears to be your very low opinion of my intelligence, I assure you that I now understand every facet of today. With great futility and dismay, I might add." Before he could comment, she continued, "But I shall strive to be civil, keep your houses in good order, and be a polite hostess to whatever parties your new title requires of you. However, that is all I can promise. No. Forgive me. That is not true at all. I shall also do my very best to capture the infuriating blackmailer, so I might throttle him myself for throwing my life into such an upheaval."

Nash jutted his chin higher and narrowed his eyes. "Then I have your word that a real truce between us is now in force? That there will be no more physical attacks?"

A wicked smile twitched at her mouth, begging to be unfurled. With more control than she realized she possessed, she held it at bay. A knee to a man's pride apparently did wonders to make him fear you. "You have my word, sir. I shall make no more attacks upon your person." She dangled her soggy footwear higher. "Now, if you will excuse me?"

He pushed past her and marched over to the settee beside the window. Defiance and determination shouted from the set of his broad shoulders. "I shall excuse you long enough to sort your"—he flicked a hand at her slippers and stockings as if shooing them away—"your situation, and then I wish to speak with you."

"A gentleman would politely ask, sir, rather than force his way into a lady's room and make demands." His condescending manner tempted her to send him to the floor again. She glared at him, fighting to control her temper.

His brow lightly puckered, whether from bewilderment or frustration, she couldn't quite decide. He apologetically tipped his head and offered her a formal bow. "Forgive me, my lady, if my behavior came across as demanding. I assure you, I did not mean it as such. I beg you to realize that today has placed a strain upon us both."

Deep down inside, the little girl whose heart he had broken so long ago wept uncontrollably because the only reason he was marrying her was to obey the queen and gain a place among the aristocracy. Sophie swallowed hard and gently shushed that poor, foolish child back into the shadows of her memories. She would deal with those silly feelings later because, in truth, she did not wish to marry Nash any more than he wished to marry her. Her past self would do well to realize that and be done with it. Neither accepting nor rebuffing his insulting apology, she went into her bedchamber.

Marie, her lady's maid, emerged from the dressing room. "Good heavens, my lady. Give me those things, and I shall have you dried and in a fresh gown quick as can be. I am sure that wet hemline is most uncomfortable."

"Sir Nash is waiting to speak with me in the sitting room." Sophie rolled her eyes to convey exactly how she felt about that.

The tiny, dark-haired maid who had always reminded Sophie of the woodland imps and fairies from her childhood storybooks shot her a mischievous look. "Shall I order you a bath drawn, my lady? For a long, hot soak after such a trying day?"

"Better not this time. I already kneed him in his pride and dropped him to my workroom floor earlier."

Marie yipped a sharp laugh before clamping her mouth shut to prevent more from escaping. She tried to calm herself but sadly failed. Her shoulders shook as she sputtered with hissing giggles. "I shall make haste, then, to get you sorted in no time at all, my lady."

True to her word, the maid had Sophie changed into a lovely muslin gown in record time. She emerged from the bedroom, hoping her future husband had changed his mind and departed. He had not.

"Shall I ring for something?" she asked, attempting to sound as serene and in control as her mother always did. "Tea or something stronger?"

"Not for my sake, thank you. But if you wish for something, then by all means, do not abstain on my account." He wandered around the room with his hands clasped to the small of his back and the muscles in his jaw flexing as though he was grinding his teeth.

Sophie yanked on the bellpull. This conversation required something stronger than tea. When Thornton opened the sitting room door, she made her wishes known in a single word: "Brandy."

The butler nodded and left.

"Brandy?" Nash repeated, eyeing her as if she had requested poison.

"Do none of your ladybirds ever drink brandy?" She couldn't resist goading him.

He narrowed his eyes at her. "I have no ladybirds—nor will I ever have any ladybirds."

"Never say never, Sir Nash. From what Maman tells me, every man has his needs. Except for priests or monks, of course. Or is it your intention to take a vow of celibacy?"

His expression shifted to one that sent a sudden surge of heat through her and made her swallow hard. "As my wife, you shall fulfill my needs, my lady." He gave her a smile that made her wounded past self swoon. "As I will fulfill yours, I assure you."

"I understand the need to consummate the marriage," she managed to say in an even tone that made her quite proud of her control. "But after that, further"—she flipped a hand—"whatever you wish to call it, shall be unnecessary."

"We shall see." He steered his meandering path to encircle her, keeping his gaze locked on her as he walked.

"Must you pace like a caged animal? Circling me as if I am your prey causes me to wonder if our truce was agreed upon too soon."

He directed her attention to the settee by the window. "Then sit with me, my lady. After all, a true gentleman does not sit while a lady stands."

She took a seat in the chair beside the settee and folded her hands in her lap. With an overly gracious nod at the settee, she smiled. "Have a seat, Sir Nash."

He sat on the end closest to her, perching on the edge of the seat as if ready to spring upon her at a moment's notice. "Do you ever do as you are asked, my fractious swan?"

"It depends on who does the asking."

"As your husband—"

"You are not my husband yet, and might I ask why you called me a *fractious swan*? The fractious part is self-explanatory, but the reference to a swan bewilders me. You have done it more than once now, and I wish you to define it so I might know whether to be insulted."

A daunting look flashed in his eyes, like ripples of lightning warning of a coming storm. She found it both seductive and disconcerting. She was out of her element here. Men were not her expertise.

"Well?" she prodded.

The smile he gave her not only brimmed with mischief but was also dark and dangerously delicious. It sent a series of shivers through her. "Even though I am sure it will nettle you, since everything I say does, I will tell you."

She adopted an aloofness, determined to never allow him to see how he still affected her even after all these years. "Go on."

"All those years ago, you reminded me of an awkward duckling just at the point of getting its feathers. Not ugly, but clumsy and determined for everyone to believe you were grown and ready to fly." He paused and took in a deep breath, possibly bracing himself for a well-deserved slap. "But when I first saw you in the queen's cottage, you took my breath away. The gangly young thing always squawking and causing trouble had transformed into a stunningly beautiful swan who behaved with such regal grace, I struggled not to kneel at your feet."

The awkward duckling, as he had so ungraciously called her, longed to treasure his words about becoming the beautiful swan, as if they were priceless gems mined only for her. But she knew better. She might not be experienced when it came to men, but she was with this one. Never would she believe any compliment falling from his lips. She gave him an unimpressed look. "You should write poetry. Or perhaps romantic stories for ladies to enjoy reading on rainy afternoons."

A knock at the door interrupted them.

"Come in," she called out, noting Nash's irritated expression with no small amount of smug satisfaction.

Thornton entered with a silver tray that contained a decanter of brandy and a pair of glasses. As he set it on the low table in front of them, he proffered a polite nod her way. "Shall I pour, my lady?"

"No, thank you. That will be all."

With the soundless steps of the perfect servant, Thornton left the room and closed the door behind him.

"I know you declined before," she said to Nash, "but would you not care for a drink after all?"

"Yes—and do not be stingy with the pour, my lady."

CHAPTER FOUR

H E HAD UNDERESTIMATED winning her over but would not err in that estimation again. Nash accepted the glass of brandy with a polite nod and relaxed back into the settee, whose delicate design had never been intended for a man his size. It crackled and groaned every time he moved. If the thing didn't collapse into a pile of yellow damask cushions and splintered mahogany kindling, he would be surprised.

The rich, fruity aroma of the drink warned him the spirits were more than likely the highest quality of brandy his modest palate had ever enjoyed. Possibly even cognac, but he was not an expert on such indulgences. He held it on his tongue and breathed it in to savor the flavor while plotting the next skirmish of words with his lovely swan. She might assume she had won the battle, but the lady would do well to realize he intended to win the war.

"Your mother informed me about your placing marked banknotes in the ransoms you paid so far," he said. The reason for his calling her swan had failed to impress her or soften her resolve against him. It was time for another tactic. "Quite brilliant of you."

Sophie acknowledged the compliment with the barest tip of her head, clearly conveying she was not the vain sort who hungered for any form of flattery. "It is not brilliant until it traps our enemy. As of yesterday, no one has attempted to cash them out."

"Were each of the payoffs made at the same place?"

"No." She sipped her brandy while staring off into the distance. "Four different addresses with no similarities at all. The only thing the five letters seem to share is the author."

"I don't suppose the handwriting is familiar to you?" As another sip of brandy warmed his tongue, he feasted his eyes on the delightful flush of color rising along the curve of the lady's lovely throat and across her high cheekbones. The one or two sips of brandy she had taken so far were hardly enough to warrant such a warming to her fair skin. She must have partaken in a drink or two while visiting the Duchess of Hasterton. Lady Rydleshire had also apprised him of Sophie's close friendship with Her Grace.

When she didn't answer, he stretched out his long legs, crossed them at the ankles, and openly stared at her. His swan appeared quite bemused as she gazed off into space with her glass partially lifted to her lips. "Lady Sophie? Have you thought of something?"

"All the letters were sent from a location fifty miles from here. Thornton specifically reported each of them cost the same to receive. The postage was two shillings and fourpence." She blinked and looked at him as if suddenly remembering he was there. "And no, I do not recognize the handwriting. Nor can I discern if the author is male or female."

"So, no suspects?"

"No. And the nature of the beastly thing cripples my resources, and the blackmailer knows it. I cannot very well make use of the Bow Street Runners or any of my private investigators. They all believe my fictitious brother Solomon is quite real."

"Solomon?"

Sophie huffed a humorless laugh that made his heart go out to her. "My father's name was David, so Maman felt the name *Solomon* quite fitting." She set her glass on the table and frowned down at it. "After my father's death, Maman became quite pious. I believe she can still quote several chapters of the Old Testament word for word. Especially the ones about King David." She pressed a hand to her forehead and bowed her head. "I really am quite tired, Sir Nash. Might we continue this conversation at another time?"

He shifted to rise from the settee, but the thing gave way with a groaning crash, just as he had feared it might. "Bloody hell!" He slammed to the floor atop the cushions that had thankfully protected his arse from any sharp stabs of broken wood.

Sophie snorted with laughter. "Oh my heavens, are you all right?"

He stared up at her, then couldn't help but laugh himself. "A fitting tribute to today. Would you not agree?"

"As long as you are not injured." She pushed the low table bearing their refreshments out of the way and moved closer, reaching down to assist him. "Here. Let me help you. Who knows how many splinters are waiting to impale you?"

"Thank you, my lady, but I can manage. I do not wish to pull you down on top of me." Well, he did, but he was now quite convinced that he had a great deal of reparation to do before that delight would be his. Gingerly, he shoved himself up from the mess, then stared back down at it. "I apologize for destroying your sofa. Apparently, I am more solid than I realized."

"Do not apologize." She wrinkled her nose at the ruined settee. "I never liked that horrid thing. It was a gift from one of Maman's admirers from King Louis's court. She had it placed in here because it reminded her of that odious little man who always reeked of soured wine, pungent garlic, and rotted onions."

Nash tried to be inconspicuous and take a sniff of his own scent to ensure the lady would not find him just as offensive as the malodorous Frenchman. He smelled of leather, perhaps a bit of wet horse, and then, thankfully, the clean citrus and sandalwood of the soaps and oils he had used this morning. He nudged the toe of his boot against the broken leg of the sofa and offered her a smile. "I assume your mother rebuffed the man gently, since he was one of King Louis's courtiers?"

Sophie pursed the supple bow of her tempting mouth into a thoughtful grimace. "I believe she convinced the king to have the man executed, but I am uncertain about that." Her grimace became a proud smile as she tipped a nod at the ruined bit of furniture. "Never underestimate or anger Maman."

"Duly noted." He studied her for a long moment, realizing this was the first time the two of them had managed a conversation that was neither stilted nor filled with animosity. "This is nice, my lady."

Her reddish-blonde brows drew closer, turning her expression into a lovely furrow of confusion. He rather liked that look on her. It somehow made her endearingly quizzical, like a kitten trying to decide whether to pounce. "I have confused you," he said.

She twitched the slightest shrug. "I must admit, you have. What are you referring to as *nice*?"

"Us." He motioned at the two of them. "At this particular moment. Talking to each other without it becoming a battle."

"Oh." She stared at him. The uncomfortable tension returned to the set of her shoulders, and her chin shot back to its defiant angle.

Damn and blast it all. He had ruined the moment by drawing attention to it. He could be such a fool at times. "I am sorry, Lady Sophie."

Leeriness darkened the velvety brown richness of her eyes. "And for what are you apologizing, might I ask? I already told you that piece of furniture would not be missed."

"I am apologizing for everything. For the way I hurt you in the past with my boyish stupidity. For unintentionally usurping the world you and your mother created and cared for since your birth. I am not sorry for kissing you, but I should not have done it without your permission, and I swear I shall never do so again. Kiss you without your permission, that is. I would very much like to kiss you again as much as you will allow me to." The way she caught her hand to her throat made him ache to reach out and take her into his arms, but he didn't.

"I am not so certain I can trust you," she said so softly it was as though she spoke more to herself than him. "You broke my heart all those years ago—without even trying. Or caring that you did so, for that matter."

"You were the daughter of my mentor, and please do not take offense when I say that at the time you still seemed to be a child. At least, to me you did. I saw you as a mere slip of a girl not yet old enough for a man's attentions. I respected you and your mother too much to insult either of you with what I felt would be unseemly behavior toward you."

She stared down at the floor, slowly shaking her head. "I was a horridly late bloomer. Maman used to try to console me by saying she had been the very same." She lifted her head to settle a narrow-eyed gaze upon him. "But you were still insufferably mean. Teasing me. Calling me names whenever I bested you in training."

"You irritated the bloody hell out of me," he said before thinking better of it. "How was I expected to act when a mere child made me look like an incompetent fool in front of my peers?"

"I suppose that would be rather uncomfortable." The leeriness in her eyes turned to mischievous pride. "But as the older of us, and a gentleman, you should have been more mature. Handled the situation better."

"Yes, well… I should have done a lot of things differently in my past." He resettled his stance, bracing himself. "That is why I apologized. Do you accept it, my lady, and can we move forward and leave the past behind us where it belongs?"

She studied him while working her clasped hands together, as though kneading a tiny ball of dough between her palms. Eight loud, distinctive pops sounded off as she flexed each of her fingers at the knuckles. She wrinkled her nose. "Sorry. Terrible habit I have whenever I am thinking."

An amused snort escaped him. "That is not very *countess-like* behavior."

She rolled her eyes. "You sound like Maman."

"You are avoiding giving me an answer, my lady. Do you accept my apology?" He eased closer, close enough to breathe in her delectable scent of jasmine, and this time, not a furious woman but one who was even more delicious and desirable.

She narrowed her eyes again, but her expression held no animosity. "I accept your apology. At least for now. We shall see if I can learn to trust you."

"I hope you can. I much prefer us to be friends rather than enemies."

"Friends," she repeated.

Was that disappointment in her tone, or was he imagining it? Had he erred and said the wrong thing again? He took her hand, praying he wasn't botching this as well. "Friends at first. And with any luck, and some time spent together, maybe more."

She allowed her hand to remain in his for a moment longer, then gently slid it out of his grasp. "We shall see."

"I understand you planned to retire for the evening and dine here in your rooms, but might you consider dining with me instead?" He felt compelled to nurture this tenuous bond they had formed. He wished to strengthen it.

She tortured him with another long moment of pensive silence, then finally eased his mind with the slightest inclination of her head. "I think that would be very nice, Sir Nash. I will dine with you."

"And would you do one thing more for me?"

She arched a brow, daring him to ask.

"Would you please call me Nash?"

"Yes—but that is the last request I will grant you for now." She leaned toward him, a thrilling wickedness in her smile. "Nash."

The way his name rolled off her tongue made him pull in a sharp intake of air. What he wouldn't give to hear her cry out his name while she lay beneath him sprawled across his pillows. His body agreed, hardening immediately. He offered her a gracious bow. "Thank you, Lady Sophie."

"Sophie," she corrected him as she poured them both another brandy. She handed him his glass, then lifted hers in a toast. "To prosperous alliances."

He touched his glass to hers. "To prosperous alliances."

"By the way, my dear friend Celia"—she interrupted herself with a shake of her head—"the Duchess of Hasterton has offered to be our witness and also volunteered her husband for the post as well." She cringed and stared down into her glass. "I wonder how long it will take for the special license to be delivered to us."

"With the queen behind it, I am surprised we have not already received it." He set his glass down on the table and offered her his arm. "Shall we return to your workroom and have another look at those letters?"

To his delight, she accepted his offer and allowed him to escort her into the hallway. But then she slowly shook her head. "I doubt you will find anything. I promise, I have studied those insufferable things backward and forward and still have made no headway regarding who wrote them or their origin. All I know is that they each required the same amount of postage one would pay for a letter coming from fifty miles away in any direction. Whoever this is, they are very cunning."

"Did the same post office collect each letter? Do they all bear the same inked stamp?"

"No. A different post office processed each of them."

"Quite cunning, indeed."

Thornton met them at the bottom of the stairs with a silver tray bearing a single large envelope. "The royal seal, my lady," he said in an ominous whisper.

She stepped back as if the parcel held a poisonous viper. "You open it," she told Nash. "Although I am quite certain we both know what's inside."

"Yes. I am sure it's the special license." He opened the envelope and removed the contents. "It is, and a letter from Her Majesty."

Sophie groaned and dismissed Thornton with a nod. "Now what does Her Royal Highness command?"

Nash squinted at the page. The flowery writing of the queen's secretary was not the easiest to decipher. He snorted out a deep huff before catching himself and stopping it. Her Majesty left nothing to chance. "Queen Charlotte has graciously invited us to have the ceremony at Kew, so she might enjoy it in the comfort of her own surroundings and help us celebrate our union."

"In my eye," Sophie growled. "She wants the marriage there to make sure we go through with it."

He offered her a sympathetic nod. "I believe you have the right of it there." He tapped the gilded edge of the parchment. "And tomorrow is the date she has chosen."

"Tomorrow?"

The panic in her tone was disappointing, yet understandable. As a military man and then a knight, he might not initially like the orders he was given, but he had learned long ago to accept them, make the best of them, and move on. While he had not planned on marrying anytime soon, now that he found himself royally betrothed to this fiery beauty, he was ready to see it done. In fact, he rather looked forward to it.

"Tomorrow." He tapped on the letter again. "With the queen and her daughters, Princess Augusta and Princess Sophie, as our witnesses."

"And Maman, of course."

"I am sure that goes without saying. Shall we find her and let her know? She was in the parlor before I came up to speak with you." He folded the papers, slid them back inside the envelope, and tucked it inside his waistcoat.

With her scowl locked on something off in the distance, Sophie worked her fingers as though trying to make her knuckles crackle once more.

"Sophie." He reached out and gently touched her arm. "We

cannot avoid this, but everything will be all right. I will make it so."

She turned her scowl on him, then dropped her hands to her sides. "Do not make promises about things you have no power over. I am not one of those ridiculous women who think every word that falls from a man's lips is as reliable as pure gold."

He caught hold of her hand and kissed it. "Then let me re-word my statement so I am quite clear. I shall do everything in my power to make our future together not only bearable but also pleasant." Still holding her hand, he stroked his thumb across the silkiness of her fingers that were tightly grasping his. "I swear my vow is as reliable as pure gold."

"There you are," the dowager countess called out as she emerged from the front parlor. "Thornton said an envelope had arrived bearing Queen Charlotte's seal?"

"Thornton gossips worse than the maids," Sophie grumbled as she snatched her hand out of Nash's grasp and tucked it behind her back.

"Thornton merely keeps me informed."

Slightly amused that Sophie didn't wish her mother to witness the intimacy of his holding her bare hand, Nash pulled the envelope from his waistcoat and held it out to the dowager. "The special license Her Majesty promised, as well as a command for the ceremony to take place at Kew. Tomorrow. In her presence, along with Princess Augusta and Princess Sophie."

Lady Rydleshire did not appear surprised. "Queen Charlotte has never been known for her patience or for leaving a plan to chance."

"Sophie's and my sentiments exactly."

The lady eyed them both as though sizing them up, her expression thoughtful and something more. Something Nash couldn't quite identify.

"I find myself overly tired today," she said. "You will forgive me if I dine in my rooms? Especially since tomorrow is now to be quite full as well. I find I need more quiet moments to reflect and ponder things, especially with the onset of the recent threats."

"Are you unwell, Maman?" Sophie drew closer to her mother as if ready to defend her against the world.

"I am merely tired, sweet child." The dowager touched her daughter's cheek. "And I need time to think. Do not worry."

Nash felt like an intruder. The close bond the pair of women shared was one he had never known with his family. His mother had died when he was quite young, and his father still behaved as though the very sight of his only son filled him with revulsion.

"Good evening to you both," Lady Rydleshire said. The woman was as beautiful as ever, even though a bit of silver highlighted her reddish-gold hair. She gave him a pointed look. "Take good care of her this evening, young Bromley. She has a great deal on her mind, and I do not wish her overset any more than she already is. Is that understood?"

"I shall take good care of her, my lady." He underscored the promise with a formal bow, then moved to Sophie's side and subtly rested his hand on the small of her back.

To his surprise, she didn't move away from his touch. Instead, she clasped her hands to her chest, almost curling into herself as she drew closer to him while watching her mother ascend the stairs.

"This has been so very hard on her," Sophie said, her words laced with worry.

"I am sure it has been difficult for both of you." He gently turned her toward the workroom, then halted. No. The black-mailer could wait. Sophie had endured enough this day. "Come. Let us sit in the parlor and speak of other things before dinner. Shall we?"

She nodded and slowly headed that way. "Poor Thornton. We have divided on him. That sometimes sends him into a spin."

"From the man's expression when he brought you that letter, I am sure he will understand." Nash glanced around the parlor, gauging the French-style furniture with a critical eye. He did not wish to land on the floor again. The light-colored wood of the tables, chairs, and settees appeared sturdier, even though the legs curved inward and ended in feet shaped like a lion's paws.

"Maman selected this furniture," Sophie said as if reading his mind. Her smile somehow seemed sad. "She said it was much like a woman, delicate and lovely in appearance but strong enough to withstand whatever comes its way." She lowered herself into a chair near the front window and gazed outside. "I fear I shall not be fit company this evening, Sir Nash. If you wish to rescind your invitation to dine together, I understand completely."

"Nash." He selected the chair closest to her. "And I find your company—"

She looked at him when he paused and smiled. "You cannot finish that sentence, can you?"

He rose and knelt at her side. "But I can, my lady. I find your company as exciting as a stormy sea and as intoxicating as the brandy we shared in your sitting room." With the lightest touch, he stroked a single fingertip across the back of her hand. "But you do not like or trust flowery declarations. So I find myself at a loss when attempting to speak from the heart."

She stared down at him, not quite frowning, but only just. "Why are you doing this?"

"Doing what, my lady?"

"Trying to win me. It is unnecessary. I am yours, whether or not either of us wish it." She flicked a hand as if shooing him away. "Courting. The flirtatious games. The *flowery declarations*, as you call them, are all unnecessary." Her mouth tightened. "We have received our sentence, Nash, and the queen has never extended clemency to condemned prisoners."

"Hard words from such a delicate swan." He rose and returned to his chair, sensing he had lost ground, and she had slid back to her original low opinion of him. "Prisoners often find their sentence easier to bear if they make the best of things. In fact, it often saves their sanity. Helps them survive."

She deflated with a heavy sigh and bowed her head. "I am sorry, Nash. I warned you I was not fit company this evening."

"What can I do to make this easier for you?" He ached to ease her turmoil, make her see him as he was now: a gentleman who admired and respected her. No more was he the insolent arse of his youth. Or, at least with her, he would do his level best not to be. "Tell me how I can help you, Sophie. I truly wish to."

She slowly shook her head and straightened in the chair. "There is nothing you can do. I must come to terms with this in my own way. My own time." Her focus shifted back to the window, and she narrowed her eyes as though studying something off in the distance. "Maman came to terms with her circumstances when Papa died, and I was born a girl rather than the son she needed. She never complained. Not once. I need to be like her."

"Do you still ride?"

"What?" She turned and eyed him as if she thought him suddenly off-kilter.

"Do you still ride?" Changing the subject and catching her off guard was the only thing he knew to do. As best as he could remember, all those years ago, she had loved riding and excelled at it.

"I do." She flicked a quick look at the rain-streaked window. "Weather permitting, of course. Why?"

"I remember you always seemed happiest whenever you were riding." He couldn't help but laugh. "It was also when you were the least annoying."

"I can still be annoying, if necessary," she warned.

"Of that, I have no doubt." He settled deeper into the chair and patted the armrests. "Quite solid, thank goodness. Just as you said." That won him a smile from her—a genuine smile.

Thornton entered the room. The stoic man appeared decidedly unhappy as he hurried to Sophie's side and held out a small silver tray bearing a note. "Forgive me, my lady. Another has arrived."

"Another what?" Nash rose from his chair.

"Are you certain it is from them?" she asked the butler while staring at the small letter as if it were about to burst into flames. She clutched her fists to her breasts as though determined not to touch it.

"The same postage was required to accept it, and the handwriting appears much the same as the others." He stood there, partially bent and holding out the tray, waiting for her to pick it up. "Would you prefer Sir Nash examined it?"

"Most definitely," she whispered. "I fear this day has drained me of all courage and determination. Forgive me."

Nash snatched up the letter. "Thank you, Thornton. By the way, Lady Sophie and I would like to dine in here, since it will just be the two of us this evening. It is my understanding that Lady Rydleshire intends to dine in her rooms."

"Yes, Sir Nash. I shall see to everything personally." The butler bowed and hurried out, closing the set of double doors behind him.

Sophie rose and stood beside him, peering down at the note in his hands. "Thornton was correct. The handwriting is the same. Well, go on, then. Open it."

Opening the intricately folded paper that was tucked into itself, Nash clenched his teeth as the single sentence jumped out at him. *I know your plan, and it will fail.*

At Sophie's strangled gasp, he caught her to his side and supported her. "Let me help you to the settee."

"I…I am all right." But she clung to his jacket as he led her to a nearby small sofa and settled onto it with her. She didn't release her grip on his coat, just thumped her fist against him. "How can they possibly know? Is it someone in our household? Someone close to the queen?"

"The queen requested the special license, which would require both our names. But those outsiders would not know about the Rydleshire title or what she planned regarding that." He silently listed everyone who might be privy to the queen's intentions.

"Servants hear everything," she whispered.

He refolded the letter. "Yes, they do. But to travel to a post office fifty miles away and make it back here without their absence being noticed would be quite the feat."

"And we only found out today what we were expected to do. How could the blackmailer discover everything so quickly?" She not only popped every finger but also cracked the knuckles of her thumbs.

If the situation weren't so dire, he would have playfully scolded her. Instead, he ignored her nervous habit. "It has to be someone in the queen's household," he said. "There is no other answer."

CHAPTER FIVE

SOPHIE SET THE quill aside and stared down at her signature on the parish registry that the queen had so astutely commanded the clergyman to bring along. It was done. She turned away, the vows she had just taken still ringing in her ears.

Thank heavens Nash had held her unconventionally close during the ceremony, or she would have surely swayed off balance and toppled over in a dead swoon. She swallowed hard. That thought shamed her. A swoon. Indeed. She, who feared nothing, succumbing to such a ridiculous spell of weakness. She was tempted to snort at the very idea, but didn't dare, since Maman and the queen stood close enough to hear. But in all fairness, she had every right to faint if she so wished it. Not only was she now married to the man she had once loved beyond all imagining, but someone in this very room might be the blackmailer threatening them all. How had her carefully orchestrated life spun out of control so quickly?

"You are even lovelier today than you were yesterday. How is that possible, my swan?" Nash's warm breath tickled across her bare shoulder. His tender kisses along her nape sent a series of shivers rippling through her. "You need to breathe," he whispered, "or I shall be forced to sweep you up into my arms to prevent you from injuring yourself when you wilt to the floor."

"I am fine," she muttered. Her maid had tied her corset so tightly that her breasts nearly touched her chin. If he dared lift or jostle her, she would surely spill over the top of her gown. The revealing creation in her favorite shade of violet was shot through with silver threadwork that formed lilies, vines, and an abundance of delicate foliage. Tiny pearls encrusted the lace around the neckline that exposed her shoulders. The same stiff, pearly lace created the band around the empire waistline and hemmed the short, puffy sleeves.

She should not have chosen this garment from her wardrobe of finery that was worn to only the most formal of occasions. The abundance of lace stiffened with pearls and silver threadwork tickled and scratched as if she'd fallen into a thicket of nettles. She subtly rolled her shoulders, trying to soothe her poor, itching flesh with a surreptitious wriggle. The uncomfortable gown also weighed as much as a small pony, and she couldn't draw in a deep breath to save her soul because of the tightness of her infernal stays. The physical discomfort only worsened the disquieting uneasiness that she was now married to a man who had never wanted her.

"Sophie?" He lightly kissed her shoulder again.

"Stop distracting me!" she hissed through clenched teeth. "I am trying to espy the blackmailer." She partially turned and shot him a glare she hoped he would take to heart. "As you should be doing, my dear husband. Remember Maman's training?"

The smile he gave her triggered another tingling shiver that pooled into a longing ache in her center. *Merciful heavens!* Why did he have to look at her that way?

"*My dear husband,*" he repeated in a low, seductive rumble. "I rather like the sound of that."

"It thrills me to no end that you enjoy being leg-shackled," she said, without looking back at him again. She couldn't concentrate because of his present behavior. The man had no shame. He should be alert and looking for the scheming devil that created this mess, not putting on a show for Maman and the queen.

He gently spun her around to face him. "Those in this room

are the queen's most trusted. Not only did she vouch for them after we shared the latest note with her, but I met them all years ago." He arched a brow. "Her Highness is quite shrewd, I assure you." He tucked a finger under her chin and forced her to look at him, something that infuriated her to no end and made her twitch to slap his hand away. She was not a child. How dare he treat her that way?

"Think about it, Sophie," he continued. "The blackmailer is a coward working in the shadows to benefit from everyone else's fears. No matter what rumors they attempt to spread, we have completed the first step in disproving them and preventing a scandal." He leaned in closer, making her heart pound harder. "And it must have occurred to you that the best way to oust someone such as our blackmailer is to act as though we couldn't care less about what they have threatened. It angers them because we dare them to prove they will do what they say." He brushed the lightest of kisses across her cheek, yet it was powerful enough to steal every breath from her lungs. "Play the part, my precious swan," he whispered against her ear. "Do not allow them to control the situation."

"I knew the two of you would suit," Queen Charlotte proclaimed as she swept up to them in a stunning gown of gold and shimmering silver. "You may thank me now."

"We are ever so grateful, Your Majesty." Sophie curtsied low and kept her gaze downcast, struggling not to choke on the lie. Yes, she had once loved Nash, but it was far too late to indulge in those feelings now. She had to maintain control.

"Indeed we are," Nash echoed with an obedient bow. "Most grateful."

The queen beamed at them. "You may show me your appreciation by naming your first daughter Charlotte. You have my blessing to do so."

Sophie forced a smile that made her cheeks ache. "Thank you so much, Your Majesty. It will be our delight."

"Charlotte Lavinia does have a ring to it," the dowager countess said as she joined them. "We must take our leave now, my dear children. Our beloved queen grows weary and should seek her rest." She cast a concerned glance at the monarch's slightly swollen hands. "Thank you so much for today, Your Majesty. Your kindness and generosity are more appreciated than you could ever imagine."

Queen Charlotte acknowledged the dowager's sentiments with a regal tip of her head, then glanced around and motioned for them all to move in closer. "The announcement will happen tomorrow," she said in a hushed tone. "Edwards has seen to it, as well as to the erection of the headstone in Calais where the *fourth earl* wished to be laid to rest. A coffin of an appropriate weight to be convincing shall be sent there, guarded by two of my best, of course." The queen lowered her voice even more. "A carriage accident brought on by highwaymen giving chase is how the poor earl died." She cast another covert glance at the servants tending to the elaborate tea she had provided, then turned to Nash. "You will receive Georgie's proclamation naming you the new Earl of Rydleshire week after next in a letter bearing his seal and mine. Even though the family will still officially be in mourning, there is no need to wait to announce the new earl because of the possibility of there being another heir. All will be complete then, and the blackmailer can say whatever they desire."

"I still mean to capture the devil," Sophie couldn't resist saying.

Maman cleared her throat. "Thank you again, Your Majesty. Please try to rest now, my precious queen. I worry about you."

Queen Charlotte reached out and took the dowager countess's hands. "You are one of the few who does indeed worry about me for me and not for what I can do for them. Your friendship is priceless to me, Nia."

"As is yours to me, dear lady," Sophie's mother whispered.

Sophie realized Nash was gently tugging for her to join him and give the two women what little privacy a room full of servants might grant them. She hooked her arm through his and released a heavy sigh that did nothing to ease her tension as they stepped out into the sunshine. "Queen Charlotte is not well."

"No. She is not."

"Maman has a wedding supper planned for us. Nothing large, mind you. A small something for those not invited to join us here at Kew. Friends whose company we enjoy and those we must invite to anchor our marriage in Society's minds." Sophie popped her knuckles, then cast a quick glance back to make sure her mother wasn't close enough to hear what she had done.

"It would be wiser for you to check for your mother's where-abouts *before* making that hideous noise rather than after. You do realize that, do you not?" He grinned down at her.

She found his lightheartedness difficult to understand, then realized the probable cause. In a short time, the man would be an earl, a member of the aristocracy—a rare advancement in status for someone who was not a member of the royal family. As much as she did not want to believe that was the real motive for his *making the best of things*, as he kept telling her to do, it had to be a factor. After all, he had never loved or wanted her as she had wanted him. Why would he do so now?

"Sophie?" His amusement vanished, replaced by gentle con-cern as he took her gloved hand and held it between both of his. "Many marriages have started far less amicably than ours, my swan. Do not worry. At the very least, we will be lifelong friends."

She didn't want another friend. She wanted to be loved and adored the way Maman still loved and adored Papa. With a forced smile, she offered him a subtle warning. "I have heard it said that swans can be very vicious creatures."

"They are also known to be true to their mates for life."

"A pity the same cannot be said for people. Especially men. I am sure Lady Margaret Shireton would agree with me, as well as several other ladies of your acquaintance."

He released her hand and stepped back, making her immedi-ately regret the childish retort. It was too late now. After all, there was no such thing as un-ringing a bell.

She turned and scowled at the door. "Where is Maman? She was the one urging us to leave the queen in peace." She shaded her eyes and glanced skyward, then gathered up her full skirts and stepped up to the carriage. "Do help me inside, Nash. The sun is quite warm, and I left my parasol at home."

"As you wish, my lady."

All friendliness and good humor had left him, and it was her fault. She clenched her teeth, scolding herself for allowing the situation to turn her into an ugly, waspish little wretch. Her irritation with herself swelled to epic proportions when he sat in the seat opposite her rather than beside her.

"Nash?"

He glared at her with the barest level of civility. "Yes?"

She chided herself without mercy. She hated apologizing, but he deserved it. "I am sorry I offended you. That was not my intent."

"Indeed, it was your intent, Sophie. Pray, do not further insult me by feigning otherwise and expecting me to accept it." He dismissed her with a frustrated shake of his head and shifted his focus to something outside the window. The resentment in his tone made the scolding sting even more.

She had earned that dressing-down, and now needed to find a way to make amends.

The sunlight streaming in brought out the coppery hues in the autumnal gold of his stylishly cropped hair and enhanced the strong, angular cut of his jaw. The man had aged so well. Too well. His youthful softness of ten years ago had become the captivating hardness of the present. He was breathtaking in military dress, resplendent with gold braid and medals, his sword, and highly polished Hessians.

She clasped her hands in her lap, fighting not to work her fingers and make her knuckles pop. She could not condemn him for his irritation. After all, she deserved it. What was it he always said? *Might as well make the best of things?* How might she make the best of this? She leaned forward and peered at the palace's doorway. Perhaps if she changed the subject, his ruffled feathers might slowly smooth back down. "Should we go back inside and see if everything is all right?"

"No."

A frustrated huff slipped free of her before she could stop it.

He tore his glare from the window and locked eyes with her. "Forgive me. No, *my lady.*"

"That is not why I huffed. I am frustrated because I allowed my foolish emotions to take control of my tongue for a mere second, and now we are at odds even though you have been nothing but thoughtful and kind to me since our reunion." The longer she thought about the entire situation, the more overset she became. "But you must admit, it is only natural for me to believe that the primary reason you are being so infuriatingly pleasant is that, in a short time, you will ascend to the aristocracy as an earl. Quite the feat for a knight. Would you not agree?"

He stared at her, slowly narrowing his eyes as if homing in on his prey. His anger made his glare even frostier.

"Well, why else would you be so happy today?" she asked when he remained silent. *In for a penny, in for a pound.* "It is certainly not because you are thrilled to be my husband. You rarely noticed me when we were younger, and when you did, it was only to be mean and try to shoo me away. You yourself admitted you found me dreadfully annoying."

"Why can you not let go of the past? We are no longer those two people."

"You hurt me."

"And I have apologized. Repeatedly," he growled. "What more can I do? I cannot take us back in time and do things differently to change your memories or your low opinion of me."

"Bellowing is not necessary." She popped her knuckles.

"Apparently, it is," he said, still speaking quite loudly. "Because you act as if you have never heard me say any of this before."

"Deny that you are pleased to become an earl," she dared him.

"Bloody hell, Sophie! You cannot be that deluded. What the blazes do I know about being an earl? From everything I ever observed, I want no part of your Polite Society. I wanted a career in the army, and yet, because I managed to calm the king one fateful afternoon, here I am in the bloody thick of things, right where I never wished to be. My father's saying is undeniably true."

"What saying?"

"No good deed goes unpunished."

She had never seen this side of him before. Vulnerable. Uncertain. Anxious. She caught her bottom lip between her teeth and chewed on it, uncertain what to say to repair the damage she had done.

"I am sorry," she finally whispered.

He remained silent, his jaw flexing as he resumed staring out the window.

"I am not an expert either when it comes to Polite Society," she continued. "I snort when I laugh, crack my knuckles when I am nervous or thinking, and would rather be riding than enduring an evening at Almack's."

He still did not speak. Nor did he look at her.

She didn't know what else to say, so she returned to watching the doorway for her mother. "For all the good it will do, I will try to help you all I can. Maman will too. She likes you very much. Always has."

Ever so slowly, he pulled his gaze from whatever he had been staring at and settled it on her. "You truly felt the only reason I was doing my best to be pleasant today was because of the title?"

"I did."

A frustrated groan rumbled free of him, and he sagged forward, propped his elbows on his knees, and scrubbed his face with both his hands. "You and I appear to have a great deal to overcome, my lady."

"It would seem so." She tucked the fullness of her gown's voluminous skirt tighter against her and patted the seat. "Please sit beside me. I shall do my very best to be the devoted swan rather than the vicious one."

He lifted his head and studied her with such weariness that her heart ached for him. "Will you also do your best to remember that I will never intentionally do anything to cause you harm or pain?"

"I will." She patted the seat again and offered him what she hoped he would take as a smile from the heart. "You have been extremely patient and kind, while I have…not been. But I shall do better. I promise."

"Forgive me, my lady, but I will believe that when I see it." He switched seats and settled down beside her.

While she did not appreciate his candor, she understood it and refused to take offense. She had been insufferably mean to him today. "I shall prove it to you, my dearest cob. Just wait and see."

"Dearest cob?"

"Of course." She couldn't resist a teasing smile. "A male swan is a cob."

The way he arched his brow made him even more handsome. "Then that would make you my precious pen."

"Indeed, it would."

The carriage door opened, preventing further reparations as Maman stuck her head inside. "Her Majesty has requested my company for a while longer. Go along home and ensure that Thornton and Mrs. Thornton have everything ready for this evening. I am sure they will, but they appreciate it when we consult with them. I shall be along as soon as Her Majesty tires of me."

"We shall send the carriage back for you," Nash promised.

The dowager accepted with a nod, then waved. "On with you now, my children."

"Goodbye, Maman." Sophie offered a less-than-enthusiastic

wave out the window as the carriage lurched into motion. Something was amiss, and she neither liked nor appreciated being left wondering what it might be.

She ran her gloved finger under the vicious lace of her sleeve, trying to soothe her poor, itching flesh. "If I ever mention pearl-encrusted lace to the modiste ever again, remind me of the torture of this dress."

Nash set her ablaze with a devilish smile. "Never fear, my lady. I shall endeavor to have you out of that dress as quickly as possible once we reach home."

She found herself at a loss for words. Apparently, his ill mood had vanished, and he had heartily returned to his *make the best of things* demeanor. An astonishingly hot flush ran through her, and she knew she must appear as red as a beetroot. Without a thought of what it might look like, she ran her finger behind the lace along her low neckline. "Oh my. I am suddenly quite warm, and that makes me itch even more."

"Shall I help you with that, my precious pen?"

"Uhm…here? In the carriage? Absolutely not, but thank you—dear cob." She fanned herself with her hand, wishing she had brought along her sturdiest fan. Surely he had not meant to… That they would… Surely not here in the carriage, where anyone bothering to glance into the windows as they passed through the streets of London could see?

She swallowed hard and stole a glance his way. He *had* meant to right here in the carriage. She could see it in his eyes. "Oh my," she repeated on a breathy exhale.

The rumble of his deep, satisfied laugh chased all lingering doubts from her mind. He lifted her hand for a kiss, then paused and frowned down at it. "The first thing I shall do when we are alone in our bedchamber is rid you of these annoying gloves that bar me from the sweetness of your silky skin." A thrilling hunger smoldered in his tone, making her catch her breath again. In a voice husky with even more intent, he continued, "Of course, the sweetness of your hands is merely a start. I fully intend to taste every delicious inch of you."

"But we…we have guests coming. R-remember?" Since when had she developed such an embarrassing stutter? He would surely think her the silliest of ninnies.

He boldly traced his fingertip along her neckline, stroking her flesh and making her completely forget the scratchy lace. "Our guests will not arrive till supper. That leaves us plenty of time to acquaint ourselves with each other and forge a much stronger truce between us." He cupped her cheek and leaned closer, trapping her in the intensity of his gaze. "I want you so enamored with our present that you never allow the past to come between us ever again." His fingers slid up into her hair as he leaned in and kissed her with such tenderness that she prayed he would never stop.

She almost cried out when he lifted his head and looked down into her eyes again.

"We could be very happy together, Sophie," he whispered. "Would that be such a terrible thing?"

She reached up and touched his cheek, losing herself in the brilliance of his eyes that were no longer icy. "Happiness would be quite nice," she said. "Happiness for both of us."

As he took her mouth once more, he slid his arms around her and gathered her close. The hunger in his kiss claimed her heart and soul, rekindling every fierce yearning she had ever possessed for him. It was everything she had ever dreamed a kiss from him would be and even more.

The intensity of the feeling terrified her. If she opened her heart to him, she would be even more vulnerable than that silly, wishful girl of ten years ago.

"Let it go, Sophie," he whispered across her lips as if reading her mind.

She pulled back and stared at him. "How did you know?"

"You tensed, my precious swan. Almost recoiled within your-self. Like a soldier raising a shield to deflect the attack."

"I find the fact that you read me so easily on just the second day of our reacquaintance quite disturbing." She ran her thumb along his jawline, enjoying the way the barely emerged stubble caused her glove to drag. The satin would be irreparably roughened, but she didn't care. "I do not recall your being so astute when Maman tested us on our lessons."

"Shall I share something with you that I am sure you will find most amusing?"

She slid her hands downward and rested them on his chest, enjoying that he made no move to release her from his embrace. "Please do."

"Your mother intimidated the bloody hell out of me."

If not for the solemness of his expression, she would accuse him of mocking her. But the look in his eyes gave testament to his every word.

"Maman always instructed us with the greatest patience. How could you find her intimidating?"

"Her reputation preceded her. Not only that, but she always seemed to know what we were thinking."

"She still does." Sophie couldn't agree more on that particular talent of her mother's.

"Might I have another kiss now, my lady?" he asked. "While your mother is a most interesting topic of conversation, I would rather we concentrate on each other."

Sophie's heart beat faster, making it quite difficult to breathe. "I do enjoy your kisses. They are the best I have ever had."

"You have kissed another?" His muscular arms tightened around her, flexing in the most delightfully possessive way.

She was tempted to lie to tease him but thought better of it. "Yours are the only *real* kisses I have ever experienced. So, of course, they are the best because I have nothing with which to compare them." Unable to keep from smiling at his reaction, she continued, "If I didn't know any better, my fine cob, I would say you were momentarily jealous."

"I want to be your first," he said, all levity gone. "In every-thing."

"I see." She leaned in, breathing him in as she pressed her cheek to his. "I only know what I have read," she whispered against his ear. "But do not tell Maman I found her books. She would not be pleased."

This time, he was the one who drew back. He lifted both his brows. "Books?"

"Some would consider Maman's collection quite scandalous. Well, most would, actually." Sophie felt the heat of another furious blush rising. One that promised to turn her entire body red and make her wish she had not broached the subject. She patted his chest. "Manuals, you might say. In fact, I believe that is what Maman called them when she caught me with them once."

"Manuals about…?"

"Well, what do you think they were about?" she whispered without really knowing why, since it was just the two of them in the carriage.

His slow smile made her flush even hotter. Merciful heavens, she would surely burst into flames soon. She cleared her throat and struggled to assume a level of sternness. "And what is *that* smile supposed to insinuate?"

"It insinuates I am looking forward to learning about your studies."

CHAPTER SIX

WELL BEFORE THEY reached Rydleshire House, Nash yearned to take Sophie right there in the carriage. But he forced himself to behave. This would be his lovely swan's first time. Christening their life together by taking her on the narrow bench of the coach would be immensely selfish. He had never struggled with restraint so much in his life, but he refused to put his wants above her needs. Especially since the infernal past still crouched between them like a snarling dog. He fully intended to tame that beast and convince it to be on its merry way, never to return again.

"Lady Sophie and I are very weary and wish to rest until time for our guests to arrive," he informed the butler and housekeeper before the front door fully closed behind them. "Lady Rydleshire will be along as soon as Her Majesty allows it. All of us are quite certain you have everything under control. Please see that Lady Sophie and I are not disturbed."

Thornton and his wife exchanged knowing glances. Nash detected the faintest of smiles from the two, but they quickly recovered their composure.

"Rest assured that we shall see to everything, Sir Nash." Mrs. Thornton curtsied before hurrying away.

"Indeed, we shall," her husband reiterated, then bowed and followed her down the hallway.

"Is there a modicum of subtlety anywhere within you?" Sophie asked him, her embarrassment palpable.

He loved the way her crimson blush made her decolletage even more tantalizing. He pulled her close and nibbled kisses along the silkiness of her shoulder. "We have limited time before the party. I intend to make the most of it, and standing in the hallway chatting with servants is not the way to do that." He wrapped his left arm around her waist, took her right hand in his, and swept her up the stairs as though they were dancing. At the top, he halted. "I never thought to ask if our things had been moved into the master's chambers."

"Since the master has not yet officially *died*," she said with an air of annoyance that almost made him laugh, "I suppose mine will have to do." Her fiery red blush deepened. "Marie will help me out of my gown, and then I shall ask her to leave us. You may wait in my sitting room."

"No, my swan." He escorted her into her suite of rooms. "You shall excuse Marie until it is time to dress for supper. I shall help you out of your gown, your stays and petticoats, and any other article of clothing that happens to come between us. I hunger to undress you one layer at a time."

She fanned herself again. "I need a very large brandy. Would you mind pouring while I inform Marie?"

"I would be happy to, dear wife. After all, this day calls for a toast."

"Indeed," she said with a nervous squeak that made him smile.

He crossed the room to a cabinet bearing several sizes and colors of decanters. As he unstoppered one and sniffed the contents, he noticed the settee that had collapsed beneath him had been removed and replaced with a sofa that appeared to be much sturdier. Good. Perhaps after this evening's supper party, they might put that sofa to good use, if sweet Sophie was so inclined.

After he filled their glasses, a realization hit him, halting him with the bottle still raised. Gads, he wanted her with an unquenchable fury. More than he had ever wanted any woman before. Maybe it was her fire. Or her wit. All he knew without a doubt was that it wasn't merely a physical need because of her stunning shapeliness, the perfect pout of her full lips, or the luxuriousness of her glorious red hair. It was more than that, something he couldn't quite define. His precious Sophie was, for lack of a better word, incomparable in every way, and that was how he wanted her—mind, body, heart, and soul bound to him completely.

The bedroom door softly clicked behind him, and he turned to find her nervously chewing on her lip as she leaned back against it.

"Marie has gone and will not return until time to help me dress for the party." She wrinkled her nose. "She was quite smug about it, too. Everyone knows what we are doing." She rolled her shoulders and pinned him with a displeased look. "It is most unsettling."

He sauntered toward her while holding out her drink. "Did you wish them to believe you intended to maintain your virginity?"

Her mouth flew open. "I cannot believe you said such a thing." She grabbed the glass from him and indulged in a hearty gulp.

"We are husband and wife now, my swan. We can say anything to one another—whenever it is only the two of us, of course. I would never embarrass you by speaking in such a manner when we were not alone." He lifted his glass. "To many years of happiness."

With a sudden shift to a timidity he had never seen in her before, she lifted her glass as well. "To happiness. Many years of it."

"Sophie." He set his drink on a nearby table, took hers, and set it alongside it. With her hands in his, he gently pulled her closer. "You do not have to be afraid."

"I am not afraid." But her voice quivered. She cleared her

throat and thrust her chin upward. "I am not afraid," she repeated. "I am just...just..."

He released her and returned her brandy to her. "You are just afraid."

"Yes," she admitted quietly. Her forlorn look almost undid him.

Retrieving his own drink, he took her by the hand, led her to the sofa, and gently but firmly tugged her down to sit beside him. "I will never do anything to hurt you. Nor will I ever do anything you do not wish me to do." He leaned closer, forcing her to look him in the eyes. "If you wish to remain a virgin until you are more comfortable with our situation, I will not lie to you and say that I'll like it, but I will respect your decision. I would never force myself upon you. The choice is always yours."

"But wouldn't that cause you harm?" She appeared to be almost cringing.

He frowned, not quite certain what she meant. "It would not make me happy or at all comfortable, but it would not cause me any harm."

She took another deep gulp of her brandy, glanced at the tightly closed hallway door, then inched closer to him. "But what about the risk of *things* falling off?" she whispered.

"Things falling off?"

She affirmed his question with a rapid nod. "I read it in one of Maman's manuals. If a man does not—" She fluttered her fingers as if to help her find the words. "If he does not find his *relief*, certain parts of his anatomy risk becoming unattached from his person." Concern shone in her ever-widening eyes. "I would never wish to cause you such harm." She offered a sheepish tip of her head. "I know I kneed you there in a fit of anger, but I do not wish you any permanent damage."

He clamped his mouth shut and held his breath to keep from laughing. After regaining enough control where he thought it was safe to speak, he took her hand in his. "I fear you are misinformed, my swan. While a man's parts might throb so badly that they feel as though they are about to fall off, I have never heard of them actually doing so. At least not from the lack of coupling."

"There are other reasons they might fall off?"

"Injury…disease… Might we get back to the subject at hand? I do not expect you to submit to me like some sort of—like someone who has no choice in the matter." He rose to refill his glass, then turned back and held out his hand for hers. "More?"

She handed it to him. "Most definitely."

As he poured, a tense pause filled the room, creeping up behind him like a fiend about to pummel him in the back of his head. "Speak your thoughts, Sophie. Your silence is deafening."

She wet her lips as she accepted the drink from him. "Perhaps Maman's books were not entirely accurate." Her eyes slowly narrowed. "But Maman is not a fool. Why would she keep such books for me to find?"

He simply had to smile. "Perhaps she wished to keep her daughter innocent and untouched? Although, if you were the compassionate sort, her methods could bring her more trouble than good by your thinking you could save a man from losing his *parts* by allowing him to have his way with you."

"Compassion has never been my strongest trait, and Maman knows it." Sophie hung her head. "She knew I would think of it as a weapon."

A laughing snort burst free of him. He couldn't hold it back any longer.

"It is not funny."

"Indeed it is, my swan."

She took another deep drink of her brandy, then rose from the sofa and set it aside. With a boldness that thrilled him, she spun around and gave him her back as she started removing the pins from her hair. "Well?"

"Well, what?" The way her coppery locks cascaded down her back entranced him into a stupor.

"You promised to rescue me from this dreadful lace. Can you manage the buttons and hooks, or shall I call for Marie?"

He lifted the heaviness of her hair, draped it over the front of her shoulder, and allowed it to tumble out of the way. "I am quite able for the task, my sweetness," he said while grazing his lips along her exposed back. He flicked his tongue across her skin while peppering a trail of kisses along her shoulders. "I knew you would taste divine." A smile came to him as she shivered.

"And what should I do?" she asked in a breathy whisper. "I no longer trust those *manuals*."

"Relax and allow me to adore you."

"I see." A surprised squeak escaped her as he undid the last of the buttons and opened the gown to make it fall away. She caught it to her chest as though suddenly loath to be free of it.

He stepped around and kissed her barely parted lips while burying both his hands in her hair. She tasted of brandy and breathless excitement, of everything he had ever wanted and more. When she opened her mouth wider and flicked her tongue to his, he almost groaned.

She released the dress and wrapped her arms around his shoulders, tiptoeing as she pulled herself closer.

He drew back the slightest bit and allowed himself to drown in her rich, dark eyes. "You are sure of this, my swan?"

The tip of her tongue raced across her lips, wetting them. She gave a quick nod. "I am."

He swept her up into his arms, kicked the dress aside, and carried her into the bedroom. "I thought we might be more comfortable in here. At least at first." This first time needed to be wonderful for her. He would allow nothing less.

"At first?" she repeated as he lowered her onto the bed and tugged off both her elbow-length gloves.

After pressing a kiss into each of her palms and along her wrists, he folded her hands across her middle and moved to untie her slippers. "Relax and allow me to adore you. Remember?"

"I am discovering that is easier said than done." She shivered and squeaked again as he tossed her slipper to the floor and gently massaged her foot.

"You have the tiniest feet." He removed the other slipper and slid his hands up her leg to the ribbon securing her stocking. "And the loveliest legs."

"Your hands… I mean… Your touch is very nice."

After removing her stockings, he gently took hold of her hands and helped her sit upright. "And now for the rest."

A shuddering breath left her, making the swell of her breasts rise above the neckline of her corset in a way he could not resist.

But rather than bury his face in those luscious mounds, he forced himself to move around her and undo the laces of her stays. He tossed them aside, then eased her back into the pillows. While he preferred her completely bare to his gaze, he would leave her with her chemise—for now.

"You are so beautiful," he whispered between kisses.

"What about you?" She tugged on his jacket with both an exciting and endearing clumsiness. "I wish to see your beauty too."

"Do you?"

"Most definitely." She chewed on her lip again, drew in a deep breath, and huffed it out. "I have only seen a man unclothed in works of art." Her head coyly tilted with the shyness of her shrug. "Is it wrong of me to be curious? Brazen or whorish?"

"I find it exciting that you are curious." He shed his jacket and waistcoat after silently damning all the dratted buttons on the uniform. Neckcloth and shirt came next, but he paused and stood there bare-chested before removing his boots and pantaloons. The blush across Sophie's cheeks was alarmingly bright.

"Sophie? Are you all right?" He sat on the edge of the bed and gently touched her cheek.

She blinked as though waking from a dream. "I…uhm…yes. Forgive me, but you are nothing like the statues or paintings."

He hoped that was a good thing in her opinion. "Should I be insulted? Do you find me lacking?"

She reached out and touched his chest as though she feared it would burn her. "Your muscles. The way you are sculpted, dusted with…with all that golden hair." Both her brows arched higher. "You are quite…"

"I am quite what?"

"Nice," she whispered, and wet her lips as though hungry for him. "Very, very nice." She puckered the perfect rosiness of her mouth and blew out a long, slow breath. "Might you make sure the window is open as wide as it will go? I am finding it quite warm in here. Is it not so to you?"

"Yes, my swan. Quite warm, indeed." He smiled to himself as he did as she asked. Before returning to her, he removed his boots, then slowly unbuttoned his falls while walking toward her. "Would you like to remove your chemise so the air might cool your skin?"

With her eyes large and dark and her lips barely parted, he at first thought she meant to refuse. But then she sat up and swept the garment off over her head, arching her back as she did so. Now, he was the one struck speechless. A breathtaking woman while clothed, she was a stunning goddess in the nude.

"I never knew such beauty existed." His voice had gone hoarse with need. Gads, if he didn't dishonor himself by spilling his seed before he even reached the bed, it would be a miracle.

"Thank you." She tucked her chin and offered him a shy smile. "Might I see the rest of you?"

Her curiosity was the strongest aphrodisiac he had ever experienced. His gaze locked with hers as he let his pantaloons drop and kicked them aside.

Her eyes flared open wider. "Oh my." She pressed a hand to the base of her throat. "How will you… How will it…?"

He climbed into the bed and eased her into his arms before she could finish. "Trust me," he whispered as he kissed his way down her throat, along her collarbone, then circled her hardened nipple with his tongue. He sucked it ever so gently while cupping her other breast and pressing the hard length of himself against her.

She arched into him while tangling her fingers in his cropped hair and holding his head tight to her chest. She drew up one of her legs, wrapped it around him, and squeezed. A breathless moan escaped her, encouraging him to treat her to even more.

He cupped her buttock and squeezed, then allowed his hand to slide to the back of her thigh, where his fingertips grazed back and forth across her slickness as he kissed his way lower.

"Oh my." She writhed beneath him as he ran the tip of his tongue down the flatness of her stomach toward the lovely reddish-blonde nest of curls between her thighs. "Surely you do not mean to—"

"Shh, trust me." He throbbed with the need to take her, but forced himself to be patient, to be strong. She needed to be properly readied to fully enjoy this union. As he suckled the nubbin of her sex, he slipped a finger inside her heat.

She clutched the bedsheets, making him smile while still enjoying the taste of her and plunging his finger in and out. Her hips moved in time with his touch, rocking against his mouth with ever-increasing abandon. He slid another finger in alongside the other and sucked her nubbin harder. She was so close. Then her hot wetness tightened around his fingers, and she screamed. As she crested with her bliss, he hugged her tightly and kept his fingers buried deep inside her. When her spasms slowed, he kissed his way back up her body.

She wrapped her arms around him and kissed him between taking in great gulps of air. "I will never not trust you again," she rasped.

"I am glad to hear that, my swan." Bloody hell, he needed to bury himself in her, but gads, he had to be patient. The pain when her damned maidenhead ripped still stood between them. He kissed her deep and long, dying to be inside her. When he lifted his head to warn her of what was to come, she silenced him with a finger across his lips.

"I want you…where you are supposed to be," she said in a breathless whisper. "Frannie and Celia told me it's merely a little sting at first, and after that, it is quite nice indeed."

"It *is* quite nice indeed."

She hugged her legs tighter around him and rose to meet him. "Then take me. Show me more of these lovely feelings, my delightful cob."

"Gladly, my precious pen. Gladly." He pushed into her tightness, then forced himself to pause. "Breathe and try to relax, my love."

Instead, she wiggled, torturing him with her delicious wetness. "More," she urged. "I will relax later."

Gads, if she only knew. He shoved in deeper still and paused again.

"Oh my," she gasped. "So much…fullness. Why do you keep stopping? Is that how it's done?"

"No, my swan. Not at all." He drove in and fully buried himself, shuddering as he struggled for control. After a tender kiss, he rose enough to look down at her. "All right?"

She rocked her hips, slid her hands down his back, and squeezed his buttocks. "The sting is already gone. Please do continue."

"Happily." A groan left him as he worked his hips with a slow, steady rhythm. The ancient need to fully possess her and claim her for his own burned ever hotter, as his lovely bride became more breathless by the moment.

"Oh my, I do like this," she said, matching him thrust for thrust. "Faster. Harder."

"As you wish, my lady." He pounded with the ravenous urgency he had felt since the carriage ride home.

She dug her fingernails into his back and unleashed a delighted moan. "Yes!"

He growled and drove harder as her wet heat clutched him. Relinquishing the last of his control, he threw back his head and let free a roar. Spasms racked him as he spilled himself until completely drained both emotionally and physically. Exhaustion slumped him, but he locked his elbows to keep from crushing her. He rained kisses across the curve of her salty-sweet neck and shoulder and reveled in her wonderful softness beneath him. The way she still clutched him made him consider telling their soon-to-arrive guests to enjoy supper without them. He and Sophie would remain here.

Her pounding heartbeat barely tickled against his chest as he hovered above her. With an insistent tug, she pulled him down on top of her. "I want you pressed against me," she said with a breathless, purring giggle. "You feel so very nice this way."

He treated himself to a long, slow kiss and realized he had not felt this contented in a long while. "This is better than nice, my darling Sophie. Much better."

As she gazed up at him, her smile slipped the barest bit.

A surge of dread shot through him. "Stay with me here in the present, Sophie. Please do not let the ghosts of the past come between us again."

She barely shook her head. "It's… It is not that at all. I was just thinking we shall have to get ourselves sorted soon. After all, we must be ready to greet our guests."

She was lying. He couldn't very well accuse her of such, but he could see it in her eyes. Those same dark shadows of vulnerability and sadness she possessed whenever she lashed out about his mean-spirited ways of the past had returned. Damn his hide for being such a cocksure fool. If he had only treated that awkward young girl with kindness and consideration, how would that have changed things now?

He gently smoothed the wispy tendrils back from her face, wishing he could repair the damage between them in the blink of an eye, but knew it to be impossible. His only hope was that, in time, she would come to trust him and believe he would never hurt her again.

"Thank you," he whispered.

"For what?"

"You honored me with this moment, and I shall cherish it always."

She frowned as she touched his cheek. "You speak as if this is the only such moment we shall ever have. That there will never be another like it."

"Every moment we share is a rare and precious jewel that will never have another like it." He kissed her forehead, lingering for a long moment before lifting his head and looking back down at her. "I know that now. I just wish I had known it years ago."

The corners of her eyes flinched as if he had raised a hand to strike her. She cleared her throat and forced a cheerfulness he easily saw through. "I should ring for Marie," she said. "It will take a while for hot water to be brought up. Shall I have her tell Thornton to send a footman to your rooms with some for you as well?"

He pushed himself up from the bed and started gathering up his clothes. "Yes, my swan. That would be most appreciated." Her gentle dismissal stung him to the core. She had hoisted her shields to protect herself—from what, Nash wasn't quite sure, but he knew he was at the center of it. A heavy sigh escaped him as he yanked on his pantaloons.

"Nash?" She sat there in the center of the bed, the linens modestly clutched to her throat, seeming almost worried. "Did I not perform my wifely responsibilities correctly?"

Her words chafed him, made him clench his teeth to keep from growling a response that would not be kind or appropriate. He ambled toward her as he buttoned his falls. "You could not have possibly *performed your responsibilities,* as you put it, more correctly except for one minor thing."

She frowned. "And what was that?"

"You were not performing wifely responsibilities, nor was I claiming husbandly rights." With his hands propped on the bed, he leaned across it until his nose was within inches of hers. "We made love, Sophie. We joined our bodies and consummated our union for all eternity. *That* is what we did. Not fulfilled duties, responsibilities, or rights. We did not have relations or sex, or commit the marriage act. We made love and shared an unforgettable bonding."

A coldness fell across her, almost like a mask of impenetrable serenity he could never hope to breach. "It was very delightful, but love cannot be manufactured," she said, "and I do not believe we should call something love when it is not. Either it flows from your heart and soul or it doesn't. You made it abundantly clear earlier that we might become *friends* rather than the enemies we have always been. Friends is what you said, Nash. Not two people in love with one another." Her pensive gaze squeezed his heart in a merciless grip. "We are better served being honest and not calling something love when it is not. Do you not agree?"

"Why are you doing this?"

"What?"

"You know damn well what." He caught her by the shoulders and pulled her closer. "Why are you pushing me away after what we just shared?"

She stared up at him, her dark eyes deep pools filled with shadows. "I will never allow myself to love you again. Not under any circumstances. We shall be friends and work together to capture the blackmailer. That is all we shall ever be." With a gentle touch to his cheek, she offered him a sympathetic smile. "Why are you behaving this way? You have never loved me."

At that moment, confronted with that accusation, Nash understood without any doubt that he would come to love her with an all-consuming fury. But now was not the time to tell her. No. Now was the time for war, the time to battle for her heart and force her to love him again. "I simply did not appreciate your defining our marriage bed in such cold terms, because our passion is not nor ever shall be cold."

Her head tilted the slightest bit, and she narrowed her eyes. "Forgive me. I shall make you a bargain. I will always refer to what goes on in our marriage bed as a sharing of passion to strengthen our union as long as you refrain from describing it as manufacturing, excuse me, as *making* love. Agreed?"

"Agreed." *For now*, he silently added. His beloved swan had no idea how tenacious he could be when he wanted something, and he damn sure wanted her more than he had ever wanted anything before. She would be his treasured wife, the mother of his children, and the woman he loved and needed more than air to breathe. And whether she believed it now or not, she would soon love him just as fiercely.

CHAPTER SEVEN

"Y OU ARE ABSOLUTELY glowing," Celia whispered as she and Sophie discreetly moved to a quieter part of the crowded drawing room. A subtle knowing colored her smile. "I see you wasted no time in consummating your marriage." She cast a glance over at where Nash stood talking to the husbands of some of the greatest gossips among the *ton*. "I cannot say as I blame you, sister. Your description of him did not do the man justice. Are you any better about this situation?"

"If anything, I am even more frustrated." Sophie eyed the carefully selected guests, gauging if anyone stood close enough to overhear their conversation. With a forced smile that belied the chaos churning within her, she fought to keep her voice low. "I told him I would never allow myself to love him again, and the stubborn churl took it as a challenge. Men!" She huffed. "Maman was right. They always fight for whatever is denied them, whether they want it or not."

"Did he say he took it as a challenge?" Celia sipped her champagne and adopted the sort of expression one might assume when talking about the weather or the latest fashions.

"No, but I saw it in his eyes. I remember that look from when we competed on the training fields." Sophie caught the eye of the footman bearing a tray of drinks and lifted her empty crystal flute. She needed another, and another after that. Nash's reaction to their indescribable afternoon terrified her. He might think himself temporarily besotted, but she knew he would never remain that way—and then where would her poor, battered heart find itself for a second time?

"You already love him," Celia whispered, then tittered with a false laugh as a pair Sophie didn't recognize strolled past them. "How in the world do you hope to keep it from him when I can see it plain as can be?"

Sophie attempted as graceful a stance as she could manage and sent a fake look of happiness Nash's way while lifting her second glass of champagne in a silent toast to him. "I shall simply make myself unlove him."

"I do not believe *unlove* is a word, sister."

Before Sophie could argue, Celia took hold of her by the arm and steered her toward the double doors that led out into the garden. "Come. The rain has stopped, and your complexion has become as red as your hair. I noticed you ate nothing at supper, and downing champagne the rest of the evening is unwise. You might fool the others, but you cannot fool me. Some fresh air is called for before your mother gets involved."

"*Unlove* is most certainly a word." Sophie swapped out her empty glass for yet another full one. "And I fully intend to accomplish it for my heart's own safety."

"What would be so wrong with allowing yourself to love your husband?" Celia took the champagne away from her and poured it into the nearest rosebush.

Sophie worked her knuckles, flinching with every soft pop. "And then what happens to me when his temporary fascination wears off? When he gains what he thought he wanted, only to discover he did not want my affection at all? When he decides to take a mistress from all the ladybirds looking to land an earl as their next benefactor?" She peeped back in through the side window, trying to spot him. "Do you not remember what I wrote about the way he treated several of my older friends in Calais?"

"You are stronger than this, Sophie." Celia scowled at her. "I know the queen unraveled everything you and your mother nurtured all these years, but do not allow this situation to take your power from you. You have the ways and means to make that man's life quite uncomfortable should he be foolhardy enough to take a mistress, and you know it." She tipped a decisive nod. "And if you cannot make him miserable, you can certainly scare off any woman foolish enough to come sniffing around him. Since when do you allow anyone to take anything that is yours?"

"Since Queen Charlotte so easily took everything I ever worked for." Sophie blinked hard, fighting back angry tears—or maybe not angry ones. Maybe the tears came from her aching heart. Since the rain had stopped, she could no longer use that as a cover to hide any weeping. "I thought you would understand, but I should have known better. You and Elias have always loved each other."

"Not always, and you know it," Celia corrected her with a rare sternness. "I love you, my sister, but you must stop feeling sorry for yourself and take control of this situation before it makes you ill."

Something heavy and sharp hit Sophie so hard between her shoulder blades that she cried out and stumbled forward. Clutching at the trellis to keep from going to the ground, she struggled not to pass out from the pain. "Run!" she gasped to Celia. Head swimming and fighting to breathe, she couldn't move, but Celia needed to get away from whatever was happening. "Save yourself! Run!"

"Help!" Celia shrieked. "Help us!"

Strong hands closed around Sophie's shoulders, and she flailed to fight them off. It had to be the blackmailer. Who else would have the audacity to climb the wall and attack her in her own garden?

"Sophie, it's me!"

Nash's deep voice somehow made it easier for her to breathe. She closed her eyes and stopped fighting, swallowing hard to keep from becoming ill.

"Search this garden now!" he bellowed, then swept her up

into his arms, painfully jostling her as he charged back inside.

"I will be all right." She forced her eyes open and pulled in a steadier breath that helped ease the throbbing that had started in the center of her back and shot through her. "Set me down and let me gather myself while you go after the fiend."

Fury filled his face. Murder flashed in his eyes. "I will not leave you alone again. Why did you go out there without me?"

"It is our private garden," she forced through clenched teeth. "Do not scold me like a child."

He bowed his head, but his face reddened with even more rage. "Forgive me." He eased her down onto a settee but bared his teeth when he drew his arm out from around her and discovered blood on his sleeve. "Call for a physician! My wife is badly injured."

"Right away, sir," Thornton called out amid the chaos in the drawing room.

"Let me have a look," the dowager countess ordered Nash, seeming to appear out of nowhere. She joined Sophie on the settee and gently tugged her forward. "Did you hear gunfire, daughter?"

A roaring in Sophie's ears drowned out her mother's voice. She struggled to remain conscious, fighting against the dark spots swirling in her vision. A hard swallow to calm her churning stomach helped very little. "Maman, just let me breathe and calm myself. I am sure the injury cannot be as bad as all that, or I would not be speaking."

"Did you hear gunfire?" her mother repeated more sharply.

"No. Something just hit me. Is Celia all right?" She tried to roll her shoulders, but a searing burn that triggered another vicious surge of nausea made her stop.

"I am right here," Celia said from her other side. "I didn't see or hear anything. She simply stumbled forward after something struck her in the back. Perhaps whatever hit her is still out there."

"I beg your pardon, my lady," said a footman to the dowager countess as he cautiously approached. He held out a large bundle crudely wrapped in twine and parchment. "This was found close to the trellis where Lady Sophie fell."

Sophie held out her hand. "Here. Give it to me."

"I will not," her mother curtly replied. "You are not only bleeding but still quite dazed. I can tell by your eyes."

"Maman—"

"Listen to your mother," Nash said, pushing closer and catching hold of her chin to peer into her eyes. "You do appear quite dazed. I shall carry you upstairs to await the physician."

"You shall not. I want to examine that bundle." A grunt escaped her as she pulled in another deep breath that resulted in a harsher stabbing pain. "I am better already. You should not have sent for a doctor."

"You are lying, my lady." He glared at her. "You are still in pain and shall be seen to if I have to hold you in place to be examined."

A dangerous glow warmed through her traitorous heart. She tried to stanch its fickleness, but his genuine concern for her refused to be ignored. He needed to stop behaving as if he cared about her, because it would not last. He would tire of her as soon as he considered her conquered.

"I would like to examine the weapon used against me, please," she said with an imploring tone she hoped would move him. She needed something that would take her mind off him, and the way his caring weakened her defenses. "Please, Sir Nash."

He pressed his mouth into a tight, flat line that made his displeasure unmistakable, but he jerked a single nod. "A quick examination of the thing, and then I carry you upstairs. Agreed?"

"Agreed." What choice did she have, since she was hampered by no small amount of pain?

He tore away the twine, then carefully unwrapped a jagged rock that was a little larger than his fist. "You might very well have broken bones from this. We must show it to the physician." He handed it off to the dowager countess, who examined it with a grimness that sent a stinging chill up Sophie's spine.

"If this had struck you in the head, you could have been killed," the dowager said.

"But I was not killed," Sophie said, trying to keep them focused on the matter at hand rather than on what might have been. "Are there any clues on the wrapping?"

Nash opened the crumpled paper wider. His knuckles whitened as his grip on the parchment tightened. *"You will pay in more ways than just coin,"* he read in an enraged hiss. *"This is only the beginning. Be warned."*

She tried to rise from the settee, but the throbbing ache made her gulp and catch her breath. "Oh…dear."

"You will stop at once, wife," he growled. He handed off the note to the dowager countess, then gently gathered Sophie up and cradled her to his chest. "To bed with you now, to wait for the doctor."

"But we must…" She fought to catch her breath from the tearing burn ripping between her shoulders. "We must compare the handwriting with the other letters."

"I am quite certain your mother will take care of that once she sees all our guests on their way." He doggedly continued striding up the steps, carrying her as if she weighed no more than a feather. "We must see to your injury and ensure it is not grave."

"I am conscious and speaking, am I not?" She had not remembered him being this stubborn.

"Many a soldier has died while conscious and speaking. I will brook no argument on this."

She relented and rested her head on his shoulder, closing her eyes to better battle the ever-increasing urge to retch that was probably more because of her overindulgence in champagne on an empty stomach rather than her injury. "If Thornton returns with some ill-mannered quack, I refuse to allow him to examine me."

"I overheard your Celia advise Thornton to fetch her stepfather. Are you familiar with the man?"

Even through the pain and nausea, Sophie smiled. Dr. Mac-

Maddenly had married Celia's mother after saving her life. "Dr. MacMaddenly is a stubborn Scot who thinks himself the most brilliant physician in London because he studied medicine at the University of Edinburgh."

"Good." Nash shouldered open the door to her suite, stepped inside, then kicked it shut. "It sounds as if the man will do."

"Dear heavens! My lady!" Marie flitted around them like an overwrought butterfly, opening the bedroom door and rushing to turn down the bed. "Your things have been moved, Sir Nash," she said over her shoulder. "Just as you ordered."

"What is she talking about?" Sophie asked, then unleashed a sharp yelp as he lowered her into the pillows.

Nash ignored her. Instead, he turned to Marie. "Thank you. Help me get Lady Sophie out of this gown. She was attacked in the garden, and we await Dr. MacMaddenly's arrival."

"*Merde!*"

"Marie?" Sophie glared at her personal maid, who only swore in French when overly distraught or astonished. "What did you mean when you said Sir Nash's things have been moved?"

The maid avoided meeting her gaze as she rushed around to the other side of the bed and clambered up on it. "If you will support her, Sir Nash, I shall undo her buttons and laces—Oh dear, there is blood. Oh, my lady."

"Do not alarm your mistress," Nash ordered her, while gently but firmly holding Sophie as Marie had asked.

"If you two do not stop speaking around me as if I am a child or unaware of my surroundings, I am going to thrash you both as soon as I regain my strength." A hitching moan escaped Sophie as another agonizing twinge sliced through her. "Answer me, Marie. This instant."

"Your husband bade us move his things from the guest room into this suite, my lady," Marie said. "I have her undone, Sir Nash. Lift her, and I shall slide the gown and corset off her. Shall I wait to change her shift until the doctor sees her? That will cause her less discomfort for now."

"Yes." Nash gently hugged Sophie to his chest so her garments could be removed in a smooth downward motion.

Panic swept across her as a harsher ache made her gasp, "I need a basin!"

Much to her horror, he held her as she retched and rid herself of every drop of champagne she had ever thought about drinking. How much more humiliation was this night to bring her?

"A wet cloth for her mouth and another for her head," he said to Marie after handing off the basin. He eased Sophie back onto the pillows and sat beside her on the edge of the bed. "Your chemise is soaked through with blood. We should change it, rather than allow you to lie in it."

"No. Not yet." She didn't care if she was floating in blood—she just wanted to be left alone so she could cover her head and quietly die from embarrassment. Through barely opened eyes, she didn't detect a hint of revulsion from him. "I will be fine," she whispered. "I merely need a moment to gather myself."

"You keep saying that." With a touch so gentle and caring it threatened to make her weep, he wiped her mouth with the wet cloth and draped another over her eyes. "Rest now. Talking only makes you draw deeper breaths and increases your pain. Be still, my swan, so you will improve. None of us can bear the thought of life without you."

He should not say such things. That wasn't at all fair. She rested her hand across the cloth covering her eyes, willing her heart to shut him out.

The door creaked, warning her someone had either arrived or departed, but she was too overset by the evening's events to lift the cloth and look. A distinct hint of crisp, clean mint wafted across her, and she immediately knew it was Celia's stepfather. The man always smelled of freshly crushed mint. She pulled in a deeper breath, knowing it would help allay the returning nausea.

"All of ye may leave while I see to the lady," Dr. MacMaddenly announced with his usual gruff efficiency. "Now."

"I am Sir Nash Bromley, Lady Sophie's husband. I will not be leaving."

"Ye will stay out of my way, then, sir, or we shall have words in another room, ye ken?"

"I assure you, doctor, I shall not be a hindrance."

Sophie kept her eyes covered but expelled a long-suffering breath. "Dr. MacMaddenly, it was just a rock that hit me in the back. Not a dagger. Not a bullet. Merely a stone, and it knocked the wind from me. I shall be fine."

"I shall be the judge of that, m'lady," the doctor said. "If ye insist on being in here, Sir Nash, lift your wife, so I might examine the wound. I saw that missile. Such an object could do a great deal of damage."

"The intensity of her pain has also caused her to be quite ill," Nash told the doctor as he slid an arm under her shoulders and gently curled her to his chest to expose her back. "I am sorry, my love. I know it hurts when I move you."

My love? When in heaven's name had he started using that endearment? He needed to stop it. Such subtle attacks on her heart were not at all amusing. A jaw-tightening sourness pounded behind her ears, warning that more champagne was on its way out. "I need the basin!"

Once again, he held it for her as she heaved so hard it felt as though she had surely turned herself inside out.

"Marie!" he bellowed. "More cool cloths for her ladyship!"

"How many times has she been ill like that?" Dr. MacMaddenly asked.

"That is only the second time," Sophie whispered as she sagged against Nash's chest. "And kindly stop talking around me. I am quite capable of supplying you with whatever information you require."

"The bruising is quite severe and only just started," the doctor said as he unceremoniously cut her chemise and peeled it away. He gently prodded and pressed, hitting every excruciatingly tender spot.

She held her breath and buried her face in Nash's chest, willing herself not to cry out.

"Nothing can be done for the puncture wounds but to keep them clean and bandaged," Dr. MacMaddenly said. He gently squeezed her arms and hands, then tapped on the bottoms of her feet. "Any tingling or numbness, m'lady?"

"No." She swallowed hard, trying not to give in to another round of heaving. A strained groan escaped her lips as Nash eased her down among the pillows onto her side.

"Laudanum and rest. Keep the wounds clean and let her rise from the bed when she feels well enough to do so." The gruff physician rounded the bed and offered Sophie a somewhat affectionate scowl. "And none of your stubbornness about resting and healing, m'lady. I ken well enough how ye are, but Celia bade me warn ye that if ye dinna do as ye are told, she will have a bit of ye, and ye willna like it."

"Thank you, Dr. MacMaddenly." She attempted a weak smile. "I shall do my best to behave."

"I doubt that." The doctor pulled a bottle and a small vial from his black leather satchel and handed it to Nash. "A full vial of the laudanum immediately. 'Tis a large dose, but she will need it for this first time, especially. Once it takes effect, see that her maid cleans and bandages those wounds. Celia said ye were a military man, so ye ken how it should be done. After that, Lady Sophie may have more laudanum as the pain demands it, but knowing this lass, she'll not take it unless ye force her, so watch her closely. There is no reason for her needless suffering."

"I shall personally see to her care," Nash said, sounding entirely too ready to rise to the challenge.

Sophie closed her eyes and covered them again with the fresh, damp cloth Marie provided. "*Merde*," she muttered, then flinched and peeped out from under the cloth to see if anyone had heard.

Dr. MacMaddenly chuckled as he closed his satchel and tipped her a nod. "*Merde* indeed, m'lady." He offered Nash a polite dip of his chin as well. "Good evening to ye, sir. Send for me if her condition worsens, and the vomiting does not cease."

"I will. Thank you, Dr. MacMaddenly."

Sophie covered her eyes again, wishing all of them would leave along with the good doctor. But then the bed shifted and confirmed that her wish was not to be granted.

"Here, Sophie," Nash said, his tone soft and coaxing. "Down this. It will get you through what we need to do before you can rest."

She cracked open an eye and glared at him. "You have filled that vial entirely too full of that bitter stuff."

"There is no need to be overly brave. That stone cut you deeply in three places that will require a generous dousing with whiskey to ensure the punctures are properly cleaned. It will not be pleasant." He leaned closer and held the vial to her lips. "Please, Sophie. Your suffering is pure torture for me."

Then get out, she wanted to scream, but not only would it take too much effort, it would also hurt. Instead, she relented and forced down the bitter concoction that had not been sweetened with nearly enough honey. She held her breath to keep from gagging.

"Perfect." He turned and set the vial and the bottle on the bedside table. "Marie has gone to fetch everything we need, and soon you can rest." He gently brushed her hair back from her face. "Shall I remove your hairpins so they don't prick you?"

"Whatever you wish," she whispered, her heart already aching in anticipation of the day when he would consider his challenge of winning her heart achieved and then would no longer want her.

He worked his fingers through her hair, plucking out the hairpins and setting them aside. "I shall tell Marie to forgo brushing out your hair this evening. Is the laudanum taking hold yet?"

"I am sad." She frowned. Had she said that aloud? "I mean...the pain does not seem as bad."

"Why are you sad, my swan?" he asked so softly that she

wasn't sure he had really said it.

"Because I will always love you, and you will never love me." She squeezed her eyes tightly shut, then scrubbed the damp cloth all over her face. Her nose itched something terrible. "Ants are crawling all over my face and making it itch." She pawed at herself. "Get them off me."

"Easy now, Sophie." He stopped her from batting at herself. "The ants are gone now." He rubbed her nose with a dry cloth that did, in fact, rid her of all those terrible, tickling bugs.

"I hate ants. Be sure they don't get into the bed." She tried to focus on Nash's face to read his expression, but he kept swimming around the room. "Sit still. How can I tell what you are thinking if I cannot see you?"

He moved closer.

"Why do you look sad too? Do you also love someone who will never love you?" Noises behind her and something touching her back made her try to turn. "Who is there?"

"Look at me, Sophie," Nash said. "Marie is getting you ready for bed. Talk to me while she works. We were talking about my being sad, remember?"

She didn't remember, but if he said so, she supposed it must be true. "I am sorry you are sad. There are kittens in the stable. Mr. Wallace showed them to me, and I told him to be sure and see that they are made quite comfortable. You could go see them. They always make me happier." Her eyelids drooped no matter how hard she tried to keep them open. They felt so heavy. Almost as if they were weighted. "Kittens and babies," she mumbled.

"What about kittens and babies?" His deep voice floated around her like a beautiful song. "Sophie?"

"Kittens and babies make me happy," she said without bothering to open her eyes. "Babies sometimes make me sad too, though, because I know I will never have one."

"We are married now, remember? We promised the queen to name our first daughter Charlotte."

"We cannot have a daughter. Or a son. We can only have kittens." At least, she thought so. Although, for the life of her, she couldn't remember why.

"If you would let yourself love me, Sophie, we could have as many babies as you wish."

"Who are you?" The voice sounded like Nash, but it couldn't be. Nash didn't like her.

"Your husband. Nash."

"I married Nash?" She huffed a snort and batted at him but kept missing. "You cannot be Nash. He was a cruel toad who wouldn't even give me the time of day ten years ago, even if I begged him for it. Who are you really, sir? And what are you doing here? I believe I am in a bed somewhere. Why are you here in a bed with me?"

"We can cut her chemise the rest of the way off, sir," a woman said from behind her. "I have her a fresh one right here."

Something shifted around her, then slipped over her head, making her nose tickle again, but she couldn't scratch it because they kept trying to guide her hands into some sort of cloth opening. "Let me go. The ants are back."

"I shall get rid of the ants again as soon as we get your chemise sorted."

Whatever he wished. She didn't bother opening her eyes again, just allowed herself to float along on the deep voice that seemed so familiar. "You have the nicest voice. Do I know you, sir?"

"No, my lady. You do not know me at all, but I swear, as I live and breathe, that you someday will."

CHAPTER EIGHT

NASH SAT IN the chair beside the bed with his head in his hands. At least now he knew how she truly felt about him. But that precious truth was a double-edged sword. Thankfully, she loved him. Unfortunately, she would never admit it unless drugged, because she was so sure he would eventually cast her aside, or break her heart in some other manner. Her girlhood feelings had not been the stuff of childish infatuation. When his wonderful Sophie loved, she loved with all her being. And the more he was around her, the more he needed her to love him without fear because, against all good judgment and no small amount of fear of his own, he was most assuredly falling just as deeply in love with her.

He lifted his head at the sound of the bedroom door opening. "Lady Rydleshire," he said, keeping his voice low as he pushed himself to his feet. "She seems to be resting peacefully at last."

The dowager countess didn't acknowledge his presence with even so much as a glance. She moved to the other side of the bed and stared down at her daughter with something akin to sheer terror. Ever so gently, she straightened the already straight covers, brushed an errant curl away from Sophie's temple, then gently kissed her daughter's forehead. "Praise the Almighty," she whispered. "No sign of fever yet."

"She is the strongest woman I have ever met. Even with the pain making her ill, she kept saying she was fine and merely needed time to gather herself."

"Gather herself," the countess repeated with a soft, sad laugh. "My beloved girl has never been *gathered* a day in her life. That is but one of the many things I love about her. Her spontaneity. Her stubbornness. I have often wondered how she can be both graceful and yet awkward as a newborn lamb at the same time." A pained sigh left her as she pulled her gaze from Sophie and leveled it on him. "I will not rest until I have the head of the individual who did this to her. No one harms my child and lives."

"I swear I will find who did this—and with your consent, I shall enlist the help of an old friend of mine. Actually, I consider him more brother than friend. He is a Bow Street Runner. One of their finest. I trust him completely, and he is the epitome of discretion."

The dowager eyed him as if doubting his word. Or perhaps it was something else, something in the way she held herself, as if waiting to be attacked. He found the way she looked at him rather disturbing. Her expression was indecipherable. "What is it, my lady? Is there something more?"

She looked away as if no longer comfortable meeting his gaze. "Forgive me, young Bromley. I am not myself this evening." Once again, she leaned over Sophie and lightly touched her daughter's abundance of curls splayed across the pillow. "I will sit with my darling child while you examine the garden and the perimeter of the street side of the wall. Find out how they accomplished this." She spared him another glance. "And by all means, have your friend help us—if you are certain he can be trusted."

"I do not feel comfortable leaving Sophie, my lady."

The dowager rounded the bed with a quickness that bespoke of rage simmering just beneath the surface. "I am her mother and would never harm her." Her furious scowl threatened to reduce him to ash.

He backed up a step, lifting his hands in confused surrender. "No, my lady. That was not my meaning at all. Please do not think such." The lady had to realize Sophie's feelings about him, all the reservations her daughter harbored. The two shared such a closeness. How could she not know of Sophie's fears? He turned and gently touched his sleeping wife's cheek, then bent and pressed a kiss to it. "I fear if she awakens, and I am not here, she will think even worse of me than she already does."

His mother-in-law bowed her head and pressed a hand to her heart. "I must beg your forgiveness, Bromley. As I said, I am not myself after this evening's events." She reached out and gave his arm a gentle pat. "I know her fears. Unfortunately, my Sophie shares my greatest fault. She never forgets anything that hurts her. Try to be patient with her. All you can do is show her you are no longer that unlicked cub determined to bed every young beauty he meets. She will eventually come to see you as the honorable man you have become."

"I hate it when I see the past in her eyes."

"Then you must do everything possible to keep her anchored here in the present." She pointed at him, reminding him of how she used to give pertinent instructions during training. "No flummery. She has little patience for overt flattery."

"Yes. I am well aware of that." He would not go into detail how he had already erred on that front.

She smiled down at her sleeping daughter, then turned back to him. "Her laudanum rest seems quite deep. But she'll not stay that way long. She never does. Please have a look at the garden and the outer wall. Your eyes are trained far better than those who have already looked over the area."

"As you wish, my lady." He turned back and kissed Sophie again, lingering for a moment with his lips pressed to the coolness of her forehead and willing her to find the courage to trust him. "I shan't be long from your side, my swan," he whispered. "Rest easy."

He bounded out the door without looking back. If he looked back, he would not be able to leave her. Fear that she would awaken without him would overcome his control and paralyze him. He rushed down the stairs and found himself unable to go any farther without knocking the Duchess of Hasterton, Sophie's friend Celia, out of the way.

"I simply would not leave without speaking to you first," she said as she snagged hold of his jacket and tugged him over to one side of the hall. "Thank goodness you finally came down. Elias and I really should get home to little Oliver soon. He has been quite fractious with Nanny of late."

"What can I do for you, Your Grace?" He itched to examine the outside wall as expeditiously as possible to get back to Sophie before she awakened.

The duchess stared up at him, frowning as if not quite able to settle on how to broach the subject she wished to discuss.

He expelled an impatient huff, not giving a damn if he appeared rude or not. "Forgive me, Your Grace, but I am not comfortable leaving Sophie's bedside for any length of time. I am merely headed to examine the grounds at the behest of her mother. Might you get to what you wish to discuss? Please?"

The lady's eyes flashed. "As you wish, Sir Nash." She resettled her grip on her closed fan as though preparing to smack him with it. "If you hurt my beloved sister again, you will regret the day you were born. We of the Sisterhood take care of each other, and you will not only have me to answer to but also the Duchess of Lionwraith. And *she* threatened to shoot her husband on their first meeting, so do not mistake her for a helpless female who will tolerate the mistreatment of a dear friend." Her scowl hardened even more. "And do not underestimate Sophie or myself. We lead. We do not follow. Nor do we meekly retire to our parlors and bemoan unfortunate circumstances brought on by the carelessness of men. We take action. Am I quite clear, Sir Nash?"

"Madam…" Nash paused, fighting his temper and the urge to use words not appropriate for a lady. "I understand you and Sophie are quite close. Close as sisters, even. But I refuse to stand here and discuss my relationship with my wife. To put it as plainly as possible, Your Grace, it is none of your affair."

Rather than fly into a petulant rage and storm away as he had expected, the duchess became dangerously calm. Her icy demeanor grew even colder as her chin jutted higher. "So you like to speak plainly, do you? Fine. I hereby put you on notice, Sir Nash. You have just declared war against a force you will never defeat—sisters who care for one another." She spun and gave him her back, then marched down the hall while calling out to her husband, "Elias, darling. I am ready to leave now."

"Sisterhood," he repeated under his breath, then shook off the frustrating encounter and stormed out the front door. He would think about the duchess's threats and her mysterious *sisterhood* later. For now, he had to investigate the garden so he could get back to Sophie.

As he entered the dimly lit mews behind the townhouse, he halted, then backed up a few steps, pressing against the wall surrounding Rydleshire House's sizeable garden. Silent as death, he peered around the corner. A tall figure slowly moved in the deep shadows along the garden wall. Every few steps, the individual would bend and touch the ground as though in search of a fallen object.

Nash eased around the corner and followed, determined to catch the trespasser before they even realized he was there. Whoever it was had a great deal of answering to do. Before the sneak thief turned, he immobilized the fiend with one arm around the man's throat, and the other locked around his shoulder. "What the blazes do you think you are doing here?"

"Sir Nash!" Thornton sputtered. "It is I!"

"Bloody hell, Thornton!" Nash released the butler immediately. "Why the devil are you out here?"

"Because I would trust no one else with the task of trying to discover who harmed Lady Sophie." Thornton tugged his coat back into place, then straightened and squared his shoulders. "All the staff are quite concerned for our lady, but none have been with her and Lady Rydleshire as long as myself and my wife. Our footmen are ample but young and sometimes scattered. They might have missed something earlier when sent out here by her ladyship."

Nash studied the older man, sensing nothing but a deeply ingrained sense of loyalty and true concern for the mistresses of the house. "And did you find anything else that might be useful in identifying the intruder?"

The man snorted with disgust. "Sadly, no, sir, and I fear that the footmen stomping around muddled any possibility of unique footprints."

Nash turned and eyed the wall. Even in the darkness, he could discern it would be difficult to scale.

"The hawthorns, sir," Thornton said before Nash asked him his opinion. He pointed at a section of hawthorn trees that exceeded the height of the wall. "It would not be an easy climb due to the thorns, but if the person were determined, they would manage it."

"Cut them down. All of them." Nash stepped back from the wall to get a better view of its entire expanse. "Once the sun rises, I shall examine the barrier for further weaknesses."

"Yes, sir. I shall inform the gardener to have the trees removed by dawn." The butler tipped his head in a polite nod. "Is there any other way I can be of service, sir?"

"Yes." Still peering at the garden wall and scanning the entirety of the mews, Nash decided not to wait until tomorrow to contact Wethersby. "Send your most trusted and *least scattered* footman to Bow Street. Have him ask for Mr. Merritt Wethersby and request him to come immediately. Give him my name."

"Yes, sir." Thornton bowed and hurried away.

Nash moved closer to the cluster of hawthorns, but in the poor light, there was little he could make out other than a few smaller branches that drooped as though broken. The butler was right—the bold blackmailer had climbed the thorny tree and probably stayed in the safety of its branches until the deed was done. Well, there was nothing more to be done here. Time to get back to his Sophie.

He tried the gardener's gate at the back of the property and found it locked. At least they'd had the foresight to secure the only other entry into the garden. He continued around the house, hurried up the front steps, and discovered himself locked out. Before he had the opportunity to pound on the door, Thornton swung it open.

"Do forgive me, sir, but I believed you would wish it locked now that all the guests have gone home."

"Quite right, Thornton. Notify me when Wethersby arrives."

"Yes, sir."

Nash took the stairs two at a time, charged down the hall, and shot through the sitting room as if storming an enemy's stronghold. But when he came to the bedroom door, he gingerly eased it open.

Lady Rydleshire looked his way, then silently rose and met him at the door. "She has not stirred so much as an eyelash."

"Good." He went to the bedside and stared down at the amazing woman he had once been foolish enough to think of as an annoyance. He watched the gentle rise and fall of her steady breathing, finding it somewhat eased the worries of his heart.

"I shall be in the sitting room," the dowager countess said. "Call out if you should need me."

"My lady—"

"Yes?"

"I intend to make her happy." He gently tidied the blankets across his sleeping swan even though they were still quite straight.

"See that you do." Lady Rydleshire slipped out the door and closed it quietly behind her.

He settled into the chair, moving it closer so he could rest his folded arms on the bed and lay his head beside Sophie. He breathed her in, finding her scent immeasurably soothing.

"You would be much more comfortable here in the bed," she said so softly that he lifted his head and stared at her. The candle on the nightstand bathed her in an ethereal golden glow, making her seem more spirit than flesh.

"Sophie?"

She didn't open her eyes but shifted with a deep breath that caused her to flinch. "Several years ago, I suffered an injury that revealed I have a high tolerance for laudanum and such. Those medicines affect me, but not nearly as strongly or for as long as they affect most."

"How are you feeling? Do you need another vial to help with the pain?"

"No. I am still rather floaty, and if I try hard enough, I am sure I could sleep." The faintest of smiles played across her mouth. "When you rested your head beside me, your scent awakened me. Sandalwood. Citrus. And you."

He wasn't quite sure how to take that. "Are you suggesting I need to bathe, my lady?"

"No," she said as softly as a kitten's purr. "You smell like you. Like you did when we…" Her voice trailed off.

Had she fallen back to sleep? A smile came to him, but he didn't prod her to finish her thought. He knew what she had meant to say, and she needed her rest. He laid his head back down on his arms but shifted so he could watch her. Never would he tire of losing himself in the vision of her.

"If you do not wish to rest in my bed, then go back to your room," she said in a breathy whisper. "I am quite fine. Just a little sore."

"This is also my room now, my lady. Have you forgotten I am your husband?" He reached out and grazed a fingertip across her cheek, unable to resist touching her even though she needed to go back to sleep.

"Husband," she repeated in a drowsy little chant. "Most sleep in their own rooms, don't they? Celia and Elias are an exception, of course, but that is because they love each other. Frannie and Lion sleep in the same bed too because their match was also rooted in love." She went still again, breathing slow and steady as if already returned to her dreams.

"We will share the same bed too, my swan," he whispered. "When you are healed."

"Healed," she repeated on a sleepy, whispery exhale. "You fuss too much."

"I can never fuss enough when it comes to you, my lady."

She rewarded him with a faint smile that lightened his heart.

The bedroom door eased open. "Bromley," the dowager countess softly called. "Your Mr. Wethersby is here."

Nash was impressed. The footman must have gone on horseback rather than wait to rig out a carriage. And Merritt had wasted no time because knew he would never be called at this time of night unless the matter was urgent. Nash rose and caressed Sophie's cheek. "I shall only be away for a moment, my swan. Sleep and heal."

"Do not fuss," she whispered, her lashes barely fluttering. "I am fi…"

He smiled. She was indeed fine. She just didn't realize how fine and priceless she was. He hurried into the sitting room, offering the dowager a grateful nod as she went into the bedroom to take his place.

Standing just inside the door was his most trusted friend, Merritt Wethersby, the hulking blond beast of a man whose ancestors had to have been Vikings. He lumbered forward, grabbed Nash's forearm in the warrior handshake they had used as children, then grabbed his shoulder and shook him. "Married? You? I never thought that would happen."

"Yes, well, a long story, and the heart of it is why I sent for you." Nash headed to the cabinet covered in decanters. "Get comfortable while I pour. What shall it be, old friend?"

"Whatever you have is fine, since I intend to limit myself to one glass. It sounds as though I need to keep my faculties about me."

"My wife, her mother, and our queen are in danger." Nash selected a brandy he knew Merritt would enjoy. "They are the target of a blackmailer who has stepped up his scheme in an alarming manner. My new wife of less than a day fell victim to him this evening. The attack upon her person could very easily have been fatal."

"How is she?" Merritt accepted the glass but didn't drink, concern filling his eyes. "Gunshot?"

"She is very fortunate and will heal. No, it was not gunfire. She was hit with a large, jagged rock between her shoulder blades. The puncture wounds concern me most. You know how quickly infection can set in on those types of injuries." Nash set his drink aside, his thirst for vengeance far outpacing his thirst for brandy. "And the note attached to the missile warned she would pay in more ways than just coin, and that this attack was only the beginning."

Merritt leaned forward, his eyes narrowing with a hunger for the hunt. Another reason Nash had called upon him. He knew his old friend to be relentless. "Where did the attack occur?" he asked.

"In our very own garden," Nash said. "Here behind the townhouse."

"Witnesses?"

"The Duchess of Hasterton was with Sophie when she was struck, but according to her, they both faced the house with their backs to the devil. Understandably, once Sophie cried out, Her Grace's only concern was getting aid rather than looking for the perpetrator."

"How similar are the duchess and your wife?" Merritt finally sampled his brandy, then arched a brow and gave an impressed nod. "Very nice cognac, old man."

"What do you mean by similar?"

"Stature. Shape. Hair. Are they so different that the suspect would easily know which woman to target even with their backs to him in what I presume was a garden only lit by a few torches?"

Nash smiled and enjoyed a large sip of his own drink. "Think back ten years. Do you recall my grumbling about a fiery-haired brat who was more annoying than any horsefly and took the greatest pleasure in making me look incompetent in front of my chums?"

Merritt eyed him with a confused frown. "Vaguely. Why? What has that impertinent little chit got to do with this?" As soon as the words left him, his jaw dropped. "No."

Nash lifted his glass in a toast. "Yes. That impertinent little chit is now my wife in all her beautiful, fiery-haired glory. And while she and the duchess are similar in stature and shape, Sophie's hair gleams like the finest polished copper, whereas the duchess's hair shines like ebony."

Shaking his head as though to clear it, Merritt took another sip of his brandy, then frowned again. "Telling them apart would be possible, then. Even by torchlight." He thoughtfully ran his finger around the rim of his glass. "You said your wife, her mother, and the queen are all targets of this blackmailer. What do the three have in common that the suspect is trying to use against them?"

"My mother-in-law is none other than Lady Rydleshire, one of the best agents ever to serve the monarchy and the founder of the elite Rydleshire Academy, which trains the Crown's current spies." He paused and arched a brow. "I believe she is also one of the closest *true* friends of Queen Charlotte. So close that when she gave birth to a daughter after her husband's murder, and no heir was left to inherit the Rydleshire title, Her Highness delicately *looked the other way* and occasionally smoothed circumstances for the dowager countess's propagation of a fictitious son to prevent the title from going extinct and reverting to the monarchy for King George to mishandle. Once Sophie became old enough to join in on the scheme, she too supported the farce of the fake Earl of Rydleshire and took it upon herself to raise the estate to a glory it had never previously known. I have not become privy to the ledgers yet, but from what I understand, my wife is as brilliant in business as she is in horsemanship and archery." He wet his mouth with another taste of brandy. "And you remember how I always complained about her besting me in both?"

"A fake peer." Merritt's frown furrowed even deeper. "They could be hanged—or beheaded, depending on Prinny's mood." He barely tilted his head to one side, still looking confused. "That does not explain your sudden nuptials, though. By special license, I presume? Since I heard nothing of this until today."

"The blackmailer sent several notes and also received several payments, but in the face of the fiend getting bolder, Lady Rydleshire took the matter to the queen. Especially since the last missive from the devil specifically threatened Her Majesty with the exposure of her part in the scheme to Parliament and the *ton*. Therefore, our wily queen put a counterattack in motion."

"Which was?"

"My marriage to Lady Sophie. The fake Earl of Rydleshire's unexpected demise, which will take place and be announced within a few days, and the prince regent's proclamation naming me as the fifth Earl of Rydleshire. Her Majesty's ability to persuade her son has apparently returned to her in full force."

"As if she ever really lost it." Merritt snorted.

"True."

Merritt shifted in his seat, finished off the last of his cognac, then held out the glass. "Perhaps one more while you explain why our good queen selected you for this monumental and extraordinarily questionable task." He shook his head. "The legalities alone—gads, man! I understand how letters patent often leave women facing the direst of straits, but to falsify a peer? And now you yourself are in the thick of it?"

"I know." Nash allowed himself a disgruntled snort as he refilled both their glasses. "Three summers ago I happened to be at Kew when the king had one of his more violent attacks. It terrified the queen and her daughters. So much so that, without thinking, I jumped in and attempted to divert His Majesty by asking his advice on harvesting crops, seasons for planting, and the breeding of animals. I referred to him as Farmer George until he calmed enough to allow me to take the scythe away from him on the pretense of checking the sharpness of the blade. I handed it off to a servant, telling His Majesty that it was in dire need of repair or the barley harvest would surely be damaged." He scrubbed a hand across his eyes. "We talked for hours, he and I, and the sad thing was, he made perfect sense about everything to do with farming. It was as though he had never been king and was quite happy about that fact." He lowered himself to a chair across from Merritt. "That day sealed my fate. The queen forbade me from ever traveling farther than a day's ride from her and her family. Gone was my hope to defend my country by land or sea. I am called upon whenever His Majesty's days are more difficult than his staff can manage. She cannot bear to see him handled as roughly as was required before I arrived on that fateful day."

"And as an earl, you would usually be right here in London. At her call year round, if need be."

"Exactly."

"And now you are well and properly leg-shackled. No good deed goes unpunished." Merritt gave him a sad smile. "Isn't that what your father always said?"

"Yes." Nash decided not to share that his marriage to Sophie had turned out to be the silver lining of the complicated storm cloud he was now a part of. As astute as his friend was, Merritt would eventually figure that out for himself.

"What information can you give me that will assist my investigation?"

"All the demands were posted through different offices. The postal stamps attested to that, and yet each of them required the same amount of postage to receive, postage for a distance of fifty miles." Nash tried to remember everything Sophie had told him about the letters, since he had yet to examine them at his leisure. "Same handwriting. Blunt, aggressive wording, of course. And, according to Sophie, knowledge of names, dates, and circumstances that few would be privy to."

"Have those *few* been interviewed?"

"I honestly do not know, but I cannot imagine either my wife or her mother leaving something as simple as that to chance."

"Perhaps I should start with Lady Rydleshire. If she would be up to it this evening, of course." Merritt tossed a glance at the bedroom door into which the lady had disappeared. "Handsome woman and yet she never remarried?"

"I do not ask those questions, and if you value your life, you will not ask them either," Nash advised, remembering the fate of the malodorous French courtier. "From what I have surmised, the dowager lost the love of her life when her husband was murdered and has never considered the possibility of another."

"And some ghosts never rest."

"Most definitely." Remembering the malevolent spirits creating the barrier between himself and Sophie, Nash couldn't agree more. But he was determined to exorcise those foul memories and lay them to rest. He and Sophie could find happiness. He felt it in his bones.

CHAPTER NINE

SOPHIE PRICKED HER finger again. She popped it in her mouth and held her tongue against it to stop the bleeding and keep from staining her embroidery even more. Her poor little bluebirds were already so spotted with blood they looked as though someone had shot them several times.

"Perhaps you should discard that piece and start again," her mother gently suggested, with a sympathetic pat on her shoulder.

"Perhaps I should be out and about doing something productive rather than sitting in the parlor playing at these silly things I have never cared about nor been able to perfect." Sophie stabbed the needle into the square of material and tossed the tangled mess aside.

Maman pressed a tender kiss to the top of her head as though she were still a child. "Remember, we are in mourning and must be the epitome of propriety. And besides, it has only been a week since the attack. Mere moments ago you said you still suffered from some soreness."

"No worse than the soreness one gets from overexerted muscles." Sophie rose from the settee and paced around the room. "When did Nash and Mr. Wethersby say they would return?"

"You know as well as I that they did not give us a time frame because they did not know." Maman picked up the discarded bit of embroidery and studied it with a loving smile. "Your needlework skills have improved. Somewhat."

"You are being kind." She wasn't a fool. Maman was attempting to placate her. "I could have gone with them. I have ridden under worse conditions."

"I do not consider the painful cramping of womanly courses a worse condition than the bruising and wounds you possess. Marie described their current state to me only this morning, and Dr. MacMaddenly insists you might very well have fractured bones he is unaware of. He does not advise that you ride for a few more weeks, and you know it."

Her mother's tone did not recommend continuing the current line of conversation, but Sophie couldn't resist. "You have ridden under worse conditions than the injury I have or a bout of painful courses. You rode after being shot."

"*Sophia Davidia Redwell Bromley.* I tire of this subject, and you will change it immediately."

A heavy sigh escaped her. Even at the somewhat mature age of five and twenty, Maman's use of her full name still stung. She offered her mother a contrite nod. "Yes, Maman."

"Write to Frannie," her mother continued. "She would love to hear from you. After all, even though she adores her new babies, I am quite certain she feels removed from everything with the isolation of her lying in."

"I wrote to her yesterday. Another letter this week would smack of desperation."

"Review the ledgers? It is nearly the end of the quarter."

"I did that earlier," Sophie said as she moved to the window and peered through the sheer panels of lace hanging between heavier damask draperies in a bright shade of blue that matched the poor, ruined bluebirds of her embroidery. Across the way, in the narrow space between Hasterton House and the townhouse next to it, the shadows seemed to move. She eased back a bit to make herself less visible but kept her gaze locked on that particular spot. "Maman, did we bring my archery equipment from Calais? I cannot seem to recall."

Her mother joined her and stood just behind her, aligning her viewpoint with Sophie's. "Direct me to the spot, child. I see nothing that warrants shooting."

"The shadows. Between the buildings. Wait." Sophie moved forward the slightest bit, baiting the brazen scoundrel to move again. "Nash mentioned having the house watched over while he was away, and Mr. Wethersby said he had a pair of men he trusted for the job."

"Well, if that is one of them, I daresay they are out of range to offer much protection." Maman's tone suggested Mr. Wethersby's men had sorely failed to impress her. "They should be on this side of the street, their backs to our walls, and ready to spring into action should a trespasser approach."

"Perhaps that is the trespasser." Sophie itched to coax whoever it was out into the open. It had been a long while since she last played a rousing game of cat and mouse. "It is a lovely day. Do you not agree?"

"It is not lovely enough for you to traipse up and down Curzon Street and try to be attacked merely because you are bored." Maman snagged hold of her arm and tugged her away from the window. "Come. Higher ground might provide us with a better view and help us identify the creature." Her smile took on a decidedly wicked slant. "Or at least ease our boredom for a time."

They scurried upstairs to Sophie's private sitting room like a pair of children intent on naughtiness. No, not *her* sitting room, she reminded herself—her *and* Nash's. Not that she had forgotten she was married. How could she when every night, except for the last two because he was traveling, her handsome yet fickle husband joined her in bed yet refused to touch her until she was completely healed? Completely healed, indeed. If he insisted on behaving as if he actually cared before showing his true colors and taking a mistress, the least he could do was treat her to more of the breathtaking pleasures he had shown her on their wedding day. But no. Much to her dismay, the cruel man had chosen chivalry over passion. She had yet to figure out the plot behind his tactics, but she would. Persistence was key. She refused to allow her heart to be caught off guard again.

"I see him," Maman said soft and low while peering out the window. She eased to one side so Sophie could join her.

Sophie held her breath as she watched the man furtively peek out, glance up and down the street, then sink back into the shadows between the buildings. "I cannot decide if he is nervous, indecisive, or simply cowardly."

"I do not think *cowardly*." Her mother squinted as though sighting a target on the questionable person below. "Note his expression when he emerges again. Like a rat that cannot decide if it is safe to come out or not. I believe he is merely cautious."

"It would take no time at all for me to slip around the houses and come up behind him in the alley. This black bombazine and crepe might actually prove useful and enable me to easier blend into the shadows." Sophie cracked her knuckles at the exciting prospect, her heart beating faster.

Her mother swatted both her hands and shoved in between her and the window, completely blocking the view. "You will do no such thing, and how many times have we discussed that annoying habit? If you persist, your fingers will surely become misshapen. Do you wish your hands to become as knobby as roots of an ancient tree?"

Resisting the childish impulse to hide her hands behind her back, Sophie took a defiant stance. "I am going out there. I can tuck my throwing knives into the front of this dreadful corset and keep at a safe distance to withdraw unscathed if need be."

"As your husband, I forbid it," Nash said from the doorway.

She jumped and nearly choked as her heart leapt to her throat. "Good heavens! When did you get home?"

"Only moments ago. Apparently, just in time to prevent you from doing something quite foolhardy." Jaw clenched and eyes flashing, he strode toward her with such force that she almost backed up a step before giving herself a hard shake and holding her ground.

"I shall leave the two of you to it." Maman dismissed herself with a smug tip of her head in Nash's direction.

Sophie swallowed hard, determined not to flinch or look away from her husband's displeased glare. "There is a lurker across the way, and I am fully capable of investigating my environment rather than cowering in the parlor and waiting for you to charge home on your mighty steed and save me."

He took her by the shoulders and gently but firmly set her away from the window, then peered outside. "Where across the way?"

"The alley to the left of Hasterton House."

"I see no one."

She shoved in beside him and tapped on the window. "He was there moments ago. Did you enter the house through the front or cross the mews and come in through the garden?"

"Merritt and I entered through the garden."

She turned to look up at him and suddenly realized how close he stood. The heat of him dared her to toss all her reservations aside, push herself into his arms, and make him hold her whether he feared he would hurt her back or not. "Uhm…"

"Uhm?" He arched a brow and smiled down at her with a look that said he knew exactly what she was feeling.

She cleared her throat and adopted what she hoped was a stern air. "You left Mr. Wethersby downstairs? Alone? Is that any way to treat a guest?"

"He is not a guest. He is my oldest friend." Nash cupped her cheek and lowered his voice. "I needed to see you. How are you, my swan? Other than determined to be the death of me by throwing yourself in harm's way?"

"I am bored, petulant, and extremely dangerous. You would do well to remember that, *my lord*." She knew the formal address would irritate him, and it pleased her immensely to do so. After word of her attack had reached the prince regent and Queen Charlotte, they adjusted the timeline of their scheme and gave the title of the fifth Earl of Rydleshire to Nash before the body of her *fake* brother had time to proverbially grow cold.

To her utter frustration, he rewarded her childish prattle with a broader smile that only made him more handsome and turned her insides into an aching mess of molten yearning. She so wished it was safe to love him.

"I like it when you are dangerous," he said softly, then kissed her with a tenderness that was still somehow demanding and oh so wonderfully possessive. He lifted his head and pulled in a deep breath, as if struggling for control. "I missed you, Sophie. Did you miss me too? Maybe even just a little?"

She started to deny the truth and dash the hope in his eyes, but her heart refused to allow her to do so. "I missed you more than just a little." With a twitching shrug, she added, "The bed seems cold and empty without you beside me."

He didn't speak, simply drew her into his arms and held her close. His heartbeat thumped steadily against her cheek, filling her with a warm contentedness. She closed her eyes and tightened her arms around him. "I truly did miss you, Nash," she whispered, half hoping he wouldn't hear. She was so weak when it came to him.

"Sophie?" His rumbling voice had taken on the deep raspiness she remembered from when they had made love.

"Yes?" She swallowed hard, struggling to steady her emotions.

"I have a confession."

Her heart plummeted. Not even married a month, and he had already been unfaithful. She had known he would do it, but this soon? How much more could he humiliate her? She eased away, gently trying to pull herself free of his embrace, but he only tightened his arms around her. "What is your confession, my lord?"

He stared down at her with a slight frown. No, not a frown exactly, but a troubled look, as if he were befuddled beyond reason. His eyes reminded her of a lightning-filled horizon. He didn't speak even though his lips were barely parted. He merely drew in a deep breath, then eased it back out.

"You are tormenting me, Nash," she said as calmly as possible. "Please, just tell me. What have you done?"

"I have become impossibly besotted—fallen hopelessly in love with my wife."

She blinked several times. Was he telling her that to soften the blow of confessing his unfaithfulness? He appeared so serious—so *truthful*. "I beg your pardon?"

"I love you, Sophie." He pulled in another deep breath and snorted it out, his nostrils flaring like an angry stallion's. "My confession is that I love you and want you to stop waiting for me to break your heart again. You are wasting our life together by living in the past." He cupped her cheek once more and leaned in closer. "You need to trust me. I *need* you to trust me."

"But—"

He stopped her with a shake of his head and a finger across her lips. "There are no *buts*. Stop waiting for me to hurt you. We are not those people anymore, and I have apologized for my dreadful behavior all that I am going to, because it does no good to keep saying the words when you refuse to hear them." He kissed her again, lingering with his lips to hers as if sealing the bond and locking the bitterness of the past away to a place where it would never hurt them again. "I love you," he whispered against her mouth. "My heart is yours, whether you wish it or not."

"I wish it." She reached up and held his face between her hands, struggling to speak through the wild churning of so many emotions. "I love you and will overcome my fears. I promise."

"That gladdens my heart more than you could ever know." He kissed her again until she moaned. With a start, he relaxed his embrace. "Forgive me, my love! Did I hurt you?"

She almost laughed. If not for his remorseful concern, she would. Instead, she patted his chest. "You did not hurt me. Have you already forgotten the sounds you coax free of me whenever you give me pleasure?"

"Perhaps tonight..." He held up a finger. "If we are very

careful and handle *things* in a subdued nature, we might... Dr. MacMaddenly fears you have broken bones of which we are not aware."

"I shall be the judge of—"

Nash yanked her to one side and shielded her with his body. "Merritt!" he bellowed as the window beside them shattered.

Chaos broke out downstairs. Doors slammed. Shouts filled the halls.

Sophie tried to twist free to see what had happened, but he grabbed her by the shoulders and held her in place.

"No. Do not go near that window." He bent his head until they were nearly nose to nose. "Your trespasser had a rifle. Stay away from all the windows while I am gone. Do you understand me?"

She opened her mouth to argue, but he read her far too easily and gently shook her.

"No, Sophie! For once, listen and do as I ask. Your life depends on it. Swear to me you will stay away from every window in this house. Swear it!"

Fear for his safety filled her. "I swear as long as you promise to go by my workroom and arm yourself with extra weaponry. Pistols. Throwing knives. The bookcase behind my desk will swing inward to a concealed room filled with whatever you need. Push on its right side, the fifth shelf up from the bottom."

He gave her a quick nod and a kiss, then bolted out the door.

She sagged down onto the settee, staring at the broken glass scattered on the floor, then squinted at the wall opposite the window. A ragged hole, dark and unnerving, marred the rose-covered wallpaper just above the waist-high wainscoting. Rage fought to overcome her fears, making her heart pound so hard she became breathless. How *dare* that devil almost kill her husband? "I hope Nash shoots that fiend," she muttered, then shook her head. No. She didn't want him to shoot the assassin. She wanted him to catch the blackguard and drag him back here so she could do it.

Maman rushed into the room with Marie close on her heels.

"Sophie!" She joined her on the sofa and hugged her close as Marie stood there wringing her hands. "When I heard the shot, then Nash shouted—oh, my darling girl."

"My lady," Marie sobbed. "Oh, my lady, you might have been killed."

Sophie gently extricated herself from her mother's hold and forced a smile. "And yet I wasn't killed," she said as calmly as her quaking voice would allow. "I am quite hale thanks to Nash noticing movement outside and reacting." She pressed a hand to her still-pounding heart. "We must all gather ourselves and, as Nash said, stay away from the windows until he returns."

"Mr. Wethersby barreled out the door as soon as the shot rang out," her mother said. "I am quite sure he will have some stern words for his men about their failure as guards." She gave an angry shake of her head. "Guards, indeed. I told you they were incompetent. That lurker should have been apprehended before he had the opportunity to take aim."

Sophie further soothed herself by dissecting the situation. "An assassin with a rifle," she mused aloud while staring at the bullet hole in the wall. "Who would consider us so dangerous, such a credible threat to them, that they wanted us dead? Blackmail for money was understandable. This? I cannot imagine the motive."

"My lady, shall I get you something to drink to settle your nerves?" Marie asked, still wringing her hands. "Do you need to lie down? Shall I help you undress?"

"Some strong tea would be perfect," Sophie told her, mainly to give her something to do.

The maid dropped a quick curtsy and stole out of the room.

"Poor Marie," Maman said. "She is accustomed to our unconventional ways, but this is a strain even for her." She reached out and touched Sophie's cheek. "And for me as well. Your life has been threatened twice now. I cannot bear this. I simply cannot bear this."

Sophie caught her mother's hand between hers and held it

tight. "We are strong women, Maman. We must look at the facts rather than dwell on what might have happened." It was now easier to breathe even though she feared for Nash's safety. They needed to discover why the blackmailer had elevated himself to the level of assassin. "Who have we, or have I, angered so? I am not important politically or socially. No one stands to gain anything by my death."

Her mother clutched her hands as if fearing she would float away. "It might be an indirect attack on me. I made many enemies while working for the Crown. As did your papa, and he paid for it with his life. Perhaps they fear you now work to protect our country and are privy to sensitive information that would cause them or whomever they work for harm."

"Proper investigation would tell them otherwise. I only travel between France and England—not all over the Continent and beyond like you and Papa did." Sophie slowly shook her head. "No, this *feels* entirely different."

"Come." Maman patted her hand. "Let us go downstairs so this mess can be cleaned up. And now that Nash is home, your things need to be moved to the master suite." She cast a worried glance at the broken window. "Those rooms will be safer, since they overlook the garden and the mews rather than the street."

"Perhaps that would be best." Sophie didn't care what suite of rooms belonged to them. She was too busy trying to piece together the shooter's motives to worry about such inconsequential things. Such violent attacks made no sense whatsoever. Ransoms had been paid, although their small amounts had been almost laughable. None of the banknotes had been cashed yet, either. So money was clearly not a motive. The entire situation smacked of an irrational mind.

Rather than risk the parlor at the front of the house, she led her mother to the drawing room that opened out into the garden. After Nash's shoring up of any security weak points in that area, the back of the house should be quite safe. Also, the drawing room gave her more room to pace until he returned safe and sound.

"Sophie, do sit," Maman implored from the settee beside the double doors open to the warm day.

"I cannot." Sophie worked her fingers, slowly cracking them one by one.

Her mother blew out a heavy sigh but didn't scold—proof enough that she was terribly upset.

A door slammed hard enough to shake the sound through the house. That was followed by scuffling and a steady stream of loud, coarse French. Another door slammed and silence fell.

"They've captured him, but where did they take him?" Sophie hurried to glance up and down the hall. "They are not going to interrogate him without me—Thornton!"

"Sophie!" Maman called out. "You must stay here."

Sophie ignored her, took a few steps toward the front door, then stopped and listened. Nothing but silence filled the house, and the hall remained empty. "Thornton!"

Still no response, which was quite unusual, because the butler possessed the almost annoying habit of appearing when one even thought about asking something of him.

She returned to the drawing room and yanked on the bellpull several times while still watching the hall.

Daryl, one of the older footmen, careened into view, emerging from the stairway that led down to the kitchens. His eyes rounded with alarm as he caught sight of her standing in the drawing room doorway, the bellpull still in her hand.

"Yes, my lady?" he asked as he skidded to a stop and bobbed a contrite bow.

"Where is Thornton?"

"I am sure I don't know, my lady. Shall I search the house for him?" The young man nervously shuffled from side to side, seemingly unable to stand still and most eager to dart off in search of the butler. "Shall I?"

"No. Thank you. You may go." She waved him away. "I am quite capable of searching the house myself." She started with the main parlor, since it was closest to the front entrance. Empty. "Either the library or my workroom. They must have taken the man to one of those."

"Sophie!"

"Maman, either come with me or wait in the drawing room, but do not ask or expect me to stop until I find where they took that devil. I have a few questions of my own to ask him."

Her mother surprised her with a tight-lipped glare and a nod.

Sophie charged down the hall, paused just outside the library door, then continued on to her workroom. The library was too quiet. They had to be in her workroom. Her mother caught hold of her by the shoulder and held her back just as she went to open the door.

"Are you certain? This could be unpleasant." Maman stressed the sentiment with a gentle shake. "If you insist upon doing this, do not get close to him. Understood?"

"I understand," Sophie replied. But really, she didn't. After all, she felt sure that Nash and Mr. Wethersby had probably lashed the man to something. How dangerous could he be? She pushed inside, determined to wring every drop of information out of the assailant.

"Sophie!" Nash blocked her way. "You should not be in here."

"I beg to differ. Since the attack was upon my person, I have every right to be in here, and intend to ask a few questions of my own."

She tried to sidle past him, but he blocked her again, catching her by the shoulders and holding her in place.

"I will share what I learn. Go back to the drawing room." He cast a glance behind him. "This could become quite unpleasant."

She jerked free, feinted to the right, then darted around him to the left, scurrying between the worktable and the bookcase that hid her arsenal of weapons. But the sight of the man with his wrists and ankles tied to a chair halted her halfway around the table. "Horton Bainery?"

The man's grubby scowl hardened even more. He ducked his chin and looked away.

"Mr. Bainery, you are supposed to be dead." She angled closer to the French agent who had crossed over and sworn allegiance to England. Able to pass for an Englishman, he had once worked with Maman at the academy.

Nash caught hold of her. "Sophie. Stay back."

"You have him tied, and you are right here." She pointed at the man. "Let me ask my questions."

"He will not answer," her mother said while boldly stepping forward. "Will you, Bainery?"

The man glared at the dowager countess with such hatred that Sophie took a step back. She had never seen such loathing in the man's eyes before. As far back as she could remember, Mr. Bainery and Maman had always been quite close—more like friends instead of mere colleagues fighting for the good of the Crown. She gave her mother a gentle nudge to step aside and took her place in front of the bound man.

"Why did you try to kill me?" Sophie watched him closely for the slightest tic that might give something away. It wasn't so much *what* he might say, but *how* he would say it. "You used to tell me French fairy tales while we ate apples and cheese in the orchard, and yet today, you tried to shoot me."

"If I had intended to kill you, you would be dead, my lady," the man growled, looking far older and thinner than Sophie remembered. Of course, it had been some years since last she saw him.

"Why did you fake your death?" Sophie meandered back and forth in front of him, noting that only one of his eyes followed her. The other seemed locked in place, staring straight ahead. When had he developed that malady?

He curled his upper lip into a deeper sneer and remained silent.

Wrapping an arm around her waist, Nash drew her off to one side. "You should leave, my swan. Merritt and I cannot *encourage*

Mr. Bainery to share what he knows while you and your mother are in the room."

Sophie looked back at the man lashed to the chair. "Do not hurt him," she said softly. "He is telling the truth."

"What truth?" Nash frowned at her, glanced back at Mr. Bainery, then returned his focus to her.

"If he had wanted me dead, I would be." She peered at the man, studying him closely. The way his head sagged forward, the tensed gauntness of his features. His breathing was ragged, and his coloring had gone an unhealthy gray. She pushed around Nash, grabbed Mr. Bainery by the chin, and forced him to look up at her. "What did you take? What poison did you take?"

"Canny girl. Just like your mother. When he gave me the orders, I said you would sort it." His smirk twitched, pulling to one side in an unnaturally taut line. With a sickening gurgle deep in his throat, he stretched back and jerked as though fighting an unseen rope that was trying to separate his head from his neck. After a hard shudder, he slumped over and went as limp as a wet rag.

Nash tried to shield Sophie, but she pulled out of his arms and focused on the old man who had once been her friend. "Mr. Bainery was a master of poisons," she whispered. "He once told me he had often envisioned himself dying by his own craft." An icy shiver stole across her. "Poor man."

"Poor man?" Nash growled, sounding ready to spit. "He tried to kill you."

"Not really. He protected me as much as he could." Sophie understood now, and the knowledge cast an eerie chill across her. "This is some twisted game, and this sorry old soul got caught up in it somehow."

"He is free now," her mother said in a wistful tone. "May he rest in peace."

CHAPTER TEN

"Y OU CANNOT TRAVEL to Calais alone," Sophie told her mother. "Safety in numbers, remember? How many times have you told me we must never travel alone?"

"I am going. With my maid and an armed footman, I shall be quite safe. I am not helpless nor without my own resources." The dowager squared her narrow shoulders. Self-assuredness streamed from her like rays of light. "You forget who I am, my child."

Nash caught hold of Merritt's arm and stopped him before the fool waded into the treacherous waters of two women in the middle of a disagreement. "Let them sort it," he advised in a low voice. The lovely ladies had taught him that lesson well.

"Lady Sophie is right," Merritt said too loudly for his own good. He kept his gaze locked on the dowager countess. "Lady Nia cannot travel to France with merely a footman and a maid. Not under the present circumstances."

Both women turned and glared at him.

"You are a dead man," Nash murmured before stepping forward to sacrifice himself in his friend's stead. "If anything were to happen to you, dear mother-in-law, I should never forgive myself. Why this sudden need to return to Calais? You said yourself the academy was under the exemplary care of some of your former star pupils."

The woman eyed him as if sighting a pistol for the killing

shot. "It is best I return to Calais for several reasons. Sophie will be safe here with you, allowing me to approach this dilemma from another angle."

"What angle?" He studied her. Something uneasy brewed in the lady's amber eyes, and it was not merely concern for her daughter's safety. No, it was more than that, but he couldn't fathom what. He had always been somewhat awestruck by the powerful woman, and the more he was around her, the more enigmatic she seemed—like a mighty goddess he dared not question. But he would question her for his beloved Sophie's sake. "What angle, my lady?"

The dowager ignored him. Instead, she turned back to her daughter. "I understand what I am doing. You must trust me."

"We are in full mourning, Maman," Sophie countered with a haughty tilt of her chin. "You should not be traveling. It is not proper."

"I have been in full mourning since your papa's murder. Do not lecture me on the appropriate behavior while grieving a loved one." Not sparing any of them another look, she haughtily swept from the room and stormed up the stairs.

Sophie stared after her, looking so lost and forlorn that Nash's heart ached for his precious wife.

He went to her, took her hand, and pressed a kiss to it, pleased she had honored his request to remain gloveless unless they were entertaining or out for the day. The satin of her skin, even the simple innocence of her bare hand, beguiled him. He couldn't get enough of touching her. He kissed the backs of her fingers again. "We will convince her to stay, my swan. Somehow."

"If need be, I will follow and keep her safe," Merritt said a little too strong for one merely determined to protect a lady.

Nash turned to his friend and found himself unable to keep from smiling. "You have fallen under her spell."

Merritt glared at him but didn't protest or deny the observation.

"If you truly care for her, then go upstairs and talk some sense into her," Sophie told him. "Be firm and do not take no for an answer."

"Does she keep weapons in her rooms?" Merritt asked with uncharacteristic leeriness.

"Of course. Any table with a drawer has a pistol in it. As long as you keep her away from drawers, you should be safe enough."

He arched a brow, rolled his shoulders as though flexing for a fight, then strode out of the room.

"You have just sent my most trusted friend to his death," Nash said, only partially in jest. He had never seen Merritt so taken with a woman before. He feared it would dull the man's sense of self-preservation.

"The only way Maman will hurt him is by refusing his attentions." Still staring after Merritt, she slowly shook her head. "She has toyed with men over the years. Out of boredom, I suppose, or what she always called *keeping her skills sharp*. But I have yet to witness her allowing another into her heart. She once told me that the pain of Papa's loss never eased, and at times was almost more than she could bear." A hitching sigh escaped her as she pressed a hand to her throat. "I cannot count the many times she told me I was her only reason for living on."

"It sounds as though your mother loves hard and with all her being."

Sophie turned to him, her rich mahogany eyes filled with uncertainty. "Yes, she does." After nervously catching the corner of her bottom lip between her teeth, she pulled in a deep breath and let it ease out. "As do I."

He coaxed her into his arms and tilted her face up to his. "I am glad of that, my love. Do not be uncertain or afraid, because I promise you, that is a trait you and I share."

She touched his cheek as if convincing herself he was real. "I am glad too, then," she said softly. "I know I promised to leave the worries of our past behind, but the troubles of our present seem to keep dragging them forward."

"I understand. What with two attempts on your life, black-mail threats, and a forced marriage? Most women would find themselves so overwhelmed they would take to their beds for weeks on end." He treated himself to the lightest of kisses, unable to resist the sweet temptation of her mouth so close to his. "But fortunately for me, you are not *most* women. You have taken it all in stride even while imprisoned by full mourning. You need a diversion from all these beastly troubles, my fractious little swan. You need an outing."

"Full mourning, my lord. Remember?"

"My lord?" He tucked her tighter against him. "All because I called you fractious?"

Her crestfallen look eased the knot in his chest that always twinged whenever he suspected her old resentments had risen once again. "No—you are right. I am quite fractious." She stretched on tiptoe and wrapped her arms around his neck. "Everything is closing in around me, and this ridiculous mourning for a brother who never existed is insulting and unfair to those truly going through the loss of a loved one." She gave an irritated huff that made her delicate nostrils flare. "And now Maman has suddenly become unreasonable. I am beside myself and resent that position very much."

While Nash longed to sweep her up to the bedroom and treat them both to an entirely different position, even his aching lust sensed Sophie needed more than resuming their marital delights for an afternoon. No, as much as he longed to sink into her and never surface again, that was for later, after she'd had some respite from their current troubles. He nibbled a kiss across the rosy sweetness of her mouth, then lifted his head and whispered, "What say you to a bit of scandalous behavior?"

Her eyes lit up like a pair of the brightest candles. "Scandalous, you say?" She teased him with a suggestive wiggle that made him second-guess his decision about not retiring to their bedchamber. "Since we are married, how could anything we do together possibly be scandalous?"

"While I adore your line of thinking, my seductive swan, I had something else in mind."

Her immediate frown delighted him. "I told you I am quite well, and last night you refused me after promising…"

He silenced her with another kiss. "You had just been shot at by someone you thought was a friend and were exhausted from the day's trials." After another gentle kiss, he barely lifted his head and lost himself in her stormy gaze. "And dare I remind you that you immediately fell asleep in my arms?"

She huffed like a child about to throw a tantrum. "No."

He tried not to smile, but her wanting him with such ferocity filled his heart with joy. "Go upstairs and have Marie help you into your riding habit," he whispered. "Let the gossips be damned."

Eyeing him as though wondering what demon had taken control of his tongue, she eased a step back. "Was it not you that sided with Maman only yesterday about Dr. MacMaddenly's recommendation that I forgo riding for at least several weeks?"

Nash ducked his head, feeling like a schoolboy caught in a lie. "Yes, it was me. However, your troubled spirits concern me as much or more than your physical wellbeing. If the mind is not at peace, how can the body be?" He nodded at the sunny window. "It is a lovely day, and surely a calm, meandering ride through Hyde Park would do you more good than harm."

"And you do not mind the wagging tongues that will surely be set off by our riding on Rotten Row while propriety demands I hide at home in layers of black bombazine and crepe, respectfully mourning my brother?"

"Let the wagging tongues be damned."

Her hopeful smile started small, then blossomed into the full gamut of lighthearted joy he had hoped to coax free.

"I don't know which pleases me more," she said, "the fact that you remembered how I love riding or that I will actually be free of this Society-imposed prison for a few hours, and you refuse to let the gossips control our lives."

"*We* control our lives." Then he amended the bold statement with a humble tip of his head. "Well, we control as much of our lives as Her Majesty and Prinny allow." He gave her a quick kiss and nudged her toward the door. "Hurry now and get changed before we lose any more daylight."

"I shall be ready in no time." She gathered up her skirts and dashed away.

The sound of her skipping up the stairs filled him with joy and warm satisfaction. This was what the two of them needed—a brief escape into their own little world to strengthen their fragile bond. As he headed toward the window for a precautionary glance at the street, Merritt walked back into the parlor, scrubbing his face as if wearied to the bone.

"You survived," Nash said, unable to resist a teasing jab at his friend.

"Barely. She told me to go to the devil in no uncertain terms." Merritt shook his head. "And I believe a few of those terms were some of the coarsest French vulgarities I have ever heard anyone say, much less a lady."

"All because of your concern for her safety?" Nash eyed the man, knowing there had to be more to the story. The dowager countess never lost her temper and quite coolly eviscerated her enemies with a cutting wit that required no derogatory terms whatsoever. "What did you say to her?"

Merritt rubbed the back of his neck while staring downward and uneasily shuffling in place. "It might not have been what I said that drew the dressing-down she delivered."

Nash folded his arms across his chest and waited, knowing his friend would eventually confess all.

After a deep breath and a blustery sigh, Merritt shrugged. "I believe it was the kiss."

"The kiss?" Nash stared at him in disbelief. "You were foolish enough to kiss the woman when you knew her to be over-wrought about all that has recently come to pass?"

"It seemed like a good idea at the time."

"And now?"

"Perhaps not so much." Merritt grinned. "But at least she didn't shoot me. Maybe she possesses a growing fondness for me after all and just isn't quite ready to embrace it."

"And how do you propose to compete with the memory of her beloved husband?" Nash decided not to mention the age difference between the two. The dowager countess had to be almost two decades older than them both. "You cannot battle a ghost, old friend. Especially not one as cherished as Sophie's father."

"I have always loved a challenge. You know that." Merritt rolled his shoulders and tugged on his jacket to resettle it. "I saw the look in her eyes when I told her that if she insisted on leaving for Calais, I would be traveling with her."

"I still do not understand her need to return to France." Nash turned back to the window as if the street outside might provide him with an answer.

"About that," Merritt said as he joined him. "I believe I caught her in either a lie or a confession she did not wish to make."

"Go on."

"She said she needed to speak to someone in Calais and tell them if they did not cease, she would not be responsible for her actions." Merritt narrowed his eyes as he pursed his lips. "And then she jerked as if startled by the words she had just uttered and bellowed for me to get out, or she *would* shoot me."

"If they did not cease *what*?" An uneasiness rolled across Nash like a heavy, wet blanket smothering a fire. Suspicion filled him. "Surely she is not the one behind the assassination attempts on her own daughter." He shook his head at the silly notion. "No. She adores Sophie and would kill anyone who dared threaten her."

Merritt gave a doubtful shrug. "All I know is what she said, and how she reacted after she said it."

"Will you be able to stay close to her and watch her without getting shot?" Nash was dead serious this time. If Lady Nia knew the assassin or knew who sent the assassin, why hadn't she shared that important bit of information before now? He would be speaking to his mother-in-law after his outing with Sophie.

"I will stay close to her because I *wish* to stay close to her," Merritt said in a tone that spoke far louder than his words. "She is a woman worth getting shot for."

"Even though she told you to go to the devil?"

Merritt smiled. "It wasn't what she said, old friend, it was how she said it." He dipped a self-assured nod. "You know exactly what I mean. I've seen how you look at your wife. You are as besotted with her as I am with Lady Nia."

Nash snorted a laugh. "It appears we are a pair of fools."

"It would seem so." Merritt nudged him. "But better a happy fool than a miserable old sage, eh?"

"Most definitely." Nash glanced back at the door. "I am taking Sophie riding to get her mind off this miserable situation, even if only for a little while. Stay here and watch her mother. Lady Nia was not exaggerating when she said she was not a woman without resources. I would not be surprised if she attempted to steal off to France this very day."

Merritt arched a brow. "It also has not escaped my notice that the staff here are more devoted than most. That makes keeping her here more of a challenge." He tipped his head to one side while eyeing the stairs. "Perhaps I should stand guard at the door to her suite. I would not put it past the lady to try to escape by way of the servants' passages."

Nash clapped him on the back. "Good man."

Sophie appeared on the stairs resplendent in a dark blue riding habit.

He dismissed himself with a nod to his friend and met her in the hallway. She did not need to know Merritt's fears about her mother. He placed her hand in the crook of his arm and ushered her to the drawing room and out into the garden.

"One moment, my lady," he said as opened the back gate.

"Do not think me rude. I merely wish to keep you safe." He stepped through first and scanned the mews for anything that might be amiss. When all appeared as it should be, he held out his hand and smiled. "All clear. Come. Let us escape for a little while."

She took his hand and skipped along beside him like an excited young girl. "I so needed this. What a fortunate lady I am to have such a thoughtful husband."

He couldn't resist giving her a teasing wink. "That is exactly what I have been telling you, my swan."

As soon as they entered the stable, they halted to avoid being run over by a trio of young cats racing after something only the felines could see.

"So, these are the kittens you spoke of?" Nash laughed as one of them skittered up a wooden post, danced across the wall separating the stalls, then leapt onto its unsuspecting siblings as they rounded the corner.

"When did I tell you about the kittens?" she asked, while leading him to the stalls at the rear of the stable.

"During your laudanum sleep after your injury." Inwardly, he flinched. He should not have brought that up. This outing was to make her forget about the trials, not relive them. A sense of relief washed across him when she didn't seem at all troubled by his answer.

"Such nasty stuff that was. For future reference, I would rather be in pain." Then she tantalized him with a sultry smile and a slow wetting of her lips, making him contemplate finding an empty stall filled with an inviting bed of clean hay. "I do remember you resting your head beside me and refusing to join me in bed because you didn't wish to jostle me." She licked her lips again and lowered her voice to a seductive purr. "I am quite healed now, dear husband, and more than a little ready to be *jostled.*"

He couldn't resist pulling her into his arms and agreeing with a kiss so heated it left them both groaning. As he pressed her back against one of the posts, he deftly removed the pins holding her hat in place, swept it off her head, and tossed it aside. Nuzzling her throat, he took great pleasure in filling both his hands with her fine, round rump and pulling her tighter against him so she might feel the effect she had on him. "Are you not interested in riding, my swan?"

She worked her hips, molding her softness along his hardened ridge. "I am indeed interested in riding. Shall we not avail ourselves of that empty bench in the stall?" She slid her hands down his back and hugged him closer. "And then, after that delicious ride, if we are so inclined, we can continue on to the park to pursue the more usual definition of the word." She caught his earlobe between her teeth and drove him mad by gently sucking on it before whispering, "Forgive me if I am too brazen, but it is your fault. You made me drunk with pleasure on our wedding day, and now that I have decided to give *us* a chance, I thirst for that drunkenness again."

He stretched tall and peered across the tops of the stalls, searching for any sign of the head groom or other stable hands. Oddly enough, all seemed quiet and deserted except for the animals. Perhaps the men had paused in their labors to go and eat. After all, it was nearly time for their midday meal. Satisfied they wouldn't be disturbed, he bent his head and nibbled his way along her jawline while untying her cravat and unbuttoning her jacket. "My only regret is that we shall be unable to divest ourselves of all our clothing. I so love the feel of your skin against mine."

"And my skirts are so dreadfully long for modesty's sake," she murmured with a breathlessness that urged him on. Then she trembled with a mischievous giggle.

He lifted his head, smiling at her sudden merriment. "My lady?"

Her expression turned wonderfully wicked. "If you conquer the incredible yardage of my riding skirts, you will find nothing but skin underneath. That is—if you are so inclined."

"I am indeed so inclined." He swept her into the empty stall, undid his falls, then lowered himself to a handy bench left there by a groom. Ablaze with yearning and determination, he rucked up her skirts and smoothed his hands up the outside of her warm, silky thighs as she straddled him.

Holding tight to his shoulders, she wiggled downward and fully engulfed him while treating him to a delighted moan. "Wonderful," she breathed, then took his mouth with a hunger that threatened to make him spill himself entirely too soon. She moaned again and started rocking her hips with the perfect rhythm.

"Exemplary riding form," he rasped as he nibbled and kissed the delightful mounds of her breasts swelling above her corset.

"What?" She gave a shudder that warned him she was close to her bliss.

"Harder, my love. Ride harder and gallop to your pleasure."

"Oh yes!" She gave a gasping cry that pushed him past his limit. He rose and took her up against the wall, pounding into her with all the passion and fury she stirred within him. The side of the stall creaked and groaned as though about to give way. He didn't care. He drove harder, growling as she sank her teeth into his jacket, drowning her shout in the cloth. With a roaring thrust, he locked in and stayed, suspending them both in time as he emptied and she filled.

"Who is there?" someone bellowed from the front of the stable. "Answer, or you'll be going to his lordship on the end of me pitchfork!"

"It is all right, Mr. Wallace," Sophie called out, in a somewhat strained and breathless voice. "His lordship and I are going for a ride." She lost what little control she had mustered, erupting into a series of giggling snorts and rendering herself unable to speak further.

"All is well, Mr. Wallace," Nash said, struggling to sound authoritative rather than well bedded and looking forward to another tumble in the hay. "Go about your business. Lady Sophie and I can tend to our mounts."

"Aye, well, take care, my lord. That man what shot at the house had another one with him. We've yet to find that seedy cove, but we been a searching for him. I grant you that."

"Why are we just now hearing about this?" Sophie whispered while still pinned against the side of the stall.

"Let us sort ourselves and find out." As much as he hated to end their passionate *tête-à-tête*, he gave her a reluctant kiss, then withdrew and eased her feet to the ground. As she shook out her skirts, he suddenly realized that while caught up in the throes of their delights, he had forgotten about her injured back. "Bloody hell! Are you all right, Sophie?"

She eyed him as if he had lost all reason. "Of course I am all right. What on earth are you fussing about?"

"Your back? Hammered against those boards. Shall I send for Dr. MacMaddenly?"

"You most certainly shall not. I told you I am quite hearty, and I meant it. Now, stop being silly."

"I am never silly. Not when it comes to being concerned about your wellbeing."

"Hmmpf."

"And what does that mean?"

She rolled her eyes. "It means you should go and speak with Mr. Wallace while I finish tidying up." Her wicked smile returned. "You still owe me a ride, my lord."

"*Several*, my lady." Nash cleared his throat, adjusted the front of his pantaloons, and straightened his waistcoat and jacket with a jerk. "I shall see what Mr. Wallace can tell us."

He found the man at the front of the stable, sitting on a short stool, sharing his meat pie with the trio of kittens and their mother. "Perhaps Cook should make the meat pies larger, Mr. Wallace, so you do not go wanting while feeding your friends there."

The grizzled old man grinned as he held out a tidbit to the mother cat, and she ate it from his hand. "Aww...I don't mind none. This here girl is the best ratter in all of London." He nodded at the largest of the three kittens. "And that one there done caught him a mouse in the feed the other day. Takes after his mum, he does."

"Perhaps they deserve a meat pie all their own as a reward. Tell Cook I said so. A meat pie a day to keep the rats away." Besides, Sophie loved the kittens. Nash knew she would approve. "You said there was another man with the assassin we captured. Why did you not mention it earlier?"

Mr. Wallace, the head groom, shifted uneasily on the stool and shook his head. "Because the bastard got away. Shamed me, it did. I used to be a fair enough guard for the mistresses of the house while keeping their favorite horses healthy, and now look at me. One snuck up the garden wall and hurt Lady Sophie and the other shot at her." He hung his head and set the rest of the meat pie on the ground for the cats. "I should be let go, I should. But I am that sorry, my lord."

"No one is going to be let go," Sophie said as she joined them. "Especially not you, Mr. Wallace. I could not entrust my beautiful horses or my kitties to anyone but you."

"Why do you believe that the man who took the shot and the one who climbed the wall are two different people?" Nash asked. "Did you see them? Can you describe the second man?"

Mr. Wallace pushed himself to his feet and pointed out the door. "I guess I couldn't say that the one that done the shooting and the one who climbed the wall weren't the same, but I caught sight of the second man watching while you and Mr. Merritt dragged his partner away. Right there he was. At that corner. But by the time I grabbed my pitchfork and went to catch the bas—" He clamped his mouth shut and gave an apologetic tip of his head to Sophie. "Beg pardon, my lady. By the time I went to catch the fiend, he'd done took off quicker than a fox. Tall man. Older. Dark-headed, with some gray. Had an odd look about him."

"Have you seen him around here since?" Nash asked, wondering if taking Sophie to the park was such a good idea after all.

The old groom shook his head. "No, my lord. And the other grooms are watching for him as well. Anybody comes around here will be set upon right quick, so they best have a good reason for being here."

"Good man," Sophie said as she bent and stroked the mother cat's sleek back. "And thank you for taking such good care of Mama here and her babies."

"I wish I'd done better with that there cove, my lady." Mr. Wallace seemed to sag as he blew out a heavy sigh. "I beg your forgiveness."

"There is nothing to forgive." Sophie gave him a stern shake of her finger. "Carry on as you always have. I rest easier knowing you are here."

He bowed his head. "Thank you, my lady. Thank you kindly." He bobbed his head again. "I best get your mounts ready. I know you said you was doing it, but that just ain't proper, if you don't mind my saying so. Be ready for you in a moment." He shuffled off down the aisle between the stalls.

"Sophie," Nash said, not wanting to disappoint her but determined to keep her safe.

She held up a hand. "We are going. I refuse to cower."

"We must be rational and safe." He braced himself for the argument he saw brewing in her eyes.

"Then fetch your pistol and have Thornton fetch mine from my bedside table. It is my favorite, and fits quite nicely in the special pocket I had the craftsman add to my saddle." She twitched a shrug that dared him to argue. "Or there is a rifle in my workroom, and all our saddles have been modified to carry them."

"And do you have shields you can lash around your body in case the miscreant shoots from a distance before we see him?"

"I daresay that my jacket, waistcoat, and the whalebone in this corset should at least slow a bullet. I am sure I will be quite fine. In fact, my greatest danger will probably be from too much sun." She gave a decisive nod. "Please have Thornton send my parasol along with my pistol."

"You cannot ride with your parasol." Nash felt himself losing this disagreement at an alarming speed.

"Have you quite forgotten my impeccable horsemanship?"

He surrendered with a bow of his head. He did not have the heart to refuse her, not when they were getting along so well. "You will stay beside me at all times and do as I ask should anything untoward happen. Agreed?"

Victory sparkled in her smile and gleamed in her eyes. "Agreed. I shall be the model of an obedient wife."

"I doubt that very much, my swan."

She snorted with mirth. "So do I."

CHAPTER ELEVEN

"IT HAS BEEN well over a month, Maman, and nothing has happened." Sophie had never seen her mother so tenacious or single-minded about anything in her life. "Please stay here so I can see that you are safe with my own eyes."

Her mother didn't answer. She merely continued inspecting the open trunks and boxes scattered around her bedchamber, supervising while her maid packed them.

"Maude, please leave us for a moment," Sophie said to the maid. "Perhaps treat yourself to a cup of tea?"

The silver-haired matron who had served Sophie's mother since the beginning of time folded her hands across her thick middle and arched a brow at her mistress.

"Yes, Maude," the dowager countess said. "I understand there is still much to pack, but please give us a few moments. I shall ring for you once I fully impress upon my daughter that I know best."

"There should be time for two slices of cake, then," the woman said as she toddled out the door.

Sophie glared after the maid. "Was that bit of wit aimed at your ability to make a convincing argument or my stubbornness?"

"Both, I would imagine." Maman idly pawed through an open box on the bed, frowning at the neatly rolled fichus and lacy handkerchiefs. "Some of these must be yours. I cannot imagine any good reason for possessing so many." With a flip of her hand, she huffed, as though dismissing the items from her presence. "Wasteful extravagance."

"Stay," Sophie said, not giving ground or allowing time for Maman to launch into another rebuttal. "Mr. Wethersby wants you to stay as much as I do. So does Nash." She decided to use the last possible weapon that might convince her mother to remain in London. "What if I am with child? I will need you here to help me."

Her mother narrowed her eyes the slightest bit. She meandered closer, then slowly walked around Sophie, studying her from every angle.

Sophie clenched her teeth, forcing herself not to fidget. Maman could sniff out a falsehood better than any hound on a hunt.

"When you do discover yourself blessed to be in the family way," her mother said, "I shall return well before my grandchild arrives. Do not lie about such things, Sophie. It is bad luck." She softened the scolding with a smile. "I have delayed returning to Calais as long as I am willing. Without me here in the house, you and your husband will have the privacy you need to grow closer and, if you are very fortunate, forge the kind of love your papa and I had." Her smile turned somewhat cynical. "And Mr. Wethersby is coming with me—even though I advised him his efforts are wasted."

"He is quite smitten with you." Sophie hated to see Nash's friend crushed, but she hated seeing her mother's loneliness even more.

"The man will eventually come to his senses and find a young woman who can give him children," Maman said quietly. "I find my own company pleasant enough after all these years and have no desire to watch pity and revulsion replace the admiration in his eyes as I age."

Sophie caught hold of her mother's hands, not knowing any other reason that might change her mind. "Please stay, Maman.

Please? It is almost August, and crossing the channel will be safe enough, but with fall and then winter coming—it could become too treacherous for you to return before spring. Please stay."

Her mother's expression hardened. "If I stay, the attacks upon you will not stop."

"How do you know that?"

"Because I have dealt with these situations before and will be better suited to deal with this one from Calais."

Sophie released her mother's hands and widened her stance as if ready to come to blows. "That argument makes no sense at all. If you can only suitably deal with this from Calais, then why did we come to London in the first place? Why did we not attack the matter from France?"

"We had to protect Her Majesty, and you know that. Do not attempt to trap me with my own words." Maman strode over to the bellpull and yanked on it. "We are done here, child. I love you, and it is because of that love that I am leaving this afternoon. This conversation is over. You may leave immediately." Her mouth tightened into a hard, displeased line that warned any further argument would be most unpleasant.

Sophie managed a nod, then left the room without another word. She hadn't been dismissed from her mother's presence because of her parent's anger since the time she had accidentally shot another student at the academy. The bullet had only grazed the poor young man, but Maman had been incensed, and rightly so. Sophie had ignored instructions, and someone was hurt because of her carelessness.

Rather than go to the parlor, she went down to her workroom. After lighting a single candle, she dropped into the worn leather chair in the corner. Perhaps she could think better in the shadows.

It was the end of July, almost August, and nothing had happened since the shooting well over a month ago. No threatening messages. No lurking strangers. Nothing. Perhaps the man spotted by Mr. Wallace had only been an assistant to the marksman and took off to save himself. Even so, an uneasiness had remained in the air, an eerie quiet—almost like waiting for the unknown evil to exhale. But couldn't that merely be because they were all so obsessed with the frustrating situation?

"Sophie?" Nash's deep voice echoed through the dimly lit room.

"I am over here. In the corner."

He lit the rest of the tapers on the candelabrum in the middle of the worktable, then joined her. "And why have you put yourself in the corner, my love? And in the dark, no less?"

"I had hoped it would help me think." A disgusted groan escaped her. "She is going. This afternoon. There is nothing I can say or do to delay her further. It's a wonder she remained here this long."

He pulled up a stool and sat beside her. "Merritt will keep her safe."

"She will never allow herself to love him. She told me so herself." The entire situation lay heavy on Sophie's heart, making it hard to breathe. "She doesn't want to watch his love turn to pity and then revulsion. Her words. Not mine. Well, she didn't say *his love*. She called it *admiration*."

Nash took her hand like he always did whenever trying to console her. "He will still keep her safe, and as for the other, we have to let them sort that out for themselves."

"I don't want to let them sort it out for themselves. I want her to stay here and allow herself to love Merritt, and for all of us to live happily ever after."

"It is never that simple, dear one." He gave her hand a gentle squeeze. "Life is more like a war to survive, and we must make ourselves happy by winning one battle at a time and celebrating each victory as it comes. That is what enables us to persevere through difficult times."

She scowled at him, knowing he spoke the truth, but hating it just the same. "When she leaves, I will be the mistress of this house, and that terrifies me."

The golden glow of the candlelight shone upon his confused frown. "Why? From what I have seen, she always leaves the running of the household to you. You usually instruct Thornton and his wife on all matters."

"You misunderstand. It is not so much the running of the house that bothers me. I know I am the countess now—even though I should be the earl." Guilt pinched her for her pettiness, but it was true. Had she been born a male, she would have been the earl. "I am the countess now," she repeated, pushing through her guilt. "I am the lady of the house, your wife, and someday, maybe, a mother. I do not excel at those roles as well as I do espionage, horsemanship, and weaponry. With Maman here, I am still the daughter, the child who plays at those things whenever it suits her. Sort of, anyway." She allowed herself another groan, even though she hated sounding like such a petulant ninny. "I suppose you find me a spoiled, selfish wife and most disappointing. I am sorry and ashamed of being the way I am."

"I find you honest and never disappointing." He offered her an endearing, lopsided smile. "Did you ever pause to think that maybe the true reason your mother is returning to Calais is because she feels the need to push you, her beloved fledgling, out into the world? She knows you will not only fly but soar."

Rather than admit he might be right, she rolled her eyes. "Why must you always compare me to some sort of bird?"

"Because you have the spirit of a bird, my dear one. The courage of an eagle, sauciness of a wren, and the loveliness of a swan." He grinned. "And *sometimes* even the wisdom of an owl."

"Tread lightly. I am in no mood to be trifled with." If he had a bit of sense about him, he would leave her to her sullenness and save himself. She eased her hand out of his and curled deeper into her chair, tucking in for a good pout. Tomorrow, she would strive to be a better person. Today, she was what she was. "Now, if you will excuse me, I intend to sit here and fume until time to bid Maman farewell."

"The post just came. Do you not wish to go through it? There are two letters, one from your Frannie, I believe. There is also a smattering of invitations. It appears your refusal to return to mourning dress after our ride in the park has been not only noticed but accepted—oddly enough."

"We are somewhat of an enigma with those of the *ton*, what with most of our time spent in Calais. Since none of them ever *met* my dearly departed brother, it appears that poor, fictitious Solomon and his untimely passing have been easily forgotten."

"Or the gossips simply wish to confirm the rumors they have heard."

She was in no humor to deal with the politics of the *ton*, nor to become their latest source of amusement. As far as she was concerned, the invitations would be ignored. "Who was the other letter from?" She cracked her fingers, wishing she could make her problems pop as easily as she did her knuckles.

"The other letter?"

"You mentioned two letters. One from Frannie and the other from…?" She arched a brow, beginning to suspect he had lied to coax her out of her doldrums.

He shook his head, appearing somewhat perplexed. "I am not sure."

A suspicion, an exciting premonition, pushed her up from the chair. "How could you possibly ignore a letter when we haven't heard from our blackmailer in so long?"

"Because I had hoped, after all this time with no sinister activity, that our blackmailer's health and wellbeing had ended with the self-poisoning of Horton Bainery."

She hurried to the door, then halted when she realized he still sat on the stool beside her chair. "Well, come on, then. Let's have a look at that letter, shall we?"

He did not appear as excited as she was, but that could not be helped.

"I cannot believe you hope the blackmailer has contacted you again."

His tone struck her as slightly scolding, but she ignored it. "I am not hopeful…exactly." Well, she was a bit, but it would sound somewhat mindless to admit it. Something deep inside her, whether it was instinct, womanly intuition, or simply a *feeling*, told her the game was not over—not with so many questions yet to be answered. Gathering her skirts in both hands, she rushed up the short flight of stairs and down the hall to the table that always held the mail. The silver tray was empty, prompting her to turn and glare at Nash.

"In the library," he said tersely while pointing at the door. "Calm down, my swan. Everything is on your desk."

She wasted no time in making her way to it and the pile of correspondence neatly stacked in front of her inkwell holder. The letter from Frannie was on top. Then what appeared to be several invitations, and then the missive she sought. An exciting sense of satisfaction settled across her as she tapped the neatly scribed postage amount in one corner. "Two shillings and fourpence. Fifty miles. Just like the others."

"Bloody hell," he growled. He snatched the letter out of her hands and ripped it open. The longer he stared down at the page, his gaze racing back and forth across the few lines, the ruddier his face became. With a hard shake of his head, he bared his teeth and handed it back to her. "Your mother must not leave here under any circumstances."

Her satisfaction curdled into a lump of dread and plummeted to the pit of her stomach. Struggling to keep her hands from shaking, she smoothed out the folded paper and read:

The old one dies in the channel and the young one dies in the park. I shall let the queen rot in Kew. No money or thanks necessary. Liars and deceivers dead is reward enough.

"Quite to the point, isn't it?" She swallowed hard, carefully refolded the letter, and handed it back to him. "I am a fool and living proof of Aesop's warning to be careful what you wish for." How could she have hoped for more contact from that maniacal cove? She slowly lowered herself into the chair behind her desk, for once at a complete loss for words or what to do.

Nash leaned across the desk and propped his hands on either side of the paper. "I will send word to Her Majesty to double her guard at Kew. Your mother will not leave here even if I have to lock her in her rooms." He gently cupped her chin in his hand and lifted her face to his. "And you, my precious one, will not go near any park in London or anywhere outside of this house without me or a proper guard at your side—understood?"

"Yes." For the first time in her life, she would not be unreasonably stubborn about her independence. She would listen and pray that they caught the blackguard before he succeeded at any of his attempts. "I am so sick of living on tenterhooks, though. How are we going to stop this devil?"

"Merritt and I will call in a few favors. Several of those we served with in the army will be more than happy to help. Of that, I have no doubt." A thoughtful bitterness seemed to settle across him. "You are right about that adage, though. *Be careful what you wish for.* I once wanted to return to serving my king and country in the army, and you wanted the blackmailer to make himself known to us once again. It appears we both got our wishes." He caressed her cheek and gave her a tender kiss. "Once this is all over, we shall make ourselves content with enjoying a quiet life here in London. Yes?"

"Most definitely." She had always wanted love and the joy and contentment Celia and Frannie had found. Now she had it, and that murderous fiend was trying to take it away from her. She tightened her hands into fists and popped each knuckle, growing angrier by the moment. "No one is going to take away what I have wanted since I first saw you flirt with Lady Withrington and ignore me. I will not allow that devil to destroy us." She might sound bold, brazen, or perhaps even hoydenish, but she didn't care. "I am going to kill him before he kills me or harms someone I love."

Nash pulled her up into his arms and held her. "Let me do the protecting. It is not only my duty but my desire, and I promise you, Merritt feels the same. Did you not tell me you had maps in your workroom tracking the postal points of each letter?"

"Yes. In the map cabinet behind the desk." She eased out of his embrace and almost cringed while eyeing the door. "Maman is already angry with me. I pray she sees sense when I tell her and doesn't think this is some ploy to keep her here."

"I shall tell her."

"I am so sorry," she whispered. She was so ashamed of her petulance, selfishness, and slowness in forgiving him for the silly hurts of their youth.

He frowned at her, appearing confused. "For what are you apologizing?"

"The queen sacrificed your life for Maman and me. It is so unfair."

He didn't respond for a long moment. Instead, he resettled his stance and looked away, as if uncomfortable in his own skin. "I will admit," he finally said, "that I felt it unfair at first. Especially when you hated me so." He slowly pulled her back into his arms. "But then I found it impossible to think of a life without you. You possess my heart completely." He sealed the words with a kiss so tender and loving that it threatened to make her weep. "I will keep you safe, my darling swan. Do not be afraid."

"As long as you keep yourself safe too." She touched his cheek, thankful for his love, his patience, and his tenacity. "I hope our children are not as stubborn as you and I. We will be sorely pressed to keep up with them if they are."

"Indeed, we will." He tucked her hand into the crook of his arm. "Come. Let us go have a word with your mother."

"Would you rather I do it alone? She is already angry with me."

"I am not afraid of your mother."

Sophie forced herself not to smile at his bravado.

"I do not fear her, Sophie," he repeated in an injured tone.

"Of course you do not fear her. You merely have a healthy

admiration of her." She gave his arm a sympathetic pat. "As do I. Do you think we might get Merritt to tell her?"

Nash arched a brow but didn't quite pull off a scowl. "You must stop tossing my friend to the proverbial wolves."

"It was merely a thought." She huffed. "Admittedly, a cowardly thought, but a thought just the same."

Just as they reached Maman's sitting room door, it flew open and the dowager countess herself rushed into the hallway, mumbling something in French. When she noticed them, she halted with a startled jerk but then quickly recovered. "What is it?" she asked rather snappishly. "I have much to do."

"You do not, my lady." Nash handed her the letter. "I find it deeply concerning that our blackmailing assassin is quite informed about the goings-on of this household. Read it. I am sure you will find it unsettling as well."

Maman paled as she read the letter. "It appears we have a traitor among us," she whispered.

"But who?" Sophie asked. "Only the staff knew of your plans to return to Calais, and they have all been with us for years."

"No. There was one other." The dowager turned almost thoughtful. "The *malletier* on Bond Street knew. Two of my trunks suffered some damage in the channel crossing and required repair before they could be reused. I was not aware of this until a few days ago, when Maude started packing. I had the trunks sent to Waldreges with the explicit instruction that I required them to be repaired and reinforced for a crossing to France this week."

"Who delivered the trunks to Bond Street?" Nash asked. "And when?"

"Redmond took them last week, but he has been in our employ for well over five years."

"Someone in the shop could have overheard him passing along your instructions," Sophie said. "Especially if they were having the house watched and followed him there."

"I shall speak with Redmond and send Merritt to Waldreges

to have a word with the shopkeeper." Nash tapped on the letter and leveled a stern look on the dowager countess. "You are staying here, my lady. For your own safety."

Sophie held her breath, waiting for Maman to argue or fuss. But her mother did neither. She simply touched her brow as if suddenly overcome by a terrible headache.

"I shall inform Maude," she said in a weak voice as she slowly moved back into the sitting room. Head bowed and her usually pristine posture now sagging and tired, she let the letter fall to the floor as she crossed to the sofa, settled down upon it, and draped a hand over her eyes.

"Maman." Sophie went to her. "It will be all—"

Her mother held up a hand and silenced her. "Let me rest, daughter. Please, just let me rest."

"Yes, Maman." Sophie pulled a knitted throw from the back of the sofa, spread it across her mother, then quietly left the room and closed the door.

Nash stood in the hallway, his face shadowed with a grim look of worry. "It is not that I don't trust your mother…"

"Perhaps Merritt should take up his post outside her door just to be certain." Sophie trusted her mother too, but also knew the fearless woman was quite capable of taking extreme measures to protect everyone but herself. "I hope she doesn't choose to do something dangerous, but I cannot say with any certainty that she won't."

"That is my fear as well. I believe Merritt is in his quarters packing. I shall speak to him now."

"Here is the letter if you wish to show it to him." Sophie pressed the vile thing into Nash's hands, wishing there was a simple way of ridding themselves of this dark cloud constantly hanging over them. She stared at the letter, willing it to tell her the identity of its author.

"Sophie? Your look worries me."

"We are going to have to set a trap. You do realize that?" She knew he wouldn't like it, but surely he would agree with her reasoning. "It is the only way we will ever be rid of this black-guard. Capture him. Make sure he doesn't have any poison to kill himself with before he talks, and then deal with him. I am sure Queen Charlotte would be more than happy to have Prinny order the man either hanged or beheaded for treason and murderous threats to the Crown."

Nash scrubbed his face with one hand. "Yes. I realize that is the only way we will ever be free." He caught hold of both her arms and pulled her closer. "But swear to me you will do nothing without my knowledge and approval."

"I promise." And she wouldn't. Too much was at risk for her to rush in and be foolhardy. "I know you wish to speak to Merritt and your army chums. All I ask is that you include me in the plans. Please do not treat me like some delicate orchid that needs to be set on a shelf and isolated." She gently patted his chest. "I can help. You know I can. Please respect that."

"I will, my love." He kissed her forehead as if sending her off to bed. "I remember your brilliance at strategizing and am sure it has only improved with age."

"Such flattery will get you everywhere," she teased, hugging him closer.

"And here I thought you didn't like flattery."

"It depends on what kind." She pulled him down for a kiss filled with determination and hope for their future. When he lifted his head, she smiled. "Onward to win this war, my husband."

He nodded. "Onward, my love."

CHAPTER TWELVE

"COLONEL! GADS, MAN, it is good to see you!" bellowed Nash's former general. "Do come in, and may I say you are looking very well."

"Trevy!" scolded Lady Hampshire, the general's wife, in the shrill voice Nash remembered from his army days. "This is Lord Rydleshire now. Did you not hear Forston announce him as such?"

Sir Malcolm Trelvadere Hampshire, known as *general* to some and Sir Malcolm to all except his wife, ignored the woman's nattering. The curled tips of his flamboyant white mustache twitched upward and framed his round red cheeks as he smiled. "A colonel, a knight, and now an earl. What's next, man? A dukedom?" The portly man, confined to his chair because of the loss of both legs below the knees, stuck out his hand.

Nash gave the fearless baronet the same warrior handshake he always used with Merritt, grabbing the man's forearm and gripping it tightly. "Good to see you, general. Forgive me for not calling more regularly." He added a wink. "And call me anything you like, old man. You earned that right years ago."

"There! You see, Viola? Now toddle on and leave the colonel and me to speak of things too unseemly for your delicate sensibilities." Sir Malcolm waggled a bushy white brow at his scowling wife.

The lady puffed like a hen with ruffled feathers. "I shall have

Forston bring in your port." She dipped a curtsy in Nash's direction. "My lord," she said before flouncing from the room.

"I heard of your marriage," the general said as he rocked deeper into his chair. "Her Majesty's orders, I suppose?" With a strained grunt, he twisted to reach an ornate metal box on the table beside him. He lifted the lid, took out a cigar, then glanced Nash's way. "May I offer you one?"

"Thank you, no." He had never much cared for tobacco but remembered the general was rarely seen without some form of the leaf, whether it be pipe, snuff, or cigars.

Sir Malcolm accepted his decline with a nod before clamping the tip of a fresh cigar between his teeth and lighting it with a spill set ablaze from the candle on the table. After several deep draws that set the cheroot glowing bright red on the end, he settled back and smiled. "As I said, Her Majesty's orders? You are known to be her darling."

"A title I prefer not to use." Nash was well aware of the gossip but helpless to change it. After all, one did not refuse Her Majesty or Prinny.

The general smiled broader and chuckled, making his great white mustache quiver. "I would never insult you, old friend. Merely curious, since I never thought of you as one interested in marriage."

"No offense taken, since it *was* by order of the queen." Nash ducked his head like a naughty schoolboy. "But now I find myself even more deeply indebted to Her Majesty for matching me with such a wonderful woman."

"Ah…true love, is it?" Sir Malcolm took a long, slow draw off his cigar, making the end of it glow even brighter red. He lifted his chin and released the smoke, blowing it upward into a whirling pillar of gray. "I am glad for you, then." He patted his leg. "Viola is an irritating sort with her nagging tongue loose at both ends most of the time, but I could not have survived this, neither physically nor mentally, without her. Nothing heals the body, the mind, or the soul like a love that is real." He puffed on the cigar again, eyes narrowing as he watched Nash. "What brings you here? I wouldn't waste my time visiting an old cripple. Why would you unless you needed something?"

Guilt at ignoring his former commander filled Nash. "You are not an *old cripple*, general, and I beg your forgiveness for my thoughtless neglect of our friendship."

Sir Malcolm held up a hand. "My bluntness was not a trawling for apologies. You know me, old boy. I say what I think and fully expect my officers to do the same." He leaned forward, his eyes twinkling with interest. "Now, what is it that brings you here?"

"Merritt Wethersby and I could not locate Burns. Forthrite, Tomes, and Freedly said you might know where we could find him, since the two of you are quite close." The general had saved Burns's life once, and Burns had repaid the favor by carrying the general from the battle that had cost him both his legs. Nash went quiet and sat straighter as the butler entered the room, carrying a tray with a decanter and two glasses.

"Well met, Forston." The general patted the arm of his chair, then pointed at the table beside Nash. "The colonel can pour. That will be all, my good man."

"Very good, sir." The butler bowed, then left the room, closing the door on his way out.

Nash poured them both a generous splash of the ruby liquid, handed the general his, then held his glass high. "What shall we toast, general?"

Sir Malcolm chuckled. "Success to whatever brings you here and causes you to search out the best riflemen of our regiment."

"Still a sly old dog, I see," Nash said after taking a sip of his drink.

"My body might be broken, but there is nothing wrong with my mind." The general swirled the port in his glass, eyeing the sparkling red richness as though mesmerized. "Who is in danger?"

"My wife, my mother-in-law, and our queen."

"And the threat?"

Nash blew out a heavy sigh. "We have yet to identify the assassin. Unfortunately, I have concluded that a trap must be set."

Sir Malcolm frowned, then shifted his focus from his glass to Nash. "Is your mother-in-law not the infamous Lady Nia? The former spy most trusted and valued by the Crown?"

"She is. Though most do not remember her as such, since she remained in France after her husband's assassination." He hated to rush the general, but he needed to get back to Merritt and the others waiting for him at Rydleshire House. "Do you know of Burns's whereabouts? You know he was the best of the four."

The baronet's woolly white brows knotted together over his troubled eyes. "Therein lies the problem, old boy. Burns is working for me." He cleared his throat, downed the rest of his port, then took a long, hard draw on his cigar and blew out the smoke, filling the air with the acridly pungent scent. "He is seeing to a very personal matter of which I am most ashamed."

A deep sense of loyalty booted Nash square in his conscience. He also wanted Burns as part of his team. If he helped the general with this *personal matter*, perhaps Burns would be free to help protect Sophie and the dowager countess.

"Is there something I could help with?" he asked as delicately as possible.

The old man exhaled another roiling column of smoke while frowning off into the distance. "It is Adelaide. She has not only ruined herself but thoroughly besmirched the Hampshire name." Still scowling, he slowly shook his head. "But she is my only child. My beloved daughter whom I shall always love, no matter what. I cannot bear the thought of disowning her, even though that is what her mother wishes."

Nash remembered Miss Adelaide Hampshire well. A stunning beauty with golden hair, large, mesmerizing eyes, and curves that made her extremely dangerous, since she was the general's daughter. As he recalled, Miss Hampshire also possessed a somewhat forward nature that had ruined many a young lady who refused to listen to her elders. "How can I help, general?"

"That, I cannot say." Sir Malcolm shook his head again. "After the Duke of Winstead refused to support the bastard he foisted upon her, she would not agree to come home and send the cause of her shame to a place for foundlings. Instead, she charmed an unknown source into footing the bill for the scheme she settled upon to support herself and the child."

"And that scheme was?" Nash hazarded to ask.

"A sporting hotel on Bond Street." The general's shoulders sagged. He suddenly looked weary and spent. "My daughter is the madam of a brothel that caters to some of the wealthiest in London."

Nash was at a loss for words. There was nothing he could say that would console his old friend, and he also didn't quite know how he might help. But duty and old loyalties demanded that he try. "What can I do?"

Sir Malcolm tamped out his cigar on the plate he used to catch the ashes. He brushed his hands together, then held out his glass. "Pour me another. That is what you can do."

After refilling both their glasses and handing the general his, Nash settled back in his chair. "How is Burns helping you?"

"He is her doorman, and protector if need be. Wealthy gentlemen of Society or not, some of her clients behave as though the world is theirs for entertainment no matter the cost—or the injury to anyone else involved." He sipped his port, then cut his gaze back to Nash. "I realize my daughter is a fallen woman, but she did not get to that level by herself." He snorted out a pained growl. "And Burns reports that since her child died, Adelaide has not been the same. He said it's as though she dares fate to do something else to cause her more pain. She takes unnecessary risks." He relit his cigar and took several long, deep puffs. "She will always be my dear little Adelaide, and I want her safe. My solicitor showed her what I set up for her in Belgium, so she might start anew, but she laughed at it and refused. Said it was too modest and common, and not enough to support her for a month. She also said she needed excitement, not some paltry little cottage on the outskirts of a dull little village in the country."

The more the poor general talked about his daughter, the more hopeless the situation seemed to Nash. If the girl didn't wish to change and start anew, she couldn't be forced to do so. And there was also the matter of paying off whoever had sponsored her setting up of the *sporting hotel*. With it on Bond Street, that financial undertaking would have been quite substantial. Only one possible solution came to him, and it was a very weak one. "If she needs excitement, perhaps she should become a spy for the Crown. My mother-in-law's Rydleshire Academy still trains candidates."

Sir Malcolm thoughtfully pursed his lips and tipped his head to one side. "Considering my Adelaide's *skills*"—he abruptly cleared his throat,—"she might make quite the effective agent for Her Majesty." Then his forehead wrinkled, and he appeared about to lose his composure. "But how will that keep my precious girl safe?"

"While I cannot guarantee her safety, perhaps with time, it will enable her to forgive herself for choices she wishes she never made and accept your offer of that cottage in Belgium."

"You think it will increase her opinion of herself?"

Nash rose from his chair and set his empty glass aside. "That I cannot say, but it would provide her with the excitement she told your solicitor she needed, and a different set of acquaintances from those with whom she currently keeps company. I have also witnessed a change in those who suddenly discover they are valued and have an honorable purpose in their lives." He tipped an uncertain shrug, at a loss for any other alternatives for the wayward lady. "Burns could go along with her if he wanted. There is a nearby village where he could stay and still watch over her."

"Burns would go. The man loves her." Sir Malcolm snorted. "He doesn't think I know, but I am not a fool." He squinted up at Nash. "But what about you? You said you needed his services."

"I would like to have his services, but it appears your daughter needs him just as direly as I do. I have Forthrite, Tomes, Freedly, and Wethersby." He offered his old friend a humble nod. "I shan't be greedy."

"How do you propose my daughter learns of this opportunity? She refuses to darken our door here." Sir Malcolm rumbled with another irritated growl. "And rightly so, after the way her mother treated her the last time she visited."

"I would be more than happy to go to Bond Street and speak with her," Nash said, somewhat relieved that he'd found some small way to help his old friend. "I shall also inform Burns. Perhaps he can gently urge her to agree if she refuses at first."

"And you are certain the infamous Lady Nia will agree? It had always been my understanding that Rydleshire Academy was quite selective."

A snorting laugh escaped Nash as he remembered what his mother-in-law had said long ago. "Lady Nia accepts her candidates based on three prerequisites: drive, raw talent ready to be refined, and the ability to pay for her exemplary training." With a reassuring nod, he added, "And since you are my friend, there will be no cost for Miss Hampshire's training." He felt sure the dowager countess would waive the fees. Especially since Sophie had shown him the ledgers of all the businesses they had funded to help women support themselves and their families. He had been amazed at the Rydleshire empire and its intricate web of ventures that gave women the opportunities they deserved.

After a throaty *harrumph*, Sir Malcolm resettled himself in his chair. "I do not expect charity. I may only be a baronet and a retired general, but I am not a man without means."

"It is not charity. It is friendship. Would you not do the same for me?"

The old man *harrumphed* again. "That goes without saying, but you understand my meaning."

"I do indeed, sir." Nash held out his hand. "I shall speak with Lady Nia this evening, and pay a call on Miss Hampshire and Burns tomorrow."

Sir Malcolm clasped Nash's hand with the powerful grip of a man half his age. "Once again, our battlefield brotherhood has saved me. You have my gratitude, colonel."

"As ever, I am grateful for your friendship, sir." Nash stood at attention and saluted his commander.

The general straightened in his chair, puffed out his chest, and returned the salute. "Keep me apprised of how it goes, colonel. I look forward to hearing of your success."

"I shall indeed, sir." After a polite bow, Nash dismissed himself, eager to set in motion the plan to help Miss Hampshire and to speak with Burns about any recommendations the man might have to assist him in his own cause. He would consult with the dowager countess tonight in private after discussing the change in plans with Merritt and the other men.

As he stepped up into the carriage and settled in the seat, he debated whether to tell Sophie. The general and his wife were quite ashamed of their daughter's fall from grace and had no doubt experienced as much of the *ton*'s scathing treatment as they could bear. Society had probably ostracized them to where only their closest friends would associate with them, and that would only be under cover of darkness and, more than likely, by using the servants' entrance at the back of the house.

"Utterly ridiculous," he muttered. Out of respect for them, he would not tell Sophie, nor would he elaborate on the details with Merritt or the others. The only person who needed to know the entirety of Miss Hampshire's adventures was the dowager countess herself. Besides, a basic survival instinct warned him that his precious swan might not be especially pleased with his visiting Miss Hampshire to convince her to part ways with her current lifestyle. Hence, there was no need to upset Sophie by telling her.

As the carriage pulled up to Rydleshire House, he spotted her stepping out the door, alone and dressed for more than a simple breath of fresh air.

"Sophie!" he barked as he bounded out of the carriage.

She glared at him, clearly annoyed with the sharpness of his tone. At the moment, he didn't care. Not when her safety depended on her doing as he had asked.

"I was merely crossing the way to Celia's." She fidgeted in place, passing her reticule back and forth between her gloved hands, clearly knowing she was guilty as sin.

He stepped up beside her and cradled an arm around her waist as he eyed their surroundings for anything amiss. "You agreed to have a guard accompany you any time you stepped out of the house. Remember?" He struggled to keep his voice even and calm when what he really wished to do was throw her over his shoulder, carry her back inside, and lock her in their bedroom until they captured the devil threatening her life. He hugged her closer as they walked down the steps. "You promised me, Sophie."

"I checked the street through the windows," she weakly defended herself, then gave him a pained look. "Merritt and the others were deep in some sort of conversation. I didn't wish to interrupt them to toddle me across the way like a group of overly attentive nannies."

As they reached the bottom of the steps, he turned her to face him. "That is why I brought them here, and they fully understand that. Are you going to force me to have them guard you the way Merritt once stood guard outside your mother's bedchamber?"

"No," she said rather sheepishly while glancing aside to avoid looking him in the eyes.

"I love you, Sophie," he said softly, gathering her closer.

"Nash!" She hissed like one of the kittens while pushing on his chest. "Out here on the street?"

"To the devil with the street and everyone on it." He tilted her face up to his. "You are mine. I love you, and I intend to keep you safe. That is all that matters." He kissed her hard, pouring his love and fear for her safety into the bond. She had made him love her, and to be robbed of her now was a cruelty he was unwilling to bear.

He lifted his head and stared down at her. "Is the duchess

expecting you?"

The color rode high on her cheeks. She hitched in a shuddering breath and ran the tip of her tongue across her lips. "No. I merely thought to call upon her for a visit."

"Might you visit her tomorrow?" he whispered, while nuzzling the silky softness just beneath her ear.

She pressed closer while turning her head so he might continue his tasting of the sweet skin along her throat. "And why would I wish to delay my visit with her?"

"Come out of the street with me, my love, and I will show you." He tugged her back up the front steps and into the house.

Thornton appeared out of nowhere, his usual staid demeanor shifting to one of worry. "My lord, my lady, is something amiss?"

"Nothing at all, Thornton," Nash said before Sophie answered. Sweeping her up the stairs to their private suite, he called back over his shoulder, "We are not to be disturbed. We shall come down when we are ready."

"Yes, my lord." The butler's tone revealed no opinion whatsoever.

"Nash," Sophie quietly scolded while ducking her head. "What will everyone think?"

"They can think whatever they wish." He ushered her into their sitting room and bellowed, "Marie!"

"Marie is either downstairs or out. I am not sure which. I told her I would be out for a while and gave her the rest of the day to herself. I believe she is quite taken with Thomas."

"Who is Thomas?" Nash didn't truly care about the maid's personal interests, but now was not the time to bring a new individual into their house. No one could be trusted.

Sophie tugged on the fingers of her elbow-length gloves until they were loosened, then slid them off and draped them over the top of a chair. "Calm down. Thomas is our footman and has been in our employ for several years."

"Then why is this romance just happening now?"

"Because, unlike you," she said as she plucked out her hairpins and let her coppery locks tumble free, "Thomas appears to be painfully shy." She laughed. "But the poor man doesn't stand a chance. Marie can be quite determined."

Nash moved in behind her, combing his fingers through her luscious curls. An errant hairpin caught on his nail. "Missed one, my love."

"Thank you." Sophie took it from him and bent to place it on the table with the others.

Unable to resist the temptation, Nash caught hold of her sweet rump and pulled her back against him. "Such a wondrous woman," he groaned while pulling her harder against him and sliding a hand around to cup one of her breasts.

She reached back to pull him around for a kiss. "Undress me, my love, and we can be wondrous together."

If Nash had his way about it, he would rip off her clothes. The thought made him laugh as he undid the hooks and buttons of her gown.

"And what is so amusing?" she asked as she kicked off her slippers.

He spun her around to face him and caught her up against his chest. "I could have you as I want you much faster if I ripped off your clothes."

She eyed him with mock sternness while undoing the buttons of his waistcoat. "That could become quite costly, my dear. And besides—this is one of my favorite gowns." She tiptoed to kiss him as she shoved his jacket down off his shoulders. "I have you pinned now, my lord."

"And what will you do with me, my wanton lover?"

She reached down, undid the buttons of his falls, and slid her hand inside. "Whatever I wish," she promised in a throaty whisper.

His buttocks tightened as she treated him to a long, slow pull of his hardness, then reached even lower with her other hand and cupped his bollocks while stroking him more. An appreciative groan rumbled free of him. Her touch was perfection.

"Nakedness would be so much more advantageous," she said

as she shoved his pantaloons downward. "Oh dear. I forgot about your Hessians. Sit, so I can rid you of these dratted boots."

"I believe it would be much more efficient if we each stripped ourselves." He wanted her naked, himself buried inside her, and the lusciousness of her breasts in his mouth. "Agreed?"

"Agreed." She stepped back and shed everything—petticoat, stays, chemise, and stockings—then stood there, unashamedly nude and breathtaking.

With himself stripped down to nothing, he strode forward and clutched her close, skin to skin, glorious, hot flesh to flesh. He breathed in her delectable scent of jasmine and a woman ready to be taken as he stretched her back across the couch and settled down on top of her. "Gads, I cannot get enough of you."

"Good." With her eyes half closed and her smile seductive, she trailed her hands down his back, caught hold of his buttocks, and squeezed. "Take me to oblivion, my love. I am more than ready."

As he pushed into her hot wetness, he heartily agreed. "Pure heaven," he rasped, burying himself fully and grinding deeper. He took her mouth in a heated kiss while teasing her with the slightest thrusting of his hips.

She tangled her fingers in his hair, kissing him back just as wildly while arching up into him, matching the rhythm of her movements with his.

They clung together in the fierce bond, moving as one, skin sliding against skin, fully joined. Sophie shuddered and clutched around him, her wet hotness squeezing him, urging him to give her his all. A moan escaped her as she raked her fingers down his back and dug her nails into his flanks. Her need matched his, the ache to drive and pound until they both exploded with bliss.

Elbows locked, Nash drove hard, reveling not only in every delicious sensation but also in the sight of her lying beneath him, flushed pink with passion.

She cried out, bucked upward, then trembled and groaned while clutching him tighter.

Control shattered, blind lust and passion bade him pound,

and pound he did. A roar ripped from his throat as he emptied into her. Once spent, he collapsed, saving her from his weight by catching himself on his forearms.

"Gads," he gasped against her throat.

Her arms tightened around him, and she pulled him downward. "Indeed."

The lazy, purring way she drawled the word made him smile. He had pleased his wife as much as she had pleased him. A contentedness filled him, prompting him to lift himself enough to give her a tender kiss. "No more risks, my love. Promise me— please?"

She raked her fingers through his hair, combing it back from his forehead. "I shall try my very best to be more thoughtful about how I go about things." Her delicate brows drew together, lightly furrowing her irritated expression. "It is so hard to behave as though one might die at any moment from a villain's killing shot."

He kissed the tip of her nose and smiled. "It would help if you were a bit more fearful rather than a bloodthirsty little swan. You must not take risks. Don't you wish to spit in the fool's eye once we capture him?"

"Spit in his eye?" she growled. "I would much rather set him up as a target for either pistols or archery." Her fury quickly mellowed to a wickedly gleeful smile. "Your choice, of course."

"Whatever makes you happiest, my love." He buried his face in the curve of her neck and ran the tip of his tongue along the delicious length of her slender throat.

She stroked his sides and hugged her legs around him. "I know what would make me happiest right now," she said with a suggestive wiggle.

"I agree, my love, and we shall go slower this time and savor it." He nibbled along her collarbone and enjoyed the silky fullness of her breast in his palm. He moved lower and traced his tongue around her nipple. "To happiness."

"Uhm…to happiness and an afternoon of nothing but each other."

CHAPTER THIRTEEN

"AND WHERE ARE your guardians now, dear sister?"

Sophie cast a casual glance around as she and Celia meandered along Bond Street, idly admiring items in the shop windows. "I believe Mr. Forthrite remained close to the carriage. But the whereabouts of Mr. Tomes and Mr. Freedly escape me. I am sure they are very close, though. Mr. Wethersby spoke to them quite sternly about keeping me safe while Nash was…" She halted, searching her memory, only to discover she couldn't finish her reply with any reasonable semblance of certainty. Her dear husband had left extremely early before she came down to breakfast.

"While Nash was…?" Celia prompted while arching a brow.

Sophie shook her head as they admired a silver tea set fit for the queen herself. "He had an appointment somewhere today, but I am not certain where. He failed to say when he kissed me goodbye before I was fully awake." She squinted harder, not at the tea set but at the oddness of the situation. He had left their bedroom so very early. Where on earth would he have needed to be at such a peculiar hour?

"He probably had some boring errand not worth mentioning." Celia drew closer to the shop window and examined a long, narrow silver tray before pulling a quizzing glass from her reticule and holding it to her eye. "Oh dear, it was much prettier when I couldn't discern that those small handles on each end were writing eels rather than delicate scrollwork."

"Writing eels? Really?" Sophie took the small magnifying glass and eyed the intricate metalwork in question. "My goodness, you are right. Why on earth would anyone wish to have writhing eels for the handles of such an unusually long tray?"

"To serve eels for dinner, I suppose?" Celia shrugged as they continued on to the next shop window, enjoying the sunny day and balmy weather. "There is the parasol shop just there. Did you not say you wished to examine the newest styles and discover if they would suitably freshen your wardrobe?"

"I wondered if they might have some simple white ones or subtle prints available." Sophie lightly twirled the pale-yellow parasol she currently held in place to shield her from the sun. "I simply do not see the need for a different parasol to match every bonnet and walking dress. Not only is it wasteful, it is time consuming to ensure that every article of an ensemble is matched to the set with which it belongs."

"Have you become miserly now that you are married?" Celia teased.

Sophie couldn't resist rolling her eyes. "You know I have never condoned wastefulness. I consider it a vulgar attitude while so many are forced to do without, through no fault of their own." She halted, adjusted the tilt of her parasol, and squinted against the brightness of the day. Dread and disgust squeezed her like an overly tightened corset. "Oh dear, is that not Lady Bournebridge and her vicious little pets coming this way?"

"Indeed, it is," Celia said with what appeared to be a forced smile. "Forgive me, but we must speak to them even though she and her cronies gave our dear Frannie the cut direct at Gretna Green. Lord Bournebridge is little Oliver's godfather."

Sophie clenched her teeth and braced herself for the unpleasantness of greeting the demoness of Polite Society. Lady Bournebridge's sole purpose in life was to make everyone either find themselves owing her a costly favor or wishing they had never made her acquaintance—usually both. But if the vile woman had any wits about her, she would tread carefully. After all, Lady Bournebridge knew Sophie had discovered that her only daughter had fallen from grace and shamed the family by eloping to Gretna Green with the head groom of the Bournebridge stables.

Lady Bournebridge, Lady Essendon, and Lady Mardlebon inclined their heads in almost identical snobbish nods as they drew closer.

"Your Grace," Lady Bournebridge said to Celia before aiming a haughty curl of her lip at Sophie. "Lady Rydleshire."

"Greetings, Lady Bournebridge," Celia said, then returned the nods of the other two ladies.

"Good day, Lady Bournebridge," Sophie replied woodenly, wishing the viperous trio would move on with no further meaningless conversation. "Ladies," she said, belatedly acknowledging the other two for propriety's sake.

Lady Bournebridge idly turned and cast a glance back in the direction from which they had just come. "So here you are, Lady Rydleshire. Imagine my surprise when I saw your husband flagging down a coach with a lady on his arm, and it wasn't you." She feigned a shamefaced look. "I fear I embarrassed myself by calling her Lady Rydleshire." Her snide chortling left no doubt she relished the encounter as the latest *on dit*. "Of course, Lord Rydleshire was good enough to correct me." She tapped her chin as though struggling with a faulty memory. "Miss Hampshire, he said her name was. Imagine my surprise."

Sophie forced her smile to remain firmly in place, refusing to give the old crow the satisfaction of a reaction. "Ah yes, my husband's cousin," she lied. "Delightful lady. They are quite close." A sickening knot tightened in her middle, threatening to make her knees give out and drop her to the ground. But no, she would hold strong. Old Bournebridge would report the weakest twitch of an eyelash to the entirety of the *ton*, and Sophie refused to give her any additional fodder for her tales.

"His cousin?" the cruel woman repeated as she arched both

eyebrows to even haughtier heights. "I see." She slid a glance over to her cronies, and they all tittered behind their hands like hags cackling over a cauldron.

"Why, there they are again," Lady Essendon said, with a snobbish wave at a pair of coaches passing on the street. "Oh dear. I don't believe they saw us."

"Which coach?" Sophie snapped, no longer able to curtail her temper.

"That one right there, dear. The hackney." Lady Bournebridge directed Sophie with a subtle nod just as the coach stopped, Nash stepped out, then turned to help a rather questionably dressed, buxom blonde step down from it. The woman, obviously one of ill repute, rubbed up against him in a most unseemly manner as she took his arm and tugged him into an establishment that bore no sign.

"His cousin, you say?" Lady Bournebridge said with a malicious smile. "Indeed." She turned to her snickering companions and twirled her parasol. "Come, ladies. Bid Her Grace and Lady Rydleshire good day. After all, I am quite certain they wish to catch up with Lord Rydleshire. Perhaps even join him and his cousin for luncheon."

The terrible trio cackled in unison and swept onward down the street—no doubt in quite the hurry to spread the news of Sophie's humiliation.

She was rooted to the spot, and a sickening chill crashed across her with the strength of a stormy sea. She turned to Celia. "You saw him? It is not just their penchant for cruelty? Not their making up of unsavory stories?"

"Perhaps we are all mistaken," Celia said gently, but her pained expression left no doubt that it was Nash who had stepped out of the carriage, then turned back to help the harlot step down as well.

Struggling to stop herself from shaking, Sophie squared her shoulders and charged forward.

"Sophie!" Celia hissed while forcing a smile at passersby.

"Where are you going?"

"Where do you think I am going?" Sophie's sister by choice should know her well enough by now to realize she would not stand idly by while her husband boldly visited his whore on Bond Street in the middle of the day—flaunting her in front of those of the *ton*, no less.

Celia caught hold of her arm and vainly tried to slow her. "You cannot go in there!" she quietly scolded, still wearing that ridiculous smile to make others think nothing was amiss. "Sophie! You must not. We already have the gossip of Bournebridge and her cronies to deal with."

Sophie halted and glared at her. "No one publicly shames me." She held up her reticule. "And I do not go in there unarmed. I not only have my pocket pistol but also my dagger." She jutted her chin back in the direction they had just come from. "Go back to the carriage. I will be quite fine, I assure you." Rage paired with unbearable humiliation seethed through her. How could she have been such a simple-minded, trusting fool? How could she have lowered her guard and allowed him back into her heart?

Celia gave her arm a hard yank and prevented her from turning. "You must not be seen going in there. Nor must you cause a scene. If you do not wish to be completely eviscerated by the razor-sharp tongues of Polite Society, pretend you saw nothing— at least for now."

"Saw nothing?" Sophie choked on the ridiculousness of what Celia suggested. "You expect me to act as if I saw *nothing*?"

"I expect you to act rationally to save face and avoid even further embarrassment. Bournebridge will supply enough fodder to the gossip rags. Do you wish to feed them even more by barging into a brothel, dragging your husband out into the street, and shooting him in broad daylight in front of witnesses?"

"A brothel?" Sophie whirled about and stared at the mysteriously plain door that Nash and the woman had disappeared through. "How do you know it's a brothel? I assumed it was merely the doxy's private den of iniquity."

"You saw how she was dressed, and Elias told me that there are at least three of them here on Bond Street that are about to bankrupt one of his clients. They call them *sporting hotels.*"

"I suppose we know what *sport* they house." Sophie stared at the place, willing Nash to emerge so she could confront him. How could he do this to her? *Why* would he do this, after all that he had said about loving and needing her? If he truly loved and needed her, why did he need that woman too? She blinked against the stinging threat of tears, refusing to allow herself to show such weakness. She covered her mouth with her gloved hand. Her heart ached so badly it threatened to make her retch.

Celia wrapped an arm around her, supporting her as she turned her back in the direction of their carriage. "Come. Let us get you home. You are not well at all."

"I do not have a home," Sophie forced through clenched teeth. "It is all his now, remember? Thanks to Her Majesty, if he wishes, he can spend every last farthing that once belonged to Maman and me. He can spend it on that whore, and there is nothing I can do about it other than shoot him and then hang for it."

"You will be my guest. He will not be allowed in my home." Celia hurried her along, hugging her tighter. "I shall send for your things, and for your mother too. Elias will see what can be done legally to protect you and provide for your future."

"I have no future and nothing can be done legally. You know that as well as I." Sophie swallowed hard to keep from sobbing. All was lost. All she had ever hoped for was gone. "That was the reason for the Sisterhood of Independent Ladies in the first place. Except Maman and I failed in our endeavors by trusting the wrong people. We were such fools." She squeezed Celia's arm as she stumbled along beside her. "At least you and Frannie secured your happiness safely. I am glad of that for the both of you."

"My lady! What happened?" asked the man Nash had introduced as Mr. Forthrite. He rushed to meet them while glancing all around. "Did something frighten you? Did those ladies who stopped and talked with you warn you of some danger?"

Sophie snorted a bitter laugh. "Leave me alone. You will only side with him."

"My lady?" Mr. Forthrite gave her a perplexed look then motioned for a man across the way to join them. "Tomes! Did you see what happened?"

Mr. Tomes joined them, looking just as confused as Forthrite. "Nothing. They spoke to those three ladies and then moved on. Not a single untoward thing happened. No unsavory-looking characters lurking about. My lady?"

Sophie ignored the men, clambered into the carriage, and sagged back in the seat. How could Nash have done this to her? All his precious sentiments had been as worthless as the dust she shook from her shoes. Clenching her teeth, she stared out the window as they rolled along. She appreciated Celia's silence. It consoled her more than any meaningless words could ever hope to.

Once they arrived at Hasterton House, Celia rushed her inside, pausing only long enough to inform the butler that under no circumstance was the Earl of Rydleshire to be allowed admittance onto the property. Only the dowager countess and Miss Marie, Lady Rydleshire's maid, were approved to come in whenever they arrived.

Gransdon nodded and even bolted the door.

"Come. Let us get you upstairs to the guest room. I shall order tea strongly laced with brandy, and we shall plan your counterattack."

Sophie didn't answer, just clung to the banister to keep from crumpling to her knees and shaming herself further by releasing the painful sobs begging to be unleashed. Counterattack? What could she and Maman possibly do? Queen Charlotte had stripped them of their power, influence, and wealth. Nash had stripped her of everything else—pride, contentment, and trust—but worst of all, he had ground her love for him beneath his heel.

Once they made it into the guest bedroom, Celia settled

beside her on the cushioned bench at the foot of the bed. "Cry, Sophie," she said. "Or rant and rage. Throw things. Break whatever you like if it will help. There is no shame in it, and it is so much better than this dreadful silence that is so unlike you."

"No." A cold numbness had settled over Sophie, and she would do nothing to dispel it. It was better this way. Crying meant she cared, and had been foolish enough to love and yearn for a man who would never feel the same for her. Never would she make that mistake again. She pulled in a deep breath and let it out. "After our tea, I would like to rest for a while and would be exceedingly grateful if you would send word to Marie about my things. She will see to bringing everything over. And send for Maman too, as you suggested earlier. But if she wishes to stay at Rydleshire House under Mr. Wethersby's protection, I understand."

"And what about your protection?" Celia gently hugged her around the shoulders.

Sophie huffed a bitter snort. "Not that it matters, but if they wish to do so, they may stand guard outside. That is the appropriate place for a master's dogs, is it not?"

"I am glad you listened to reason and did not make a scene that you would have later regretted." Celia rose and yanked on the bellpull.

"I suppose." Sophie pushed up from the bench, crossed the room to the dressing table, and eyed herself in the looking glass. "Her hair was golden. Like sunshine. Mine resembles one of the queen's red Pomeranians." She cupped her breasts and turned sideways, studying herself from that angle. "Her hips and bosoms were quite a bit larger than mine, but not so heavily curved as to be considered too plump. I suppose a man can never have enough of those things from a woman?" Was that why Nash had strayed to Miss Hampshire's bed?

"Stop." Celia caught hold of her hands and squeezed them. "You are loveliness itself. There has to be an explanation for his being there today."

Sophie snorted again. "I am sure there is. She gives him delights that he apparently does not find with me. Why else does a husband frequent a brothel?" She held tightly to Celia's hands, struggling to understand, fighting to find a logical reason for this horrid pain he had foisted upon her. "Do you ever worry about Elias straying? About his taking a mistress?"

"Every woman experiences doubts at one time or another." Celia pulled Sophie into another hug. "But we must not drive ourselves mad with wonderings. Facts, dear sister. We must discover the truth about today and move forward from there."

Sophie spewed a bitter laugh as she pulled away. "Truth, you say? Do you honestly think he will fall on his knees and say, 'Why yes, my love, I meant to tell you I was going to visit my favorite ladybird today'? No. He will tell me some convoluted lie and expect me to fawn at his feet and beg his forgiveness for doubting him." She gave a violent shake of her head. "There is no such thing as the truth with Nash, and the sad thing is, I understood that. I witnessed his callous treatment of other women years ago when I first fell in love with him. His lies. His trickery. I knew, Celia, I knew." She clutched her hands to her breaking heart. "I was such a fool to think he would be any different with me."

A light knock on the hallway door interrupted them.

"That will be our tea," Celia said. "Come into the sitting room, dear one. You need a drink."

Sophie needed something, but at present, she wasn't sure what it was unless Celia knew of a way to turn back time and fix all her mistakes. She followed her into the small sitting room and sank into a chair as Celia went to the door. Sagging to one side with her head in her hand, she ignored the murmurings in the hallway. She didn't have the energy to care anymore.

"Two of your guards—Mr. Forthrite and Mr. Tomes are the names Gransdon gave—are standing outside at the front gate. I asked him about the third guard, but he had no information about that man." Celia set the tray on the low, bandy-legged table close by and filled the cups with brandy, forgoing the tea completely. She held out the delicate saucer and cup. "Here. Drink this. It will either help calm you or numb you enough so you cease to care. Either way, you need it."

Sophie accepted the cup and stared down at the pale amber liquid that perfectly matched the translucent roses painted on the fine porcelain. Peach brandy. She doubted it would help. At this point, nothing would help her feel better.

"I instructed Gransdon to send a pair of footmen across the way to help Marie bring your things over." Celia settled in a chair across from her but left her cup on the tray. "I did not, however, send for your mother. Not yet."

"And why not?" It seemed like the appropriate question to ask, although Sophie didn't particularly care whether Celia answered it. She didn't care about anything but drinking herself into oblivion and curling into a pitiful knot under the bedcovers.

"The more I pondered your mother's behavior since the two of you arrived here in London, the more questions I have thought of than answers." Celia laced her fingers together and folded her hands in her lap. "Since when has the esteemed Lady Nia, the most talented female agent who ever served the Crown, given up on a problem so quickly and sought help from said Crown when she had to have known what it would cost the two of you in the end?"

Sophie took another deep drink of the fruity beverage, inhaling the powerful fumes as the brandy warmed her tongue. Her head was beginning to pound, probably because she had not allowed herself to melt into a sobbing, inconsolable mess. "Speak plainly, Celia. I have neither the patience nor gracefulness at the moment to sort through niceties to describe the raw, vulgar truth. What do you suspect, and who has betrayed me?"

The duchess tipped a sympathetic nod, retrieved her cup and saucer from the tray, and partook of a healthy sip of the spirits herself. "Your mother and the queen betrayed you. Colluded, if you will, to marry you off and be done with the undue stress and maintenance of perpetuating the fake earl."

Sophie drained her cup, then refilled it herself while mulling over her friend's logic. "But what about the attempts on my life? Do you truly believe Maman wished me dead?" That was so unimaginable that it didn't even upset her to suppose such a thing. All her life, she had been nothing but cherished and treasured by Maman.

Celia frowned and returned her cup and saucer to the tray. "I do not believe your mother wished you harmed, but I feel it with the whole of my being that she is behind the scheme of your marriage. She surrendered too easily, sister. Recall her tenacity over the years. When has she ever given up on handling anything herself?"

"Never." Sophie stared off into the distance, sipping her brandy and wishing the numbing effect would take hold faster, because Celia's reasoning was beginning to make sense. "So you feel I have Maman to thank for marrying me off to a whore's bird?"

"Either her or the queen or both." Celia gave her a pained look. "Please forgive me for speaking so plainly when you are already overwrought. I do hope I am wrong."

Sophie topped her cup off yet again and held it up in a mocking toast. "Do me the courtesy of changing your original instructions to Gransdon about who may come in to visit me. Marie only. For now, at least. I have much to think about. Please politely decline Maman's entry until I can find the strength to speak with her about all that has come to pass and what she might know of it. You have given me much to think about." She indulged in a hearty sip, flinching as the beverage burned its way down her throat. "Maman is an expert at dancing around the truth without soiling her soul with a lie. I am currently in no condition to confront her and extract an answer I can recognize as the truth."

Celia rose, crossed to the door, then paused. "I am sorry, sister. I will help you in any way possible. Please understand that."

"Thank you, dear one. You have my utmost gratitude." Sophie swallowed hard, her throat aching as she once again teetered on the verge of tears. "Thank you for being here for me."

Celia nodded, then quietly left.

Sophie slowly stood and made her way back into the bedroom. A shuddering sigh worked its way free of her as she climbed onto the bed and curled into a tight ball on her side. She cocooned herself in the counterpane, huddling inside its sumptuous layers and wishing she could disappear. Thank heavens Celia had given her a haven, a sanctuary where she could hide and decide what to do and how to go about doing it.

A hot tear burned its way free. Another followed it, then a torrent of sobs shuddered out of her. She had been so happy. So content—so foolishly trusting and, damn her stupidity, so very much in love. Now she understood why Maman had never remarried or taken any other man seriously. Apparently, a true, lasting love between two people, a bond that kept them faithful to one another, hardly ever happened. Maman had experienced it once, so in her wisdom, she had known that in all probability she would never find it again.

Sophie shook with another hard, keening cry that came from the depths of her soul. Perhaps that kind of love didn't even exist anymore. Who was to say? She sniffed and coughed, choking on her misery. It didn't matter if it existed anymore or not—she would never attempt to believe in such a ridiculous fairy tale ever again.

CHAPTER FOURTEEN

H IS DISCUSSION WITH Burns and Miss Hampshire had gone much better than expected. Satisfaction filled Nash as the coach rolled to a stop in front of Rydleshire House. The day had been most successful, and Burns had even suggested an ingenious ploy to flush their villain out into the open. Excellent outcomes all around, indeed. He tipped the coach driver handsomely and grinned like a fool as the hackney drove away.

"Colonel!" Forthrite called out as he rushed toward him, glancing up and down the street as he crossed it. Tomes jogged along at his heels. The men's scowls shattered Nash's high spirits.

Panic and dread gripped him with icy fingers. "What has happened? Where is my Sophie?"

The two men halted and exchanged cringing looks.

"One of you better damn well answer me now."

Forthrite jabbed a thumb back at Hasterton House. "Your wife is in there, sir. Has been ever since she and the duchess got back."

"Got back from where?"

"Shopping," Tomes said. "Seemed to be looking around, mostly. They didn't tarry long or go into any of the shops. Eyed what was in the windows and spoke to some lady friends of theirs."

"But after they spoke to those women, your lady acted un-well. Like something untoward had happened," Forthrite said.

"Afraid I don't know what was said. Wasn't close enough to hear anything."

"I saw nothing happen," Tomes said. "And her ladyship refused to tell us what went wrong. Neither she nor Her Grace would tell us anything."

The back of Nash's neck tingled with an uneasiness that made him roll his shoulders to rid himself of the unholy sensation. There had been that odd encounter with those three ladies who had addressed Miss Hampshire as *Lady Rydleshire*. Had those three meddlers relayed the meeting to Sophie? "Where did this happen? Where was Lady Sophie shopping?"

"Her ladyship and the duchess were strolling along pretty as you please on Bond Street." Forthrite gave a bewildered shake of his head. "Then, after talking to those ladies, they loaded back up into their carriage, hurried to here, and scuttled into the duchess's place. Haven't been out since."

"She must be feeling poorly indeed, colonel," Tomes said. "She sent for her maid. A pair of footmen even helped the woman take several bundles over there to her."

Nash clenched his teeth to keep from bellowing at the top of his lungs. Either those vile women had convinced her or Sophie had seen him with Miss Hampshire and assumed the worst. That would be the only reason for her behavior. He charged across to Hasterton House, loped up the steps, and pounded on the door. He would explain everything and bring her home so her mother could validate the truth of his story. Then all would be well between them again—at least, he prayed it would be so.

Gransdon barely cracked open the door. "Good day, Lord Rydleshire. You are not allowed admittance, sir."

"Not allowed admittance?" Nash forced the toe of his boot into the crack so the butler couldn't close the door. "My wife is in there. You will allow my entrance immediately."

"That is not possible. Good day, my lord." The wily old man booted Nash's toe back out, slammed the door shut, and bolted it.

Nash stared at the door in raging disbelief. This could not be happening. Not when he and his precious swan had finally worked everything out and thrown themselves fully into growing their love and creating a real and lasting marriage. He banged on the door again, then rammed his shoulder against it over and over. The massive thing didn't budge. "Damned oak. Let me in, Gransdon! Now, I say! Let me in this very minute!"

No sounds came from the other side of the barrier that kept him from the woman he loved.

"This is not over!" He ran back across the street and charged up the steps. They would let Sophie's mother inside. She would plead his cause. As he burst into the house, Merritt and the dowager countess met him in the hallway. Their grim expressions made his heart plummet.

"She has barred you as well?" he asked his mother-in-law.

"Yes." Lady Nia drew in a deep breath and released it with a heavy sigh. "Celia is protecting Sophie the best way she knows how—at Sophie's request, I am quite certain."

"By keeping you from your distraught daughter? Is she mad?" He wanted to rush back over there and chop the door to bits with an ax. "Why are you not enraged?"

"Because Celia loves Sophie like a sister." The dowager sadly shook her head. "And Sophie trusts no one but her now. Not even me. I do not understand what happened today, but whatever it was, it destroyed the progress that the two of you made over these past few months." Her mouth tightened into a hard line as she tipped her head in his direction. "Would you care to share what you think overset her?"

"I think this is better discussed in the parlor," Merritt interrupted with a cautious glance up and down the hall. "Considering we have yet to discover our traitor."

Nash agreed. He followed them into the room and shut the double doors. Neither Lady Nia nor Merritt sat. Nash felt the same. The torment of this situation did not allow for sitting. "I fear Sophie saw me with Miss Hampshire on Bond Street and completely misunderstood the circumstances of my visit. And according to my men, she spoke with some ladies of the *ton* who more than likely made the situation even worse."

Lady Nia stared at him in disbelief as she slowly drifted toward him. "You did not tell her about your promise to General Hampshire?"

The accusation in the woman's tone cut through Nash like white-hot steel and accused him of being the worst sort of fool.

"I did not wish to trouble her with it." He inwardly flinched at the weakness of the excuse.

"You know she has struggled to trust you." The dowager closed the distance between them as though ready to strike him. "Did you not consider for one moment what it would look like for you to be seen with a woman of Miss Hampshire's reputation?" She clenched her trembling fists tighter. "Where did you meet with this young madam of Bond Street to discuss her opportunities?" Her furious scowl left no doubt about how deeply he had fouled this venture. "Tell me you discussed everything in the privacy of a coach. Tell me you chose not to enter her brothel during midday, when the ladies of the *ton* are known to do their shopping on Bond Street."

He bowed his head and stared at his boot tips. "I wish I could tell you all those things. But I cannot."

"*Merde.*" She turned aside with a hard shake of her head. "My child may never trust you again."

While he painfully agreed with that possibility, Lady Nia could still make all the difference in this debacle. Surely she knew that. "You can tell her of our plan to set Miss Hampshire up in a new life as my way of helping the general. Tell her I was not visiting the brothel for anything other than to speak with the woman and consult Burns about a way to trap our assassin."

"And how do you expect me to convince her of your fine, upstanding character when she will not see me, either?" Lady Nia spun around and shook a finger at him. "I will not clean up your mess for you! You are a damned fool. I cannot believe you did not tell her. Never keep secrets from your wife. Never! Have you no sense whatsoever?" She glared at him, then slowly narrowed her eyes. "Or are all your words merely that? Pretty little words. Platitudes to get what you want. Are you even capable of loving someone enough to do what is best for them no matter what anyone else thinks, or how uncomfortable it may make you?" She threw up her hands and turned her back on him again. "You may have lost her forever this time." She sank into a chair, closed her eyes, and rubbed her temples with shaking hands.

Merritt just stood there staring at him.

"Well?" Nash resettled his stance and braced himself. "Say it. I can see you are about to burst with the need to do so."

His friend slowly shook his head. "I never thought you a foolish man until now." He sauntered closer. "You tossed away the love of a fine lady just because you wished to avoid the unpleasantness that conversation would stir." He shook his head again. "I changed my mind. You are not a fool. You are a bloody coward."

Nash wouldn't argue with either of them because they were both right. He deserved everything they said and more. He scrubbed his face with both hands, hating himself more than his precious Sophie ever would. "Tell me what I can do," he begged. "Tell me how to repair this damage I have done."

Lady Nia slowly shook her head. "I am at a loss. I have no idea what my daughter might do because of this." She fixed him with a hard look. "Sophie feels foolish and betrayed. I know that much. She may run, and if she wishes to hide from us—we will be hard-pressed to find her."

"She cannot steal away. All her things are here." The ridiculousness of what he had just said settled like a crushing weight on his shoulders. If Sophie wished to run, she had the resources to do so, and Celia would do anything in her power to help her. His precious swan would want for nothing.

"Write to her," the dowager said in a tone that instilled little confidence that such a plan might work. "I shall write to her as well, and also write to Celia. All we can do is hope that one of them will read our letters and give us the opportunity to speak with Sophie and convince her that you have not strayed." She flinched as though in pain. "Have your general write to her as well. Perhaps his letter will get through, whereas ours will more than likely end up as ash in the grates of Hasterton House."

"Write to her?" He grimaced at the foolhardy plan. That could take days. He wanted things settled right now, this very hour, if possible. "I am not writing to her. I am going back over there, and, one way or another, I will see my Sophie."

"Did it ever occur to you that you are behaving like a man filled with guilt?" Lady Nia pinned him with a harsh glare that cut him to ribbons.

"I am filled with guilt, but not for being unfaithful to my beloved wife. I have not nor ever will do that to her. But I do feel guilty for not telling her of my plans before I carried them out."

Loud voices in the hallway made all of them turn and stare at the closed double doors.

Thornton opened one of them and stuck his head into the parlor while keeping his body wedged in the space to prevent whoever was in the hall from entering the parlor. "Mr. Forthrite insists on speaking with you, my lord."

"It may be too late now," the man growled as he shoved around the butler, marched to the front windows, and yanked aside the drapes. "The carriage is just now pulling away. I feared as much."

"What carriage?" Nash joined him at the window in time to catch a glimpse of a shiny black hackney as it rambled out of sight. He spun around to Forthrite. "Tell me. Now!"

"A well-dressed fellow," Forthrite said. "Tall. Older. Beady black eyes and a long nose. Real rat-faced, he was. Got out of the carriage and went into Hasterton House. In there for just a little while. When he came out, Lady Sophie was on his arm."

"He took my Sophie?" Lady Nia shoved in between them, her voice filled with panic. "Why did you not stop him? Why did you not shoot him?"

Forthrite gave her a bewildered look, then an awkward dip of his chin. "She went with him like she meant to go with him, my lady. Near as I could tell, the man did nothing to force her. In fact, they seemed right friendly with each other."

Nash caught hold of his mother-in-law's arm and turned her to face him, suspicion pounding through him. "Who is this man?"

"Virgil Nevillestone. Sophie calls him *uncle*, because he was my husband's closest friend. They were even closer than most brothers."

Something in her eyes, in the way she held herself, told Nash there was so much more that she wasn't saying. "And yet you don't seem to trust him. You even wanted him shot. Why?"

She drew herself up, lifting her chin higher. "Because he is the one behind the threats." She wet her lips as if about to double over and retch. "The man is deranged."

Nash grabbed her by the shoulders, wanting to shake her hard but somehow finding the control not to do so. "What do you know, mother-in-law? All of it! The *entire* truth, if you would be so kind."

Merritt rested a hand on Nash's arm and gripped it firmly. "Let her go, Nash."

"He has every right to be enraged," Lady Nia told Merritt. She huffed a bitter laugh. "When he learns the truth, he may kill me—and rightly so. I deserve the worst punishment that can be meted out."

As the ominous dread within him grew, Nash held up a hand and silenced them all. He jerked his chin at Forthrite. "Follow that carriage. You, Tomes, and Freedly. If you can safely get a killing shot off, do it."

Forthrite shot out of the room, and Nash turned back to Lady Nia. "Make haste, my lady. I have my love to save."

"When I created the fake Earl of Rydleshire, I unknowingly imprisoned my precious daughter. I thought I was securing a stable future for her, but instead, I created a lonely, dangerous trap." Lady Nia folded her hands and held them poised in front of herself while standing proud and tall. "Everything was fine until Sophie got older. She became so lonely when others her age debuted and found husbands. She was especially lonely after Frannie and Celia, her *sisters*, made wonderful love matches." The dowager countess frowned at the floor, her sadness aging her. "I came up with a plan to shatter the walls of my dear child's prison, and when Queen Charlotte agreed to help, I thought all would be well—especially because Sophie had loved you. Even though she never spoke of you, I knew she still cared." She lifted her gaze to his, trembling as she spoke. "But then the one whom the queen and I trusted to help us make the threats seem *real* enough to convince Sophie turned on me and revealed a side of himself I had never seen before."

"Virgil Nevillestone." Hatred and thirst for the man's blood consumed Nash.

"Yes. Virgil Nevillestone. My husband's best friend, who had always stayed close to me and Sophie. I thought it was because of his friendship with David. But as it turned out, the man possessed an unhealthy obsession for me." She bowed her head, and her voice broke. "And that obsession became quite alarming after I made the mistake of allowing him into my bed for a night that I wish never happened."

"Why didn't you tell me all this before?" Nash opened and closed his fists, aching to smash something. "You *arranged* for Queen Charlotte to make me the earl and forced Sophie to marry me with the assistance of a madman to threaten her life?"

"Sophie loved you." Lady Nia stared at him as if those three words explained everything. "I knew, if you could learn to love her, that you and she might discover the joy her father and I had." She jutted her chin upward again. "And I was not aware of the extent of Nevillestone's madness until he tried to stone her and then hired a shooter. I did everything I knew to stop him." She fisted her hands and moved closer. "I offered to marry him even, but he laughed in my face and said it was too late."

"Why did you not tell me?" Nash roared. "I could have

tracked the man down and ended him."

"I sent men after him," she said, her tone defensive and shrill. "I almost killed him twice myself, but he escaped."

He couldn't hold back any longer. He grabbed her by the shoulders and gave her a hard shake. "Why did you not tell *me?*" He shook her again. "Me? Your daughter's husband? I had the right to know!"

Her tears slipped free and rolled down her cheeks. "I didn't want Sophie to know how I failed her. How I had risked her life and lost control of the situation."

He shoved her away and turned aside, too angry to even look at her for fear of what he might do. "And now he has her," he said with a ragged breath. "He has the woman I love." He turned and jabbed a shaking finger at her. "I want you gone from here by the time I return with her."

"I want to come with you."

"You have done enough, dowager countess. Quite enough indeed."

He charged out of the parlor and headed for Sophie's workroom to load up on weapons. He selected a pair of pistols and secured them under his coat, thanking the powers that his brilliant wife always kept everything loaded and ready. He belted on a sword, snatched up a rifle, then broke into a run and took the shortest route to the stables. As he burst out of the garden and crossed the mews, he bellowed, "My horse, Mr. Wallace! Now!"

Unable to stand idly by while the groom readied his mount, Nash helped the man, stashed the rifle in the saddle's special holster, then leapt onto the horse. Just as he exited the mews and turned onto the street, Tomes galloped into view.

"This way, my lord!" The guard turned his beast in the middle of the street and waved for Nash to follow. "Forthrite sent me back to show you the way," he called out as Nash caught up with him.

"Forthrite and Freedly are still with the carriage?"

The man nodded while leaning forward to spur his animal

on. "They've gone to the park and slowed to an amble. The men are staying close and ready to fire as soon as they can get a clear shot."

Nevillestone's last threatening letter came back to Nash with a vengeance: *The old one dies in the channel and the young one dies in the park. I shall let the queen rot in Kew. No money or thanks necessary. Liars and deceivers dead is reward enough.*

"He means to kill her there!" He spurred his horse on, cursing the conveyances clogging the thoroughfare. Curzon Street led right to Hyde Park but was not close enough for his liking. He needed to be at his precious swan's side in the blink of an eye. A roiling gray blanket of clouds blotted out the sun, and rain cut loose as if the Almighty Himself had decided to punish Nash for his arrogance.

"There!" Tomes pointed as they galloped across the grounds, ignoring the paths and lanes. "In the middle of those trees. By the lake."

Nash didn't slow as he pulled a pistol free and readied it to fire. The hackney had come to a standstill beneath a massive oak. The driver sat hunched over against the storm with his collar pulled up high and his hat pulled low. The team of two horses stood with their heads lowered against the deluge.

Due to the blinding rain, Nash couldn't make out anything through the back window of the carriage other than shadows. At least there appeared to be two people in an upright position, although they both sat very still.

"Damn and blast it all!" He tossed all caution to the wind, motioning for Tomes and the other two men to cover the driver in case the man had been armed by Nevillestone. He eased up beside the carriage and drew up even with the door. When he yanked it open, his blood ran cold.

The blackguard sat with the tip of his pistol tucked under Sophie's chin. Pale as death, she stared straight ahead clutching her reticule in her lap.

"Lord Rydleshire," the devil drawled with a baleful smile.

"Virgil Nevillestone at your service, and I would like to thank you for making this part of my plan go ever so much easier." He nudged Sophie's throat with the gun's barrel and wheezed out a haughty chortle. "I had not quite worked out how to get fickle Nia's daughter to join me in a final ride." He wrinkled his sharp nose as though suddenly smelling something foul. "Lover's spat, you understand, and this upstart of a chit always sided with her mother." He chuckled. "At least, until she decided she could no longer trust her—thanks to you, my lord."

"Let her go, and I will consider allowing you to live," Nash said. "My men and I have you surrounded."

"Let her go?" Nevillestone barked with amusement. "You are most entertaining, my lord." All humor left the man, and pure evil shone in his eyes. "There is no power on this earth that could convince me to allow this spoiled bit of skirt to live."

Nash ground his teeth until his jaws ached, ignoring the sound of a horse approaching at a hard gallop. With his pistol trained on Nevillestone, he pulled his rifle from its sheath and aimed it at the man as well. "There will be nothing left of you to bury if you harm her."

"You think I care?" the man sneered, but then his expression filled with so much rage that he shook as if chilled to the bone. "I told you it was too late," he growled through bared teeth.

"Let her go and take me instead," Lady Nia called out. Her nervous mount danced back and forth on the other side of Nash's horse, mirroring the tension of its rider. "You hate *me*, Virgil. Not her."

Nevillestone made a moue of distaste and shook his head. "Decidedly wrong, my lady. I hate you both." He cast a jerking nod in her direction. "Although I do admit to hating you more than I despise her."

"But if you kill her, and her husband kills you, I live on." She fixed him with a victorious glare, then beamed a blindingly cruel smile at the man. "I shall dance on your grave in a dress of the brightest crimson, and see that your headstone reads: *Here lies*

Virgil Nevillestone—less of a man both in and out of the bedchamber."

The blackguard gave her a toothy grin. "You truly believe I would rise to such desperate bait? Have I not foiled you at every turn so far?"

Nash noticed Forthrite attempting to ease around the other side of the carriage, squeezing in between it and the tree to catch the fiend unawares.

"If he comes closer," Nevillestone warned, "I shall blow off her pretty little head much sooner than I planned." He thumbed the hammer of the pistol back another click.

Sophie closed her eyes and flattened her mouth into a fiercer line.

"Come back to this side, Forthrite," Nash ordered his colleague, itching to unload the rifle into the devil's chest. The man might be a maniacal coward, but he was no fool. Nevillestone used Sophie as a shield.

"Much better," the blackguard said with a slow nod. "It will be my choice when to end this performance. No one else's."

"In my eye," Sophie growled before two shots rang out inside the carriage.

Nevillestone unleashed a bloodcurdling scream, then fired wildly as she dove out the door and tumbled to the ground.

Nash emptied both pistol and rifle into the man. The force of the weapons' close range slammed the devil back against the seat, then he slumped into stillness.

"Sophie!" Nash leapt from the saddle and reached for his beloved swan.

"Get away from me," she snarled while scrambling out of reach, but then she looked across the way and paled. "Maman!"

Nash turned and discovered his men kneeling on either side of the dowager countess. His heart sank at the dark crimson stain slowly spreading across the front of the pale blue spencer that perfectly matched the delicate flowers of her gown.

"Maman," Sophie sobbed as she crawled over to her mother and pulled her into her lap. She pressed a hand on the stain, shaking her head as the bleeding refused to stop. "Maman, you must stop this nonsense immediately. It is no longer amusing!"

"I saw what you did," her mother said softly while looking up at her with a faint smile. "Well done, my dearest one. Shot him in his lap without taking your pistol from your reticule."

"You taught me well, Maman." Sophie gave another hitching cry as she hugged her mother closer. "Now, you must stop bleeding this instant. I cannot be without you, Maman. Not for a single second. Do you understand?"

Even though he feared it futile, Nash ripped off his jacket and waistcoat, then tore off his shirt and wadded it against Lady Nia's chest and applied pressure. He looked to Forthrite. "A physician. Now."

Forthrite offered a grim nod before mounting up and thundering off.

"Let me go, my little one," the dowager countess whispered. "It is time for me to join Papa."

"Stop it, Maman. I will not listen to such." Sophie covered Nash's hands with hers and held the shirt harder against the wound. She stared into his eyes and begged, "Save her! Please!"

Lady Nia barely lifted a hand as though trying to touch Sophie's cheek. "Papa waits for me, little one." Joy outshone the sadness in her eyes. "See him, precious?" she asked in a weaker whisper. "He is right there, and so very proud of you. As am I— always and forever."

"No," Sophie wailed, closing her eyes while rocking with her mother in her arms. She caught Lady Nia's outstretched hand and pressed it to her cheek. "I need you here with me. Please…please don't leave me."

"I love you, my precious daughter. Please…find it in your heart to forgive me. You have always been my greatest treasure." Then the dowager countess released the softest sigh, and not another breath followed.

CHAPTER FIFTEEN

TOO OVERWROUGHT AND weary to shed another tear, Sophie stared at the mausoleum through the fluttering folds of her black gossamer veil. Maman was happy now, finally reunited with Papa. She wondered if he would scold her mother for the terrible scheme that had cost her the opportunity to spend more time on earth with their only daughter, the child of their perfect love, as Maman had so often called her.

A deep sigh worked itself free, despite her best efforts to stop it. Perfect love, indeed. Such a thing only existed in fairy tales and silly romance stories read by girls too foolish and naïve to believe the cold, hard truth.

A tall, somber form quietly shifted in place to her left, pulling her from her tortured musings.

"She is at peace now, Mr. Wethersby," she gently reminded him. Even though Maman had never given him the slightest encouragement, he had remained hopeful and steadfast in his adoration.

"And her soul is now whole again," he said with a sad smile. "I am glad for her. Your mother deserves a peaceful eternity with the love she longed for with all her heart."

Sophie nodded, then turned toward him and offered him the slightest nod. "Thank you, Mr. Wethersby, for all that you tried to do. I will forever be in your debt."

The blond giant of a man smiled and returned a grateful bow.

"It is I who am in your debt, my lady. I return to London now, but if you should ever find yourself in need of me, send for me, and I will be there."

"Thank you, good sir. Safe travels and Godspeed."

He bowed again and touched the brim of his hat. "Good day, my lady. God be with you." Then he turned and disappeared into the foggy drizzle of the unbearable day.

"Come, my lady," Marie gently urged. "The carriage awaits, and the rain grows colder." She held an umbrella over Sophie and another over herself. "You will surely become ill."

"Is he still there?" Sophie asked without looking back at the gate that closed off the private memorial garden on the grounds of Rydleshire Academy at their property in Calais, France.

"Yes, my lady. Beside his carriage."

Sophie gritted her teeth and indulged in another heavy sigh. She kept her focus locked on the dates carved into the front of the mausoleum's stunning white marble that Maman had imported all the way from Italy. Nothing but the best for Papa, she had said—nothing but the best for their love.

She took the umbrella from Marie and barely tipped her head toward the carriage they had taken rather than ride with Nash in his. "Go, Marie. I am not ready yet, but I do not want you drowned in the increasing downpour. Go wait in the dry. I shall be along soon enough."

"But, my lady, you must—"

"I must do what I deem best for myself," Sophie corrected her firmly. "Now, go."

She didn't like being stern with Marie, but she had much to think about. Elias and Celia had been good enough to help her go over all her possible options before she left London to bring Maman home. Thankfully, her mother and the queen had possessed the presence of mind to ensure that the academy and property in Calais belonged solely to Maman and not the Rydleshire estate. They were now passed down to Sophie—along with funding for the property's upkeep and the school's continued operation. She had been surprised at the inheritance artfully hidden in the paragraphs of her marriage contract. She had assumed that upon the completion of her surprise wedding, everything became the property of her new husband, as per usual. Considering the circumstances of her now defunct union, the discovery of her ability to maintain an independence she had previously thought impossible came with a great deal of relief.

"Sophie." Nash's deep voice jarred her from her thoughts, twisting in her heart like a white-hot knife. "Come, my lady. The weather grows more severe."

"You go. I would not wish your driver to become ill."

"My concern is for you, my lady, not my driver."

"Rest easy, my lord. I am quite capable of looking after myself." She silently lauded herself for maintaining the detached numbness necessary for survival. She had no one now but her dear sisters of choice, and they were in England tending to their loving families—as they should be. Maintaining an aloof, emotionless presence was paramount to prevent her from shattering into shards of helpless, weepy bits. "Go, my lord. I shall be along presently."

"I shall wait here with you, my lady."

"As you wish. Your choices and actions are your own." She knew without looking that his strong, handsome jaw would be locked in that stubborn angle that made him even more irresistible. She would not succumb to him. Never again. Soon enough, he would either return to his harlot on Bond Street or take up with a different ladybird here in France. Of that, she had no doubt. Without a word to him, she turned and made her way back to her carriage. He could follow if he wished, or drown in the mud and rain for all she cared. It mattered not to her. The dull ache where her heart had once been served as a constant reminder to harden herself and nurture an unfeeling existence.

He offered his hand to help her step up into her carriage. Rather than accept his aid, she handed him her umbrella and climbed into the conveyance by herself. She needed no help—not from him.

Much to her annoyance, he climbed in and settled down beside her. Marie sat in the seat across from them, clasping and unclasping her hands in her lap.

"Do sit still, Marie," Sophie quietly admonished her.

"Beg pardon, my lady."

"Marie, would you be good enough to return to the house in the other carriage?" Nash asked. "Upon your arrival, please prepare her ladyship a hot bath to soothe her from the effects of this chilling day. We shall be along shortly."

"Yes, my lord," Marie said while avoiding looking Sophie in the eye. "Shall I instruct George as to where you would like to go, my lord?"

"Yes, Marie, ask him to take us around the grounds until I tell him otherwise."

"Yes, my lord." The maid climbed down from the carriage, her speediness betraying her desire to escape as quickly as possible.

Sophie clenched her teeth while drawing in a deep breath to brace herself against what would undoubtedly be another long diatribe of apologies, professions of love and regret, and lies about never straying in the first place. He had plied her with the sentiments at every opportunity over the past week, even left letters under her bedroom door, and tied notes of love to bundles of flowers, bottles of perfume, and meaningless jewelry.

For the life of her, she could not understand why he was trying so hard to repair something that had obviously never been a priority to him. Men strayed. She had heard servants and the *ton*'s gossips chat about it innumerable times. He was simply behaving like a normal, heartless lordling. Therefore, somehow, she would hone the art of being the cold, heartless wife. She swallowed hard, forcing the knot of torment that constantly choked her back down where it belonged.

He moved to take her hand, but she slid it out of his reach and tucked it beneath her crossed arms as she shifted to stare out the window at the dreary landscape.

His deep, frustrated sigh did not escape her. "Sophie."

"Yes, my lord?" she dutifully answered while still staring out the window.

"What happens now?"

His question surprised her. This was a new tactic for him. Perhaps a coy response was in order. They had not battled this way before. "I assume we drive around until you tire of it, and then we return to the manor, where I shall have a bath, then retire to my private sitting room to take care of necessary correspondence until time for dinner."

"That is not what I meant, and you know it."

She risked a glance his way, then looked away just as quickly. Looking him in the eyes was a mistake she would not make again. "Forgive me, my lord. Might you elaborate on your inquiry so I can answer accordingly? I truly have no idea what you wish to know."

"What happens now? Between us," he repeated quietly.

"As for you, I do not know." She stiffened her spine and lifted her chin. "I intend to take my mother's place here at the academy and continue her work."

"What about England? Rydleshire House? The queen prefers I stay close to the royal family."

She assumed a nonchalant air. "That is your responsibility, not mine, even though England and the royal family shall always have my loyalty. I am dedicated to training agents to serve them wherever spies are needed. My place is here." She shrugged. "As for Rydleshire House, it belongs to you to do with as you see fit. Either live there while you are in London or sell it." She fortified herself with another deep breath as she lifted her chin higher. "I no longer have a life in London among the gossips."

He unleashed another deep sigh, but it sounded more like a frustrated growl, pleasing her immeasurably before she reminded herself that *feelings* must not be allowed—not even feelings of victory.

"What about when we have children?" he asked, speaking a great deal louder than necessary.

"I am not with child, my lord," she answered coldly, the admission saddening her more than it should. She should be pleased her body did not nurture a baby. A precious child would only complicate this already impossible situation.

"But someday you could be with child." The heat of him so close, the scent of his sandalwood, citrus, and male musk, made all those old memories resurface, dangerous memories she could not under any circumstance dwell upon.

She hardened her heart and tossed her previous decision aside. She would look him in the eye. "I will not get with child by you, my lord. You availed yourself of other means of satisfaction, and I have accepted that, remember?" She swallowed hard again. "Quite clearly, I might add, it was brought to my attention that my services are no longer required. Our bedrooms shall remain as separate as they have been since the day of my mother's death."

"I love you, Sophie. How many times must I tell you that this was all a terrible misunderstanding? I have never been unfaithful to you, nor ever will be." Guilt and anguish filled his voice. The same guilt and anguish he had thrown at her at every opportunity ever since that fateful day. "I hold myself fully accountable for your mother's death, the sorrows of our marriage, for everything that has gone wrong." He slowly shook his head, weariness and despair making him seem so much older. "But I am so sorry, my swan," he whispered. "Please…I beg you…"

"Stop." She held up a hand as if pressing it against the impenetrable wall between them. "Repeating the same words over and over will neither dilute nor abolish my humiliation, my suffering, or the pain of your betrayal. It has been one week since you cast me aside, and I assure you, the only way I feel differently today is that grief has joined the ache in my heart. Go back to England. To your queen. Your harlot. Your friends who admire you. My place is here, and here I shall stay. Alone."

"I will never release you from this marriage," he said, his tone low and ominous. "You are mine, Sophie. For all time."

"I do not seek release from this marriage. I merely seek release from you." She needed to cry so badly, needed to throw herself into his arms and sob away all her pain while he held her like he had when she was silly enough to swallow everything he said. But if she relented now, what would she do the next time he made her look like a complete fool? "Might you signal George to take us to the manor now, my lord? I do not wish the bath you ordered for me to grow cold."

He caught her by the shoulders and turned her toward him, drawing close as though about to kiss her.

She turned her face away and said, "If you kiss me, my lord, know that you do so against my will and my wishes. You once said you would never force yourself upon me. Was that also a lie?"

They stayed in that position for what seemed like forever, as if they were frozen in time. Then he released her with a gentle shove and turned away, sagging forward to drop his head in his hands.

Hollow victory, she told herself while batting her eyes against the sting of tears begging to be shed. She turned back to stare out the window as the carriage rolled past the rear entrance of the academy, where several new admittances were overseeing the unloading of their trunks off the wagon from the docks. Two young women and three men who looked barely old enough to be out of boarding school stood on the steps, clustered beneath the overhang that protected them from the weather.

One of the women, the older one, caught her eye and made her bang her umbrella against the roof of the carriage to bring it to a halt. "Of all the audacity," she growled before pointing at the door. "Get out. Your ladybird needs help with her trunks."

Nash scowled at her, narrowing his eyes as though he feared her mad. "What are you talking about?"

With a hard jab of her finger, she pointed out the window at the disheveled blonde woman standing slightly apart from the others in the group. There was no mistaking Miss Adelaide Hampshire, even though she appeared to be dressed with a great deal more propriety than she had been on Bond Street. "Did you truly think I would not notice her among the trainees?"

"If anything, her presence here proves my innocence," he said, his voice a low, pained growl. "She is here to train, to set herself on a more honorable path, and stop debasing herself to survive. I told you of the promise I made to her father. Your mother knew and agreed to accept her into the academy." He caught hold of her shoulders again and brought her close once more. "You and your mother have helped so many like her, so many trapped in her very same circumstances. Why can you not accept she is here to change her life, and it has nothing to do with me? There never has been nor ever will be anything between us other than the fact that her father is my friend."

"I said, get out." She glared at him, refusing to be taken in again.

"Sophie—"

"All I have is your word against what I saw with my own eyes that day on Bond Street. The way she rubbed all over you like a cat in heat. The way the two of you laughed together as you disappeared into her brothel while Lady Bournebridge and her cronies watched my horror and humiliation with glee. Unfortunately, due to poor choices of her own, my mother is no longer here to corroborate your story about the esteemed Miss Hampshire's wish to change her ways. You will forgive me if I believe what I witnessed rather than what you would like me to believe."

His hands fell away from her shoulders. Ever so slowly, he closed his eyes and dropped his chin to his chest. "What will it take to make you believe the truth, my precious swan? I beg you—tell me, what it will take?"

"I do believe the truth, the real truth—not your version of it. Now, go to her. As I said, she appears to need your assistance settling into her room." Raw, razor-sharp emotions made her stomach churn. If Nash didn't get out of the carriage soon, she would surely retch all over him. Bile burned at the back of her throat, making her struggle to control the bitter sickness about to overpower her. She popped every one of her knuckles, then clutched her gloved hands in her lap while stiffening against his very convincing act of contrition.

"Sophie." Sorrow rolled off him in great crashing waves that threatened to topple her. He barely shook his head. "I love you and only you, my dearest swan."

She clenched her teeth tighter together, knowing if she tried to speak, she would scream.

He released a shuddering sigh, then dipped his chin in a single nod before stepping out of the carriage and closing the door behind him.

With every part of her aching to weep, she banged on the roof of the carriage, closing her eyes as it lurched into motion. She didn't look out the window to see the lovers' reunion. After only a week of managing her misery, she just didn't have the strength to add more torture to her poor battered heart.

As soon as they reached the manor, she jumped from the rig before it came to a full stop and ran inside. Blinded by the tears she could no longer hold at bay, she clung to the banister and pulled herself up the steps to her private quarters.

"My lady!" Marie caught hold of her and helped her into the dressing room. "Oh, my lady. I am so very sorry."

"A basin. Quickly!" Sophie grabbed the bowl from Marie, dropped to her knees, and rocked over it, casting up everything she had ever thought about eating.

Marie wiped her face with a cool cloth and offered a glass of water to rinse her mouth. "There now, my lady," she said quietly as she took the basin away. "Off with those wet things and into the tub. I placed a vial of peppermint oil beside it, and also added some to the water. I feared you might be ill after this terrible day."

"She is here," Sophie rasped as she stiffly worked with Marie to shed her damp clothing.

"She, my lady?"

"His whore from Bond Street. I saw her on the steps of the academy. Acting like a new trainee moving into the dormitory."

"Then maybe what Maude said was true." Marie helped her to the tub and settled her into the comforting warmth of the mint-scented water.

"Maude?" Sophie closed her eyes and pulled in deep breaths of the crisp peppermint oil steam. "When did you speak with Maude?" Maude had been her mother's lady's maid for as long as Sophie could remember. The old woman had become so distraught upon Maman's death that it had made her quite ill, so ill that Sophie had insisted the dear matron stay on at Rydleshire House for however long was necessary.

"Before we left London, she sent for me," Marie said as she added a kettle of hotter water to the tub. "She said she overheard Lady Nia and Lord Rydleshire talking about helping that girl from Bond Street the day before all the bad things happened, and everything became such a mess. She wanted me to tell you because she knew you were upset with Lord Rydleshire about his going there to talk to that woman." Marie returned the kettle to the hook inside the small hearth and swung it back over the fire. When she straightened, she gave Sophie a pained look. "I was afraid it was her laudanum talking, so I didn't say anything before now. But maybe he really was just helping that girl escape that awful place."

Sophie sank deeper into the water and covered her eyes with a cloth. "How much did Lord Rydleshire pay you to tell me this?"

"My lady!" Marie's injured tone was convincing enough to give Sophie a twinge of guilt. "Have I ever given you any reason to question my loyalty? If I have, then I shall tender my resignation immediately, although it will pain me greatly to do so. I care about you, my lady. You are…a…a good and fine lady."

"I cannot trust him, Marie. Too much has happened."

"But Maude said—"

"What Maude said does not matter. Why did he not tell me he was going to help that girl? Why did he not take me with him? I could have told her about the academy and reassured her." She uncovered one eye and squinted up at the maid. "But he didn't tell me, now did he? He did not want me involved, and also didn't want me to know he was going to see her. For what reason, I ask you?"

"My papa used to avoid telling my mama things to keep from getting pans thrown at his head before he had even done anything to deserve a good bump on his pate." Marie soaped a rag and reached for Sophie's arm. "He always said it was safer to ask forgiveness than permission. When things worked out, Mama never knew the difference and didn't get angry with him. When things went bad, he only had to run from her once rather than twice." She bobbed her head as she lathered Sophie's arm. "Smart man, my papa. Mama had a strong arm and good aim."

Sophie pulled her arm away and washed her face, then covered her eyes again as she leaned back and rested her head on the folded linen padding the edge of the tub. She was so confused, so torn, so heartbroken. How had life become such an unbearable torment that she didn't know what to believe or which way to turn? "If you were me, what would you do, Marie?"

"I think his lordship meant well, my lady, and the way he looks at you when you don't realize he's looking at you… I mean, I can't for the life of me remember when I saw a man who adored a woman so."

Sophie pulled in another deep breath of the minty steam and released it with a heavy sigh. "I cannot trust him, Marie. Not after all that has happened. I simply cannot bring myself to do so."

"Then I am sorry for that, my lady." Marie sadly shook her head. "I wish I could help make things better for you. Truly, I do."

"I know you do, Marie." Sophie waved the maid away. "Leave me to soak awhile, would you? I can manage if I decide I need anything."

"Yes, my lady."

For the millionth time, Sophie allowed herself to relive that terrible moment on Bond Street. The shock. The heartbreak. The humiliation. All of it came flooding back with the same sickening strength it had possessed that day. She pulled in a deep breath, then let it ease back out. *Calm yourself and look at the facts.* She needed to block out Celia's shock and the cackling cows who had delighted in her misery. "Focus on Nash and the way he acted that day," she intoned, as though reciting a bedtime prayer.

She saw him as clearly as if she was back on that street. He had helped the cyprian out of the carriage. Of course, it was a gentleman's duty to offer a hand to a lady. She draped the cloth over her eyes again and snorted. A *lady*, indeed. She scrubbed her face again and forced herself to concentrate on every detail of the memory. He had offered his hand—not caught hold of the woman by the waist, or pulled her close as she stepped down. He had merely held out his hand, and once she stepped down onto the walkway, *she* had caught hold of his arm and pulled herself up against him. He had not offered the lightskirt his arm. His smile that day—had his smile seemed strained? Had he tried to edge away from the whoring cat and attempted to put some space between them?

She narrowed her eyes as if squinting would help her focus the memory. Nash and the harlot had laughed together. There was no doubt about that. Another man she hadn't recognized had opened the door and held it for them. That was all Sophie could remember, because she and Celia had taken flight rather than wait for Nash to come back out. Grudgingly, that had probably been for the best. Or in her fury, she surely would have shot him. Not a killing shot, mind you, but one that would make him think twice about the company he kept.

Not a killing shot. At the time, she distinctly remembered wanting to kill him for hurting her so. But now? She groaned, then held her breath and submerged completely. To the devil with keeping her hair dry. She needed the water's muffled silence of oblivion. She stayed under as long as she could, then came up for air and scrubbed her scalp, combing her fingers through the tangles. Lathering her sodden mane, she indulged in the rare distraction of washing her hair by herself. Marie would not be pleased, but the dear maid would simply have to understand.

She submerged again and again until well rinsed, then relaxed back on the pillow of folded linen once more. *Not a killing shot* kept running through her mind. She stared at the islands of bubbles bobbing across the water's surface. "God in heaven, help me. I still love him." A pained groan worked itself free of her at the admission, and she thumped a fist against her chest. Yes, damn his eyes, she loved him. What power on earth had made it impossible for her *not* to love Nash Bromley? It had to be a curse of some sort—definitely a curse, because she had fallen under his spell since first setting eyes on him all those years ago.

A sad laugh hissed free of her. Loving him was the easy part. Trusting him was the impossibility. How could she ever trust him? Did wives just *ignore* their husband's questionable deeds and hope for the best?

"I cannot possibly do that," she informed the bubbles as she wiggled her toes through them and scattered them across the water. Of course, she wasn't perfect herself, and Nash had *ignored* her temper and opinionated ways on several occasions. "But that is entirely different from the matter of trust and fidelity," she said aloud. Yes, she had a terrible temper, was annoyingly stubborn, and often had a very difficult time looking at things from any perspective other than her own. But none of those things compared to the deadly sin of unfaithfulness or lying.

"My lady! Your hair!"

"I thought it might help me feel better," Sophie said, unable to keep the defeat from her tone.

"Come along, then." Marie's exasperation was obvious as she held out a drying towel. "Wrap this one around you, since I warmed it by the fire. I'll fetch another for your hair."

With the toasty linen gathered around her, Sophie went over

to the hearth and perched on a plump hassock, so Marie might have an easier time drying her hair. "I think I shall dine in my dressing room tonight," she mused as the maid squeezed the water out of her long mane. "I simply do not have the energy to deal with anything other than a quiet meal and solitude."

Marie hung the soaked drying towel on a rack by the fire, shook out another, and continued her efforts to dry Sophie's hair. "Then you have a decision to make about the folks waiting for you in your sitting room."

"What *folks?*" Sophie frowned, then flinched as Marie scrubbed her head harder.

"Lord Rydleshire, a Mr. Burns, I believe he said, and Miss Hampshire are waiting to speak with you." The maid tossed the wet linen onto the rack with the other and gently nudged Sophie to stand. "I told them I was not about to be rushing your soak, not after the day you'd had. They said they didn't mind waiting. Especially Lord Rydleshire. He said he wasn't about to leave until they spoke with you."

"Lovely." Still clutching the linen to her chest, Sophie turned and glared at the sitting room door, debating whether to lock it and let her uninvited guests sit in there until they rotted. She closed her eyes and let her shoulders sag. No, that would not do because, as much as she hated to admit it, Nash's stubbornness and tenacity rivaled her own. He *would* sit out there forever.

"Dress me for battle, Marie," she said with a weary shake of her head.

The maid eyed her with a thoughtful look. "Mourning or not mourning?"

"Stunning victory and relentless control."

Marie gave a curt nod and headed for the wardrobe.

CHAPTER SIXTEEN

"WHAT MAKES YOU think she will even agree to see me?" Miss Hampshire wrinkled her nose at the sober gown of light gray with dark blue trim that she pulled from the trunk. "Even if she does, she'll think you just paid me to say whatever I tell her."

While Nash wasn't foolish enough to disagree, he still held out hope. He would never give up, never relent in convincing Sophie that he had not been unfaithful to her. He fully admitted he should have included her in his plans and told her everything. Avoiding an unpleasant confrontation with his wife was his sin—not adultery. His precious swan had to be swayed to forgive him for his cowardice. "Burns brought the letter from your father. That will help."

With a moue of distaste, the lady eyed the pair of sedate black boots before placing them in the wardrobe's bottom. "The lady will claim it a forgery." She arched a brow at him. "I know wives, colonel. Lady Rydleshire is not the first to oust her husband after he sought a bit of fun outside the marriage bed."

"I sought *nothing* outside my marriage bed—nor will I ever." Nash yanked open the door to the small room assigned to Miss Hampshire for the length of her training. "How many times must I demand that this door be left open? Understood?"

With a wicked gleam in her eye, the girl waved a corset and a pair of shockingly pink stockings like flags of surrender. "No privacy for my intimates, colonel? Shame on you."

"Burns!" Nash stuck his head out into the hallway, grabbed the man leaning against the wall, and dragged him inside the room. "Stay in here with us."

"Need a chaperone, do you, colonel?" Burns grinned. "Addy trying to take advantage of you again?"

Nash shoved the man against the wall. "If not for the general, I'd send you both back to the hell where I found you. This *favor*, which neither of you appears to appreciate, has cost me the only woman I have ever loved."

Miss Hampshire snorted and waved away his words. "You are an earl. You're supposed to have mistresses."

"I do not want a mistress!" he bellowed. "I want my wife!"

Both Burns and Miss Hampshire glanced at each other and edged as far away from him as the small room allowed.

"Meant no harm, colonel." Burns lifted both hands while pressing back tighter against the wall. "We'll make this right with your woman so she'll know you didn't do nothing untoward with Addy or none of her girls. General wants us to make amends too. He was none too happy when I told him 'bout what went on and how things soured on you."

"You got me out of debt with Mr. Forbes," the somewhat meeker Miss Hampshire said. She hung another sedate gown into the wardrobe while offering Nash a slight nod. "I owe you, colonel, and I appreciate all you did. Truly, I do." She frowned at the items left in the trunk. "I sure miss my fancy clothes, though."

"Both of you report to the manor as soon as this room is set in order." Nash glared at them, wishing he had never gotten involved in the sorry matter. While he respected the general and considered him a friend, Miss Hampshire's lukewarm gratitude and heady regret about giving up certain particulars of her past had set his nerves on edge. That woman had cost him entirely too much. He charged out of the dormitory and stormed across the campus on foot in the driving rain.

Servants scattered as he burst into the manor, all except the butler, Clipton. The diminutive man with his black hair slicked back as if it had been painted on his head rushed forward, reaching for Nash's dripping coat and hat. "Saunders informed me your bath stands at the ready, my lord."

Nash still wasn't accustomed to having a valet who anticipated his every need. "Thank you, Clipton. I am expecting a Mr. Burns and a Miss Adelaide Hampshire. When they arrive, please see them into the front parlor, and notify me immediately."

"Shall I have refreshments prepared, my lord?"

"No. Their visit will be brief." *And, hopefully, effective*, Nash silently added as he climbed the stairs. At the top, he paused and stared longingly at the door to Sophie's suite and sent up a prayer that this meeting would repair at least some of the damage done. In his heart, he knew it would take a lifetime to win both her forgiveness and trust once more. All he asked was a chance to prove he would never hurt her again, or be so foolish as to keep anything from her merely to avoid a clash of their wills. Lady Nia had been oh so right, and so had Merritt. He had been a coward when he chose not to tell her of his plans to help the general's wayward daughter.

"Your bath, my lord." Saunders directed him to the dressing room with an efficient tip of his head. "Shall it be casual attire this evening, or do you expect guests?"

"Not casual," Nash said as he peeled off his soaked clothing and stepped into the tub. "I am dressing for war, Saunders."

"War, my lord?"

The valet's expressionless voice revealed no opinion whatsoever, but Nash knew better. Servants knew everything, and he had no doubt they were well aware that the lord and lady of the manor were at odds with one another. "Yes, Saunders, war. I am fighting for my wife."

"*For* your wife, my lord? Not *with*?" For the first time, the stoic little man appeared to be slightly perplexed and attempting to clarify matters in order to react accordingly.

"Yes, Saunders, I am fighting to win my wife's heart once

more." Nash hurried to wash, stepped out of the tub, and scrubbed himself dry. He halted as soon as he entered the bedroom and stared at the clothes laid out on the bed.

"Acceptable, my lord?"

"Yes, Saunders. Quite." His military dress, complete with medals, sword, and highly polished Hessians, bolstered his hopes further. That had been his attire on their wedding day, and Sophie had seemed to like it. This plan would work. His precious swan would be his once again, and he would spend the rest of his life proving his devotion to her.

As he finished dressing, a quiet knock was followed by Clipton's quiet announcement through the barely opened door. "Mr. Burns and Miss Hampshire have arrived, my lord. Waiting in the front parlor, as instructed."

"Good." Nash tugged his coat in place and adjusted the hang of his sword at his side. "Show them up, please. I shall be at the door to Lady Sophie's suite."

"Yes, my lord."

Nash squared his shoulders, then charged forward as though heading into battle and took his post in front of Sophie's rooms. He breathed a bit easier when he noted that Miss Hampshire had changed into one of the more sedate dresses provided by the modiste responsible for costuming the ladies of Rydleshire Academy. Burns had even combed his hair and appeared to be doing his best to look respectable.

Nash didn't speak to either of them when they reached him, merely gave a curt nod and ushered them into the private sitting room. He motioned for them to be seated on the sofa in front of the window.

Marie stepped out of the bedroom, clutching a pile of folded linens to her middle as if they were a shield. "My lord?"

"Please ask her ladyship if she is well enough for a brief meeting with myself, Mr. Burns, and Miss Hampshire."

The maid eyed the pair on the couch, then slid a doubtful look back to him. "Her ladyship has had a very trying day, my lord, and is currently attempting to repair herself with a good, long bath." She cleared her throat and took on a sterner air. "Forgive me, my lord, but I shan't be interrupting her or asking her to hurry. She has been through too much, she has."

Nash bowed his head. Unrelenting regret pounded through him, wrapping cruel fingers around his heart and twisting. "I am well aware of her suffering, Marie, but it is imperative that we speak with her. Please convince her to see us. We will wait however long it takes her to get ready—at her leisure, of course."

The maid squinted at him as if wrestling with whether to do as he asked. "I will try, my lord," she said quietly, then curtsied and disappeared back inside the bedroom.

"Colonel?" Burns said in a loud whisper while waving him closer.

Nash arched a brow as he walked toward him. From the man's expression, there was no telling what he was about to say.

"Does she still have her pistol?" Burns cast a nervous look at the closed bedroom door. "Forthrite said she separated Nevillestone from his bollocks in one shot." He gave Nash a leery nod. "After the week that lady's had, you might want to make sure she's no longer armed."

"Rest easy, Burns. If she shoots anyone today, it will be me." Nash returned to the other side of the room, then did another lap, unable to stand in one spot for very long.

"You better quit your pacing," Miss Hampshire said while tapping the toe of her boot on the lush Persian rug at their feet. "She'll be even angrier if you mark a trench in her pretty red and gold carpet." She wiggled in place and glanced at the bedroom door. "She won't be one of my instructors, will she? Showing me how to use weapons and such? I'm not so sure that would be such a grand thing."

"I have no idea," Nash said, and nor did he presently care. His sole concern was a selfish one. He wanted Sophie back in his arms and would never let her go. He continued his pacing, straining to hear the slightest sound from the next room. Nothing but silence reached him, and that was worse than shouting for Marie to tell them to all get out. Silence could be deadly.

He jerked with a start as the latch of the bedroom door clicked, then held his breath as it slowly swung open. He continued not to breathe as Sophie swept into the room, not dressed in her mourning clothes but wearing an off-the-shoulder gown of the whitest silk that shimmered with leaf work embroidered with golden threads. It was a ball gown designed to stop time and draw every eye in the room. And it did so, perfectly displaying the mounds of her creamy breasts that swelled with her every intake of breath, accentuating her long, slender neck, and showing off her lovely shoulders and narrow waist that filled his hands so perfectly. Gads, he had been such a damned fool.

Nash licked his lips, then cleared his throat. "Thank you, Sophie," he forced out in a rasping whisper.

She spared him a narrow-eyed study, then swept her gaze from the toes of his boots up to his medals, and then to his sword. "Have you been called to another war of which I am unaware, my lord?"

Time to fight for her. Time to win her back. "I have been called to war, my lady," he said while jutting his chin higher. "A war for your heart. I fully intend to win it and never lose it again."

She flattened her mouth into a taut, displeased line, then shifted her attention to Burns and Miss Hampshire.

Both jumped to their feet. Burns bowed, and Miss Hampshire dipped a curtsy deep enough to satisfy the queen herself.

"Granville Burns at your service, my lady." The man bobbed his head again. "Deepest regrets on the loss of your mother."

"Thank you, Mr. Burns." She slid her focus to Miss Hampshire and waited.

Nash held his breath, praying Miss Hampshire could convince Sophie that nothing untoward had ever happened between them.

"Miss Adelaide Hampshire, your ladyship." The girl curtsied again and kept her gaze locked on the floor. "I cannot thank you and Lord Rydleshire enough for giving me a way out of..." Her voice trailed off, and she cringed. "For giving me a way out." She nervously tipped her head at Mr. Burns. "He's brought a letter from my papa, thanking you too." She coughed and bowed her head even more. "And apologizing for all the trouble I caused between yourself and Lord Rydleshire."

"Do you think I am a fool, Miss Hampshire?"

The young woman arched both her fair eyebrows to her matching hairline. "Oh no, my lady. I told Lord Rydleshire that no matter what I said, you'd think he just paid me to say it, so he wouldn't be in the suds with you anymore." She emphatically shook her head. "But he truly did nothing untoward, my lady. All he did was pay off my debt to Mr. Forbes so I could be free. The whole time he was at our place, he pushed me and the girls away. Didn't want a thing to do with any of us."

Sophie's expression remained unreadable, but Nash sensed her aching weariness. He felt how fragile she was, and how she was barely holding herself together. "Sophie," he said quietly with a step toward her, but stopped as she held up a hand to stay him.

She approached Burns, gliding like the magnificent vision she was. "The letter, Mr. Burns."

Burns hurried to pull it from the inner pocket of his jacket and held it out. "It's no longer sealed, my lady, because it was addressed to Lord Rydleshire, and he done read it."

"Then why is it in your possession, Mr. Burns?"

"'Cause his lordship gave it back to me and said for me to bring it to you." Burns shrugged. "He knows you don't trust him anymore, and more than likely wouldn't take it from his hand."

"He is quite correct." Sophie opened the letter and stared down at it long enough to read it more than once.

Nash held his breath again, wanting to rush to her but knowing to hold fast and not overplay his hand.

She slowly re-folded the parchment and gave it back to Mr. Burns. With her gloved hands clasped tightly in front of her, she squared her lovely shoulders and turned to Nash. "Is that all?"

"Beg pardon?"

"Is that all?" she said quite a bit slower, as if she thought him somewhat dim.

Both his hopes and his heart sank like the heaviest stone, but he refused to surrender. "That depends, my lady."

"Depends on what?"

"On you, my precious swan."

Remaining as cold and unsmiling as she had been for the past week, Sophie moved to the golden tasseled cord hanging beside the hearth. With her head held high and her gaze locked straight ahead, she gave it a hard pull, then turned and faced the door leading to the hallway. She stayed as silent and unyielding as the iciest day of winter.

A few moments later, Clipton entered, looking from her to Lord Rydleshire.

"Please show Mr. Burns and Miss Hampshire out," she told the butler.

"Yes, my lady." Clipton held the door and arched a brow at the guests, who hurried to leave. The butler followed, closing the door behind him.

Nash braced himself, waiting for her to oust him next. He resettled his stance. He would not leave her this time. If he had to, he would sleep across the threshold of her bedroom door.

She stared at him, her rich mahogany eyes weary and sad. With a slow shake of her head, she turned away, went to the blue velvet fainting couch in front of the hearth, and slowly lowered herself onto it. She kept her gaze fixed on the gently crackling fire.

"You hurt me," she finally said so softly that he almost didn't hear her.

"I know," he admitted, daring to move closer. "I was a coward and a fool."

Her faint smile gave him hope. "Better to ask forgiveness than permission," she said, as though repeating a memorized verse. She turned and looked up at him, her brow puckering with the slightest frown. "But was it really better?"

He dropped to his knees beside her. "No. It was not, my love, and it has taught me that no matter how much I fear we might disagree or fight, it is much better to include you in everything rather than risk losing you." He took her hand, his heart soaring when she didn't pull it away this time. "I cannot live without you, Sophie. Please try to love me again."

A single tear escaped and rolled down her cheek as she gave him another sad smile. "That is the problem, you see. Even though I wanted to hate you for making me look the fool, I couldn't. I have loved you since I was ten and five, and you were twenty. Even then, I tried to hate you when you were so infuriating, but I couldn't." She frowned and shook her head again. "You are like an affliction I can never be rid of—one that has no cure."

Considering all the things she could have called him, he humbly accepted the title of *affliction*. At least they were talking, and she still held his hand. She could call him anything she liked.

"Might we begin again?" he asked gently. "I will do better this time. I swear it."

She didn't answer, and the deepening of her frown worried him.

"Sophie?"

"I know I am stubborn and have a temper, but am I truly so horrid that you felt forced to hide things from me?" She shifted on the lounge and leaned toward him. "Is it because I kneed you in your… Is it because I attacked you that day?"

He cupped her cheek in his hand and forced himself to speak the truth. "I was cowardly, my love. I took the easy way out because I truly did not think it would matter. I needed to talk to Burns about helping us and thought I could kill two birds with one stone—and didn't want to take the time to convince you that I needed to do it." He grazed his thumb along the curve of her bottom lip, still not brave enough to try to kiss her. "I failed you, and I failed your mother. I am so sorry for being such a fool."

"If Maman's death taught me anything, it is that we some-times make mistakes when we think we are doing what is best for those we love." She took in a pitiful, hitching breath. "I miss her so much, Nash." She touched his face as her tears overflowed. "And I missed you too."

A groan escaped him as he pulled her into his arms, rocking as he cradled her to his chest. "My darling," he whispered, hating himself for causing her so much pain and now finding himself powerless to ease her sorrow. "I love you, my precious swan, and I am here now."

She clung to him, weeping for the longest while. He hated her suffering but loved her being in his arms. Then she made a noise he couldn't define. It wasn't exactly a stifled sob, but more like an uncomfortable exasperation.

"My love?" He gently lifted her face to his.

"The haft of your sword is rather unbearable, my lord," she said, arching to one side while holding her ribs.

"Gads, forgive me!" He set her aside and removed the offending weapon. "Did it bruise you?"

She graced him with the most beautiful smile he had ever seen. "I am sure it did not." She cast a meaningful look at the door. "But perhaps we might check. After you ensure the latch is locked, of course." She sniffed and swiped at her tears. "And I would not be averse to your holding me some more once we are more comfortable—if you don't mind."

If he didn't mind? Did she think him a complete cod's head? He hurried to secure their privacy, then returned to where she sat on the floor, tilting her head, watching him with a faint smile. Without hesitation, he scooped her up, lowered them both to the lounge, and settled her on his lap. "Hopefully, your stays took the brunt of the sword's abuse," he said as he positioned her so he could undo the multitude of tiny buttons running down the back of her gown.

"I am not wearing any stays. In fact, I am not even wearing my chemise or petticoats, since I was in a hurry to dress and get your *meeting* over with." She cast a sheepish glance at him over her bare shoulder. "Please do not think me vulgar or lowly. I simply did not care at the time and was not of the mindset to force myself to feel otherwise." She held up both hands and gave a derisive laugh. "Marie convinced me to at least wear my elbow-length gloves."

Her confession about her state of undress hardened him to the point of nearly spilling himself. He struggled for control as he tugged off her gloves and tossed them aside. "You know how I feel about gloves, my lady."

She gave him a lopsided smile that turned slightly wicked. "Yes, I know. How do you think Marie convinced me to wear them?"

He ached to taste her, hold her while breathing her in and possessing her completely. But he was so afraid of stepping wrong and fouling the moment. "May I kiss you now, my love?"

"No." A warm sultriness had replaced her cold disdain, but her smile disappeared, making his heart plummet.

"No?" He swallowed hard.

She twisted to face him and plucked at his cravat, untying the neckcloth with slow, deliberate tugs. "You may not kiss me until we rid ourselves of these clothes." She arched a brow. "I do not wish to snag my gown's fine needlework on your medals, my lord."

"A prudent decision." He slid her gown down to her waist and leaned forward to bury his face in the warm, silky curve where her neck met her shoulder. He breathed in the delicious-ness of her jasmine scent and groaned. "Pray, let us make haste, then."

She rose and let her gown fall away into a froth of snowy silk around her ankles. Without taking her gaze from his, she untied the shimmering gold ribbons tied just above her knees.

Nash reached to help remove her stockings, but she backed up a step and shook her head.

"No, dear husband. You have fallen sorely behind in divesting yourself of your clothing." She stood before him in all her naked glory, idly plucking the hairpins out of her curls and allowing the coppery waves to tumble free. As she ran her fingers through her hair and fluffed her tresses, she frowned. "Have you changed your mind? You appear to be frozen in place."

"You have bewitched me, my love." He yanked off his coat and threw it aside, then kicked off his boots, stripped off his waistcoat, and sent his shirt sailing through the air. "You outshine Botticelli's Venus," he whispered as he shed his pantaloons. "You are my goddess."

"I do not want to be your goddess," she said quietly as she seemed to float toward him. She rested her hands on his shoulders and kept a frustrating amount of space between their naked bodies. "I want to be the woman you cannot live without." She smiled as she traced the outline of his ear, then combed her fingers through his hair. "Even though I have a terrible temper, no patience whatsoever, and make my knuckles pop at the most inopportune time…" Her smile faded. "Can you please try to love me as much as I love you?"

"I love you more." He pulled her into his arms and covered his mouth with hers while pressing her tight against him. Her warm, satiny softness drove him mad with more desire than he had ever possessed before.

She clung to him, opening her mouth and inviting him to deepen the kiss by tangling her tongue with his. She wrapped a silky leg around him as she raked her hands down his back, then clutched his buttocks and squeezed.

The smoothness of her belly rubbing against the hardness of his length made him groan. "I need you, my love," he rasped. "I fear I cannot go slow this time. I have longed for this for too long, feared I would never know the treasure of your embrace ever again."

"Then take me, my love. On the lounge, on the floor, on the sofa, or in the bedroom." She squeezed his buttocks again, harder this time, the same desperate need echoing in her tone. "I do not care where you take me. Just take me. Make me forget my sorrows for a little while."

"We shall start with the floor," he said as he lowered her onto the Persian carpet in the middle of their discarded clothes.

She smiled as she wrapped her legs around him and arched to meet him. "A promising start, but mind your elbows, my love."

He sank into her with a rumbling groan, burying himself completely. "Elbows?" he rasped as he slid back out, then drove in deep again.

"Rug burns," she said with a gasp as he pounded into her faster.

"To hell with the rug burns," he growled, then set into a rhythm that made further conversation not only impossible but unnecessary.

CHAPTER SEVENTEEN

NASH KISSED EACH of the dimples centered above her fine, round buttocks, then licked his way up her spine, smiling as Sophie wiggled beneath him. "Be still, my lady. I have not finished tasting every bit of you."

"Are you quite certain, my ravenous lord?" she asked with a lazy giggle as she rolled to her back and guided him to her breasts. Arching into him with a satisfied moan as he tongued her nipple, she wrapped her legs tighter around his hips. "I feel as if I have been thoroughly worshiped by that wonderful mouth of yours."

After sprinkling a trail of kisses across the swell of each of her breasts, he raised his head and smiled. "I will never finish worshiping you, my love. Never."

A quiet pecking on the private servants' door made him bellow, "Enter and die!"

"Nash!" She shook beneath him with a laughing snort, then cleared her throat and called out, "I shall ring when I need you, Marie."

A subdued "Yes, my lady" came through the closed door.

"It is hours and hours past dawn, you know." Sophie treated him to a long, slow kiss that encouraged him to settle back between her legs with a satisfied growl.

"Alas, my wife tires of me," he said, jutting his hips and rocking into her hot wetness with insatiable greed.

"Never," she groaned, matching him thrust for thrust. "Oh, never!"

He rode harder, feeling her bliss building and clutching to reach its pinnacle. "Take it, my love, take your pleasure."

She cried out and bucked with a wildness he couldn't resist.

A triumphant roar tore from his throat as he pumped harder, then poured into her until he was left shuddering. He collapsed, barely saving her from being crushed by catching himself on his forearms. With his forehead pressed to hers, he kissed her nose between gasping breaths. "My precious love," he whispered.

She hummed a pleased sound, reminding him of a purring kitten. "We do have a precious love between us."

"We do indeed."

A strained growl rumbled up between them and made Sophie gasp. "Oh dear. I am mortified."

Nash chuckled. "Why? Because you are hungry and need food?" His stomach chose that moment to make its wishes known with an even louder grumble than hers. "We did miss our dinner last night."

She eyed him with a wicked arch of her brow. "Do you resent the sacrifice?"

"Not in the least, my love." He nibbled a lingering kiss across the sweetness of her ruby lips. A heavy sigh escaped him as he lifted his head. "I suppose we must eat though to keep up our strength."

"Yes, my lord, we would not wish to become weak and listless."

He kissed her again, then gently stroked her cheek. "During breakfast, shall we discuss where to live and how to go about forging our future together? Are you up to that, my love?"

She smiled up at him, her eyes glistening with unshed tears. "I do not care where we live or what we do, as long as we are together and as happy as we are at this very moment."

"I adore you, my precious swan," he said in a rasping whisper, his heart and soul teeming with relief, thankfulness, and more love than he ever thought possible.

"I adore you more," she said, then pulled him down for a long, slow kiss. As he went to lift himself off her, she pulled him back. "Once more before hot chocolate and toast?"

"As many times as you like, my love—as many times as you like."

EPILOGUE

Rydleshire Manor
Calais, France
June 1823

"And the little boy thanked the pirate king for seeing him safely home."

Sitting beside Sophie in the nursery, Nash tried his best not to smile at their five-year-old son's obvious displeasure as his mother closed the book and returned it to the nightstand shelf. The perpetually adventurous lad with hair as fiery as his mother's and a healthy share of both their stubborn personalities hated when bedtime stories ended because it meant he was expected to lie still and go to sleep.

"Solly did it, Maman! I pwomise he did!" Charlotte Lavinia Sistine, Solomon's precocious three-year-old sister, shouted the accusation from her cot in the opposite corner of the nursery. "I saws him!"

Nash clenched his teeth and didn't dare meet eyes with Sophie or he'd laugh. They both knew Solomon had stolen the last bowl of raspberry crowdy off Cook's shelf, even though he had already devoured one for dessert. The enterprising young lad had erred and left a trail of the sticky raspberry drippings that led to his favorite hiding place under the stairs. When presented with the evidence, he had stood in front of his tiny lair and unabashedly blamed his sister, vowing to one and all that *Sissy did it.* The only problem was that Sissy couldn't reach Cook's shelf, nor did she yet possess the coordination to push one of the stools across the kitchen floor, climb up and retrieve the bowl, then successfully descend without a sound or dropping her stolen treasure.

"Sissy, my cherub, it is time to sleep." Sophie gave her daughter a loving smile and kissed her on the cheek as she tucked her back under the covers.

"The piwate king didn't lie like Solly does," the golden-haired moppet vowed with a harsh glare in her brother's direction.

Nash kissed his beloved daughter on the forehead, then gave her a wink as he whispered, "Maman and I know. Go to sleep, my sweet girl."

"Maman?" Solomon called out.

Sophie arched a brow at Nash, signaling that perhaps their son was finally ready to confess. "Yes, dear one?"

The child clasped his hands together on top of the covers, wringing his little fingers as if trying to pop his knuckles like his mother. "I understand that the pirate king never lied, but that was just a story. You and Papa lie sometimes. Don't you?"

"When have we ever lied to you?" Nash asked, unable to imagine where his son had gotten such a notion.

The boy shrugged. "Well…maybe never to me or Sissy, but to old people like you. When you needed to—right?"

"Have you been sneaking over to the academy again?" Sophie asked with motherly sternness.

Solomon twitched another shrug, which meant that he had, in fact, slipped into the spy classes again even though he knew he wasn't supposed to.

Nash scrubbed a hand across his face while blowing out a weary snort. He had to admit, though, that the lad retained every tidbit he heard—even better than many of the students. A sense of pride laced his frustration with his stubborn child. "An agent pretending to be someone else to protect our country and our sovereign is not a liar. They are assuming a role for the greater good." He leveled a stern glare on his son. "And you have been told several times that you are not to go over to the academy. I shall have a word with Nanny and Miss Amy as soon as we leave this room."

"Sorry, Papa." Solomon had the good sense to look ashamed, but Nash knew it was an act. The imp would be back over to the training rooms as soon as he found a more creative way to slip away from poor Nanny and the maid assigned to help her. The boy lifted his gaze to his father, then cut a sly glance over at his mother. "But Papa *never* lies to you? Not ever? Arby's papa lies to his mum and gets in trouble whenever he gets caught."

Sophie looped her arm through Nash's and gave it a loving squeeze. "Papa *never* lies to me. I trust him completely."

Nash's heart swelled near to bursting, making him send up a prayer of gratitude. It had taken time, patience, and a great deal of understanding to get their love to where it was today, and he cherished every precious moment he had been granted with this wonderful woman. "We would like to trust you, Solomon, because we love you." He hugged Sophie closer and rested a hand on the pronounced swell of her rounded middle. "You are the eldest, my son, and must protect and set a good example for Sissy, and for this one too."

"Solly lies!" Sissy sang out.

"Shut your gob, Sissy!" Solomon shot back.

"Solomon," Nash said. "Did you take the dessert after being told you had already eaten enough sweets for the day?"

"It wasn't for me," the boy halfheartedly admitted. "Kitty was extra hungry because of her babies."

"Kitty?" Sophie asked.

"Babies?" Nash repeated. "What are you talking about?" The only cats in residence were those in the stables, and the boy had not been out there today.

"Kitty is my new cat from Arby's place. His papa was going to kill her and her babies, so me and Arby saved them. She's under the stair because the other cats in the stable acted like they were going to be mean to her when we tried to take her there."

"How long have you had her under the stair?" Sophie asked.

Nash wrinkled his nose, imagining the mess that a trapped mother cat and her kittens would create.

"Three days now," Solomon said. "I loosened a board on the back wall so she could come and go through the servants' hall. I didn't want her thinking she was in prison or nothing." The lad grinned. "She caught a mouse yesterday and made Miss Josie squeal and drop all the folded linens."

"Where in the world was Nanny while you were doing all this? Where was Miss Amy?" Sophie fixed a bewildered frown on her son.

"Nanny's getting kind of old, Maman. She naps a lot." His grin widened to a proud smile. "And Miss Amy likes cats too, and thinks Arby's dad is an arse."

"Solomon." Nash arched a brow at his son. "We do not use vulgar words in the presence of ladies."

"Sorry, Maman."

"Apologize to your sister too," Sophie advised.

"Sissy isn't a lady. She's a—"

"Solomon!" Nash pointed at the boy. "I think it best that you go to sleep now before you get yourself into even more trouble."

"Sorry, Papa." The lad obediently pulled his covers up under his chin and faked a yawn. "I love you, Maman. I love you, Papa." He turned his head toward his sister's cot and raised his voice. "I even love you, Sissy."

"Don't love you at all, Solly. You got me in twouble."

"*Charlotte Lavinia Sistene.*" Sophie huffed a weary sigh. "You were not in trouble at any time for the missing dessert. Now forgive your brother and tell him you love him, because you know you do."

"Love you, Solly." Sissy's tone denied the sentiment, and made Nash bite the inside of his cheek to keep from laughing.

"Papa and I love you both. Now to sleep, my angels," Sophie said as they moved toward the door.

Nash extinguished all the lights except for the gentle night lamp glowing on the mantel. Then he and Sophie left the nursery.

As Solomon had earlier stated, in the attached sitting room, Nanny was sound asleep in her chair by the fire, but Miss Amy was wide awake and reading in the chair opposite her.

"If they call out, fetch us," Sophie said as she and Nash crossed the room.

"As always, my lady." Miss Amy nodded, then looked back down at her book.

As soon as they stepped out into the hall, and Nash had closed the door behind them, he started chuckling and couldn't stop. Sophie joined in with a fit of snorting giggles, covering her mouth to keep from getting too loud.

"Your son," she said, her shoulders trembling with uncontrollable mirth.

"Your daughter," he countered, pulling her into his arms and rocking from side to side. "Gads, I couldn't be any happier if I tried, my love. You and our children make my life joyously complete."

She leaned back and gazed up at him with a loving smile. "I love you, my joyous husband."

"And I love you more, my precious swan." And he sealed the vow with a kiss.

The End

About the Author

If you enjoyed TO STEAL AN EARL, please consider leaving a review on the site where you purchased your copy, or a reader site such as Goodreads, or BookBub.

If you'd like to receive my newsletter, here's the link to sign up:
maevegreyson.com/contact.html#newsletter

I love to hear from readers! Drop me a line at
maevegreyson@gmail.com

Or visit me on Facebook:
facebook.com/AuthorMaeveGreyson

Join my Facebook Group – Maeve's Corner:
facebook.com/groups/MaevesCorner

I'm also on Instagram:
maevegreyson

My website:
https://maevegreyson.com

Feel free to ask questions or leave some Reader Buzz on
bingebooks.com/author/maeve-greyson

Goodreads:
goodreads.com/maevegreyson

Follow me on these sites to get notifications about new releases, sales, and special deals:

Amazon:
amazon.com/Maeve-Greyson/e/B004PE9T9U

BookBub:
bookbub.com/authors/maeve-greyson

Many thanks and may your life always be filled with good books!
Maeve